Lee pulled her close, holding her as if she were made of flower petals.

She didn't want this dance to end. Jenna wanted to keep her eyes closed and keep moving in Lee's arms.

But of course it had to end. She was acting like a silly, addlepated girl, and she would never be that young again. She was wiser now. She knew better than to let herself become involved with a man. It never turned out the way you thought it would.

The musicians started to pack up their instruments, and the crowd thinned and then began to disperse.

Lee kept her hand in his as they walked back to the wagons. They had not spoken to each other all evening, had not needed to. But there were things that had to be said out loud, and it was going to be tonight.

Author Note

My great-grandparents came to Oregon in a covered wagon along the Oregon Trail from Independence, Missouri, to Oregon City and the Willamette Valley. Great-grandfather Edgar Boessen was an immigrant from Germany; Great-grandmother Maia Bruhn came from Denmark. Their descendants now number in the thousands.

There is an old, very romantic family story about how Edgar and Maia met and fell in love; I'm sure it is probably little different from hundreds of other treasured family tales. I hope you will find Jenna's story, told here, to be one that touches your heart.

Typical of those intrepid travelers who came west on the Oregon Trail is the following diary entry:

"Friday, October 27. Arrived at Oregon City at the falls of the Willamette.

Saturday, October 28. Went to work."

—James W. Nesmith, 1843

LYNNA BANNING

Baby on the Oregon Trail

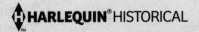

ISBN-13: 978-0-373-29911-9

Baby on the Oregon Trail

Printed in U.S.A.

www.Harlequin.com

Lynna Banning combined a lifelong love of history and literature into a satisfying career as a writer. Born in Oregon, she graduated from Scripps College and embarked on a career as an editor and technical writer and later as a high school English teacher. She enjoys hearing from her readers. You may write to her directly at PO Box 324, Felton, CA 95018, USA, email her at carowoolston@att.net or visit Lynna's website at lynnabanning.net.

Books by Lynna Banning

Harlequin Historical

The Ranger and the Redhead
Loner's Lady
Crusader's Lady
Templar Knight, Forbidden Bride
Lady Lavender
Happily Ever After in the West
"The Maverick and Miss Prim"
Smoke River Bride
The Lone Sheriff
Wild West Christmas
"Christmas in Smoke River"
Dreaming of a Western Christmas
"His Christmas Belle"
Smoke River Family
Western Spring Weddings
"The City Girl and the Rancher"
Printer in Petticoats
Her Sheriff Bodyguard
Baby on the Oregon Trail

Visit the Author Profile page
at Harlequin.com for more titles.

To those from the many countries
that make up America who have had the
courage to forge new paths and start new lives.

Chapter One

Oregon Trail, 1867

"Miz Borland?"

Jenna smoothed the threadbare apron over her swelling belly and turned to see Sam Lincoln, the wagon train leader. The big man removed his stained leather hat and stood uncertainly beside the wagon.

"Hello, Sam. Would you join us for supper?"

"No, thanks. I—" His sunburned face looked strained, and suddenly Jenna's breath jerked inward.

"Sam? What is it?"

He turned the hat brim around and around in his hands. "Don't rightly know how to say it."

Oh, God. Something had happened. "Is it about one of the girls? Ruthie?"

The leader took a step closer. "Not the girls, no."

"Mathias?" she whispered.

"'Fraid so. He's…well, he's been shot."

"Shot!" Jenna closed her eyes. Surely she was dreaming.

Sam stepped forward and laid both his weathered hands on her forearms. "He's dead, Jenna."

She felt suddenly cold, as if all the blood in her body was draining away. "What?"

"He was caught stealing a horse. The owner killed him."

She pulled away from Sam's steadying grip and abruptly sat down on the bare ground. Dead? It wasn't possible. And stealing a horse? It made no sense.

"Where is he?" she asked, her voice unsteady.

"In our wagon. My Emma's, uh, laying him out. I expect you'll want to see him."

"Not yet. I have to tell the… His daughters."

"Ruthie's over visiting with the Langley girl," Sam volunteered. "The two older ones are down wading in the creek."

She nodded. *Dead*. Mathias was dead. Dear God, what would they do now?

"I'll tell 'em about their pa if you want, Jenna."

Jenna fought waves of blackness at the edge of her vision. "No. I'll tell them, Sam. Just…just give me a minute."

Ten minutes passed before she could stand and make her way to the Lincolns' camp. She hesitated before the large canvas-covered wagon and clenched her jaw so hard her teeth ached. She couldn't look at him. Then she resolutely mounted the step, drew back the curtain and stepped inside.

Round-faced Emma Lincoln rose and without a word laid her freckled hand on Jenna's arm. The older woman tipped her head to indicate the still form stretched out on the bedroll, and Jenna forced herself to look.

She hadn't remembered Mathias being so tall. Or so pale. In death his features had relaxed from the perpetual scowl he had worn; now he looked almost peaceful. She scanned his body for signs of blood but saw no stains. At her questioning look, Emma took her hand.

"The bullet entered his temple, Jenna. Killed him instantly. I cleaned up the… I cleaned him up."

"Thank God," Jenna murmured. *Oh, yes, thank You, God.* There would be no messy remains for his daughters to see. An unnatural feeling of calm flowed over her, along with an inexplicable sense of…what? Relief? Dear God, how could she feel this, as if a huge weight had suddenly lifted from her shoulders? It made no sense.

Or maybe it did. Mathias had not been pleased with her of late. Maybe he had never been pleased with her.

She drew in several deep breaths before she risked speaking. "Emma, thank you for doing this for Mathias. I must find the girls and tell... They will want to see their father."

"Sam says if it's all right with you, they'll bury your husband at dawn, before we pull out. And tonight Sam and I will sleep under our wagon."

Jenna nodded and climbed down from the wagon to do what she must. She'd gone only a few yards when Ruthie danced up. "What's wrong, Jenna? You look all white and funny."

She knelt before her stepdaughter and struggled to compose herself. "Ruthie, I want you to find your sisters. I have something important to tell you all."

"Dead?" Tess screeched. "What do you mean Papa is dead?"

Eleven-year-old Mary Grace began to sob.

"I mean..." Jenna began. She glimpsed Ruthie's stricken face and the words froze on her tongue. She swallowed hard and knelt before them.

"Your father has been killed. Accidentally shot by... well, it doesn't matter who."

Tess swayed forward and Jenna reached up to support her. Mary Grace wrapped her thin arms around her middle, but Ruthie just stared at her with horrified blue eyes.

"You..." Jenna's voice broke. "You girls can see him if you wish. He's laid out in the Lincolns' wagon."

"I don't want to see him," Mary Grace sobbed.

Jenna folded her into her arms. "You might want to, honey. You will want to have seen him after we leave in the morning." She pressed her lips shut and walked them over to the wagon, where she stood with them beside their father's body in the fading light.

"Papa don't look dead," Ruthie said after a time.

"Doesn't," Tess snapped.

"Well, he do—doesn't. He looks like he's sleeping."

Jenna patted Ruthie's thin shoulder. "Let's remember him that way, as if he is just…asleep."

At her side, Mary Grace jerked. "How come there's no blood or anything?"

Jenna drew in an unsteady breath. "Well, Mrs. Lincoln said the…the bullet hit his temple, so there wasn't very much bl—" Her voice choked off. What could she say to them?

"Come on," Tess said, her voice tight. "Let's go back to camp." Without waiting for Jenna, she herded her younger sisters outside and started across the compound.

Dear God in heaven, what should she do? The girls had resented her from the moment she had married their father, and now she was solely responsible for them. By the time they reached Oregon they would hate her.

A cold chill snaked into her belly. And they would hate her baby.

Chapter Two

The following morning, Sam Lincoln and four other men dug a grave and laid Mathias to rest. Jenna watched them, her hands curved around Ruthie's narrow shoulders, while Mary Grace and Tess looked on in stony silence.

Reverend Fredericks read some verses from the Bible, something about there being a time for everything under the sun. Then clods of earth thudded onto the blanket-wrapped corpse of her husband. It was an awful sound, terrible and final. Jenna clamped her jaw shut and pressed her palms over Ruthie's ears.

Finally the last shovelful of fresh earth was heaped onto the mound and her fellow travelers drifted back to their wagons. Ruthie stepped forward and laid a ragged handful of scarlet Indian paintbrush on her father's grave. Jenna's heart lurched as if cracking into two jagged pieces.

"Come, girls," she managed. "We must pack up our things."

Ruthie turned her face into Jenna's blue homespun skirt. "I don't want to leave Papa here all alone."

Tess leveled a venomous look at her sister. "Then you're nothing but a big baby."

Jenna fought an urge to sharply reprimand the girl, but concentrated on wrapping her hands around Ruthie's quivering frame. She had never disciplined Mathias's daughters, and besides, what good would it do now?

"Tess." She addressed the girl over Ruthie's blond curls. "That is unkind. Your sister, all of us, are hurting. You know how hard it is to leave your father here."

Tess bowed her head. "Sorry, Ruthie. You're not a baby, I guess. Come on, Mary Grace." The two older girls walked off, leaving Jenna standing by the grave with her youngest stepdaughter.

She stared at the wildflowers, wishing she had thought to gather some as well, but she'd been so busy frying the breakfast bacon and rolling up the bedding inside the wagon there had been no time. And anyway, Mathias would not care. The flowers were really for Ruthie, a way to say goodbye.

Jenna closed her eyes briefly, then turned toward their camp. She felt numb, unreal, as if this were happening to someone else.

Emma Lincoln stopped her. "Jenna, at the meeting this morning, Sam asked the men for a volunteer to drive your wagon. In about half an hour the man will come to hitch up your oxen. If you'd like to be alone for a while I could take the girls in our wagon."

Jenna studied the woman. What a kind soul the trail master's wife had been, right from the very beginning. How she wished some of that generosity of spirit would rub off on Tess!

"No, thank you, Emma. I am quite all right." She wasn't, really. She dreaded the days ahead, but she could not admit this to anyone. How would she manage without Mathias?

A blade of anger sliced into her belly. Mathias had talked and cajoled and pushed until she finally agreed to join the wagon train and come west. And now here she was, embarked on an unwanted journey she had no choice but to continue; once a wagon train started out across the prairie, there was no way to get off. No way to go back to Ohio.

Another woman, Sophia Zaberskie, thrust a loaf of fresh-baked bread into her hands. "You eat," she grated in her perpetually hoarse voice. "Keeping belly full makes to heal."

Jenna pressed Sophia's meaty arm. Sophia should know; she had lost one child to cholera before the emigrant train was even under way, and another child, a boy, died two weeks later when a wagon wheel rolled over him and crushed his chest. If Sophia could survive, so could she.

She took Ruthie by the hand and walked to their camp. Tess and Mary Grace looked up but did not speak, both keeping their faces resolutely turned away from her while she moved about packing the skillet and the Dutch oven inside the wagon. Tess grumbled at her request to fill two buckets with springwater and dump them into the water barrel strapped to the wagon box; Mary Grace walked listlessly at her sister's side, kicking at stones.

When the last of their belongings were stowed away, Jenna surveyed the tangle of ropes and harnesses and wood oxen yokes stashed under the wagon and her heart sank as if weighted with lead. She had no idea how to hitch up the team. Mathias might have taught her. Why hadn't he?

It was hard to accept that he was gone, that he would never again snap at her for forgetting to fold a blanket in his particular way or serving him dumplings with his stew when he preferred biscuits. She knew she had been a disappointment to him; she often felt small, as if she didn't matter.

Ruthie's small hand patted her skirt. "Jenna, are you crying?"

"N-no, honey. I'm not crying, just feeling a bit sad."

"Me, too. Tessie won't talk to me and Mary Grace is too busy. And I'm scared."

Jenna went down on her knees before the girl. "I'm a little scared, too. But we will be all right, just you wait and see."

A shadow fell over her. "Mrs. Borland?"

She jerked to her feet. The man was tall, with overlong dark hair and steady eyes that were a soft gray. He held his broad-brimmed hat down by his thigh.

"Sorry to startle you, ma'am. My name's Carver."

"I know who you are, Mr. Carver."

He'd joined the wagon train at Fort Kearney. A former Confederate soldier, Emma had confided. A Virginian. From a slave-holding plantation, no doubt. Jenna's father had fought for the Union; he'd been killed at Antietam.

"I've come to yoke up your team."

Her stomach clenched, and it must have shown on her face.

"Ma'am? Are you unwell?"

"Mr. Carver, surely someone other than you volunteered?"

His gaze flicked to the back of the wagon, where Tess's face was peeking out from the curtain. "Mrs. Borland, is there someplace we can talk in private?"

"Why?"

Gently he grasped her elbow and moved her away from camp. "I want to tell you why I volunteered."

"I don't really care why, Mr. Carver."

"I think you may when you hear what I have to say," he said quietly. "You see, it was my horse your husband was stealing. I was the one who shot him."

Jenna stared at him until her eyes began to burn. "Dear God in heaven, why would I want anything, *anything at all*, to do with the man who killed my husband?"

A flash of pain crossed his tanned face. "You probably don't, Mrs. Borland. And I can't blame you. But I'd sure appreciate it if you'd hear me out."

Shaking with fury, Jenna propped her fists at her waist and waited. She could scarcely stand to look at him.

"I didn't know who was taking my horse," he said after a moment. "Didn't recognize the man. But I knew my horse. The rider was heading hell-for-leather— Excuse me, ma'am. He was riding toward the trading post we passed yesterday morning. I fired my rifle and he went down."

"You killed him."

"Yes, I did. I'm sorry he turned out to be your husband, and the father of your girls there." He inclined his head toward the wagon where three heads now poked out from the rear bonnet.

"'Sorry,' Mr. Carver, is not enough," she snapped.

"I realize that. I know nothing can ever replace your husband, but I'd like the chance to do what I can to make it up to you. That's why I volunteered to drive your rig."

"You cannot 'make it up' to me, Mr. Carver. Ever. Don't you understand that?" She clamped her lips together, afraid she would cry.

"I mean to try, Mrs. Borland. Where's your yoke and the harnesses for the oxen?"

"Did you not hear me?" Her voice went out of control, rising to a shout. She hated him! He was a cold-blooded killer. "I do not want your help!"

He turned his back on her and peered under the wagon. Mary Grace stuck her tongue out at him, but he paid no attention. Instead, he snaked an arm out to capture the tack and moved off to where the oxen grazed inside the circle of wagons. He moved with such assurance she wanted to toss the hot coals from her morning cook fire into his face.

The instant he was out of sight, Tess scrambled down and planted herself in front of Jenna. "You can't let him do this!" she screamed. "He was my father, and that man killed him. He has no right to be here, touching Papa's animals."

Jenna sucked in an uneven breath and wrapped both arms across her waist. "Perhaps not, Tess. But neither of us can yoke up the oxen, and he has volunteered. I will speak to Mr. Lincoln tonight and ask for someone else."

The girl's face flushed, but Jenna was suddenly too

weary to care. Her shoulders ached. Her head felt as if it were stuffed with sharp-pointed rocks.

"Take Ruthie down to the latrine, then get in the wagon."

She paced around and around their small campsite until Tess and Ruthie returned and Mr. Carver appeared, tugging the oxen, Sue and Sunflower, by their lead ropes. He said nothing, just moved past her, positioned the two animals in front of the wagon and went about jockeying the yoke into place and adjusting the harnesses, his motions unhurried.

Jenna stepped closer to watch what he did.

He paused and his gray eyes sought hers. "Want me to teach you and your oldest girl how to do this?"

"I— No. I mean, yes. But not my oldest girl. Tess would find such a task beneath her."

His dark eyebrows went up, and then he nodded. "My little sister never wanted to curry her own horse. Same reason." He went back to adjusting Sue's harness.

"How did your sister turn out?" she blurted out. "Was she spoiled?"

He straightened, a look of such naked anguish on his face that Jenna winced.

"My sister was killed when Sherman's men reached Danville and marched through our plantation. Some Yankee soldier bashed her head with his rifle butt. She was eleven years old."

Stunned, Jenna stared at him, a choking sadness knotting her chest.

Mr. Carver shuttered his features and bent over the hitch again. "Watch now, Mrs. Borland. You have to pull this ring tight, or it'll work loose."

"Mr. Carver, I—I am sorry about your sister."

"War is ugly, ma'am. We did some awful things to you Yankees, too."

"But a child! Dear God, what is the world coming to?"

"Wondered that a lot when I was in the field. And later,

fighting the Sioux." He finished tightening the jangling metal, patted the heads of both animals and turned to her. "What are their names?"

"Tess, Mary Grace and—"

He smiled, and she was struck by how white his teeth were against the tanned skin. "I meant your oxen, Mrs. Borland. Helps to know how to address them."

"Address them? Mathias never talked to the oxen."

"Lots of folks don't. I do."

"Sue and Sunflower. Sue is the one on the left."

He nodded and scratched Sunflower behind one ear. "If you're ready to pull out, I'll go get my horse."

A horse! She was terrified of horses. One had bucked her off when she was eight; she'd never forgotten it.

"Aren't you going to...? Mr. Lincoln said the volunteer would drive our wagon."

"I will do that, ma'am. I'll just bring my horse and tie it beside the wagon."

Jenna checked on the girls. "You two can walk along-side the wagon if you wish. Or you can ride inside, but it will be hot when the sun is high."

"I'll walk," Mary Grace said.

"Me, too," Ruthie chimed.

"I'd rather die than see that man driving Papa's wagon," Tess muttered. "I'll stay inside."

Jenna found her sunbonnet and a blue knitted shawl, then climbed up onto the driver's box. She supposed she could learn to drive the oxen. She'd never liked the two animals. She'd never liked horses, either. But she supposed she could stand Mr. Carver until they stopped for supper tonight and she could speak to Sam Lincoln about a re-placement.

Within ten minutes he returned, mounted on a huge, gleaming black horse. He tied it to the wagon, climbed up beside her and lifted the reins. Then without a word he lowered them again and eyed Ruthie, who stood clutching Mary Grace's hand.

"You want your little one to ride up here?"

"Why?"

"It's safer," he said.

"Very well." She dropped onto the ground and handed Ruthie up onto the box beside Mr. Carver. She didn't really want her sitting next to that man, but he was right; it was safer. She wondered why Mathias had never thought of that.

Slowly the circled wagons peeled off into a ragged line and amid the creak of huge oak wheels and the clank and groan of mule and ox teams, the train rolled forward. Their wagon took its designated place at the end.

Rather than ride next to Mr. Carver, Jenna set out on foot, walking an arm's length from a downcast Mary Grace, who twitched her spare body away from her. She tried to say something, but the girl cut her off. "Just leave me alone," she hissed.

Suddenly the girl yelped and darted forward to her father's grave. The wagon train wheels were now rolling over the mounded earth, and Jenna could see that Mr. Carver intended to do the same.

"Stop!" Jenna screamed. He reined in and waited.

Mary Grace reached him first. "They're driving right over Papa's grave!" she wailed.

Mr. Carver tied the reins around the brake and jumped down to face the girl. "Miss Borland, we do that of necessity. If the grave looks fresh, wolves will get at it."

"Wolves?" Jenna shuddered.

He went down on one knee before Mary Grace. "I know it's hard to watch, miss, but it has to be done unless you want your father's grave desecrated."

"What's des-crated?" Ruthie piped from her seat on the driver's box.

Mr. Carver pushed his hat back and stood. "Desecrated

means something spoils a grave. Digs it up, maybe. You wouldn't want your papa to be disturbed, would you?"

Fat tears stood in Ruthie's blue eyes. She shook her head. Lee Carver glanced over at Mary Grace. "You understand, miss?"

The girl nodded.

Lee Carver looked to Jenna. She stood close to her daughter, but he noted that the girl hitched herself away from her side. Odd.

"Mrs. Borland?" he prompted. "Would you like me to drive around the grave site? This is the last wagon, so it'll be pretty well dusted over by now."

She stared at him, her face so white it reminded him of the stationery he'd used to write Laurie during the War. After a long moment she gave a short nod.

"It is all right, Mr. Carver. I would not want their father's grave disturbed by animals."

He wondered why she put it that way, "their father's grave." Why was it not "my husband's grave"? All at once he realized that the girls were not *her* daughters; they had been *his*.

He glanced up at the smallest girl. "Ruthie?"

"It's all right, mister. Papa's in heaven anyway."

His heart thumped. Oh, God, what had he done? He'd shot a horse thief, but the man had been a father. A husband. No horse was worth that, not even his black Arabian.

What the hell had the man intended to do with his horse? Where was he heading? And why?

He clenched his jaw, then climbed back up onto the box and picked up the reins. No matter what he did to make amends, Jenna Borland would get rid of him the first chance she got.

Chapter Three

Tess spoke not a single word to anyone all morning, and when the sun burned high over their heads, she refused to offer Mr. Carver even a tin cup of water.

Ruthie's nose and cheeks got sunburned, despite her floppy calico sunbonnet, and halfway through the long morning her tired little body had tipped sideways against the upright frame of Mr. Carver. To keep her from toppling off the bench, he curled his arm around her and went on driving the oxen, the reins looped over his long-fingered hands.

Jenna pressed her lips together and brought him a cup of water from the water barrel lashed to the wagon.

By the time the train stopped for their nooning, Jenna was half-sick from the heat and dust. She had walked beside the rank-smelling oxen for hours after Mary Grace had given up and crawled into the wagon bed, and when the train pulled into a shady grove of ash trees, every muscle in her legs was trembling.

She rested for an hour in the cool shade, letting the breeze dry out her sweat-sticky cotton dress and soothe her overheated body. Then she packed away the lunch makings and when the train was ready to pull out again, she resumed her position beside the wagon. She stiffened when she saw Mr. Carver approaching.

"Mrs. Borland, if you think you could drive the oxen, I'll walk. I can keep one hand on Sunflower's yoke just to make sure she—"

"No," Jenna interrupted. "I don't like those two animals. Horses, too, if you must know. I would rather you drive the wagon."

"Wouldn't you rather rest inside the wagon instead of walking, ma'am?"

"Again, no thank you. The girls will be inside and they… Besides, it's stifling in there. I don't know how they can bear it."

He chuckled. "I wouldn't even ask, if I were you. Mary Grace and Tess, isn't it? The older one would rather bake like a biscuit than look at me."

Jenna blew out a weary sigh. "I'm sure part of it is because of their father, but the rest is because… Well, I don't pretend to understand them."

He regarded her with a flicker of emotion in his eyes. "Could be they resent having a stepmother."

"When Mathias was alive, the girls tolerated me, up to a point. Now that he's gone, they can't bear to be near me. Except for Ruthie, that is."

Why was she telling him this? She'd never confessed to anyone how Mathias's daughters treated her, not even to Emma Lincoln. Perhaps the midday heat was softening her brain.

"I'd think not being their mother would be difficult."

"Are you married, Mr. Carver?" Too late she realized how rude the question sounded. If he had a wife, surely she would be traveling west with him.

A veil dropped over his gray eyes. "I was married once," he said, his voice quiet. He said nothing more, and Jenna knew she couldn't ask. But she did wonder about him.

Near sundown, a shouted command from Sam brought

the wagons into a wide circle, and men began unhitching their tired animals and leading them into the grassy area in the center to feed. Forage was lush, and there was plenty of water from a tumbling creek. The mules and oxen gulped greedily. Jenna longed to splash some over her face and arms, but first she had to make supper.

A grumbling Tess lugged two brimming buckets of water and plunked them at Jenna's feet so hard they slopped over onto her leather shoes. Biting her tongue, Jenna stepped around the lanky girl and enlisted Mary Grace to help her drag three flat rocks together to make a crude fireplace. She sent Tess and Ruthie for kindling and firewood—buffalo chips, if they couldn't find any downed tree branches.

When the fire was crackling, Jenna settled the iron kettle on the rocks and began slicing up potatoes and wild onions and dried venison. For seasoning she added a generous dash of salt and the last of the dried rosemary. Then she mixed up plain flour and water biscuits and patted circles of dough onto the hot rocks to brown while the stew bubbled. The smell was mouthwatering.

She kept a wary eye on the black stallion, still roped to the wagon, and wondered why Mr. Carver didn't release him to graze with the other animals. She found out when he strode into camp, scooped out a double handful of oats from a burlap bag tied to his saddle and offered it to the horse in his cupped hands. He talked to the animal in low tones while it ate.

Jenna shook her head. *Mercy, he treats that animal like it was almost human!*

Men. Back in Roseville, Mathias had once adopted a mongrel dog. He'd fussed over it plenty, but he'd never hand-fed the mutt. Jenna had hated it because it nipped at Ruthie's bare toes. When they joined the emigrant train, Mathias had left the dog behind to fend for itself. Even Jenna had wept.

"Mary Grace, would you please tell Mr. Carver supper is ready?"

"I'd rather let him starve," the girl announced. Her hazel eyes flashed with anger.

Jenna dropped the iron ladle into the stew and spun to face her middle stepdaughter. "I can understand how you feel, Mary Grace, but the man has driven our wagon all day in the hot sun while you and your sister lazed inside. It would not be kind to refuse him food. He has certainly earned it."

"You tell him, then!"

"I am busy with supper." She worked to keep the annoyance out of her tone, but from the rebellious look on the girl's round face she knew she hadn't been successful. She laid her free hand on Mary Grace's plump shoulder, but she jerked away.

"I know you do not like Mr. Carver, Mary Grace, but do as I ask. Now," she added. "Unless you don't wish to eat supper." She leveled the threat calmly, but she'd had enough. Putting up with hateful treatment took energy, and her strength was just about depleted.

Mary Grace threw her a dark look and stomped off to where Mr. Carver stood brushing the stallion's hide.

"Why do we have to be nice to him?" Tess demanded from behind her.

"Because." Jenna sighed. "Feeding your enemies is the Christian thing to do."

"Huh!" Tess clattered the tin plates and cups onto an upturned apple crate. "I hope he chokes on it."

"Hush, now. Here he comes."

Ruthie danced up from washing up in the creek, her face and hands still dripping. "We're having ven'son stew, mister." She blotted her wet cheeks with the sleeve of her dress.

"Smells good," Mr. Carver said. "I've been eating hardtack for so long I forgot how good real food smells."

"What's hardtack?" Ruthie asked.

"Kind of a thick dry cracker."

"What's it taste like? Is it good?"

"Not too good. It tastes a little like sawdust, I guess. Mostly you just roll it around in your mouth until it softens up, then you swallow it quick."

Jenna ladled the thick stew onto the plates. "Pass the biscuits around, please, Tess." She tipped her head toward Mr. Carver.

To Jenna's embarrassment, Tess pointedly bypassed him and instead scooped biscuits from the crockery bowl onto her sisters' plates.

"Tess." Jenna kept her voice calm but inside she was seething. "If you would honor your father's memory, you will behave as he would want you to. And now, because he is gone, you will behave as *I* want you to."

Mr. Carver solved the problem by standing up and reaching a long tanned arm for the bowl. Then he settled back on the ground, dropped the biscuit into his stew and mashed it up with his spoon. Jenna hid a grin. Tess's rudeness didn't seem to matter one whit.

She set a bucket of water onto the coals to heat for washing dishes and ate her supper in silence. When she had downed her last bite, she licked the spoon, laid it on the tin plate and handed it to Mary Grace.

"Would you rather wash the dishes tonight or roll out the bedding in the wagon?"

"Dishes," she said with a grimace. "Let Tess make up the beds."

Jenna nodded. Tired as she was, she tried to smile at the girl. "Ruthie, your cheeks are sunburned. I'll put some ointment on before bedtime."

"Where's Mister gonna sleep, Jenna?"

Ruthie's question stopped her cold on the way to the wagon for the medicine kit. Yes, where *would* he sleep? Up until tonight, she and Mathias had slept together under the wagon, but now what?

Out of the corner of her eye she caught Mr. Carver studying her. Would he sleep in their camp? Under the wagon, where she slept? Absolutely not. She must speak to the wagon master right away.

"Girls, I'm going over to talk to Sam Lincoln." She pressed the bottle of ointment into Ruthie's small hand and untied her apron.

"Can I come with you?" Ruthie begged. "Missus Emma gives me cookies."

"Not this time, honey. I have some…business to discuss with Mr. Lincoln. You stay in camp and help Tess make up the beds."

Mr. Carver rose and stood looking at her, his hands on his slim, jean-clad hips. The back of her neck grew hot, so she turned away from him and marched out of camp.

"Mister?" Ruthie gazed up at Lee with a question in her sky-colored gaze. "How come nobody likes you?"

Son of a gun. Even a child sensed the resentment against him. It wasn't just the Borland family; everyone in the entire emigrant train had avoided him since the day he joined them at Fort Kearney. The thick hatred in the air because of his Confederate service followed him everywhere, and now, after killing Mathias Borland for stealing his horse, the heavy fog of dislike felt suffocating.

He knelt down to Ruthie's level. "There's lots of reasons they don't like me, I guess. For one, I'm a Southerner. A Confederate."

What's a 'Federate? Is it bad?"

Lee exhaled and thought how best to answer her. "A Confederate is someone who thought it was worth a fight to keep their way of life. I'm from Virginia, and that's a Confederate state. Or it was, anyway."

"Did you fight?"

"Yes, I did." He'd fought alongside Bobby Lee, not because he thought slavery was right, but because he loved the South and his heritage. General Lee had felt the same.

"Did you win?"

"Nobody wins in a war, Ruthie. It's a bloody, senseless way to solve a disagreement. The North won. That's your side. But soldiers I commanded probably killed some of their kin, and that's why nobody on this train likes me much."

"Did you ask 'em to kill those people?"

Lee shut his eyes briefly. "Yes, I did. That's what soldiers do, and I was a soldier. Was your daddy a soldier?"

"Nope. Papa didn't like fighting. He was a..." Her voice faltered. "A..."

"A Quaker, maybe?"

"Nope. Tess says he didn't want to go off to war an' leave us."

Lee sensed there was more to it than that. There was something odd about this family, and he sensed it was more than just the loss of their father. The girls resented Jenna, that much was clear. Maybe because she was going to bear a child? Or maybe because Jenna had replaced the girls' real mother.

What little he'd seen of Mathias Borland made him wonder why Jenna had married the man. What was she, twenty-three? Twenty-four? She was too pretty not to have had other offers, plenty of them. Why would she choose a blustering loudmouth like Borland? Unless she was pregnant and he had been her only option.

Ruthie held up a dark bottle of something. "Would you put this on my face? It's stuff Jenna made to help my sunburn."

"Wouldn't you rather wait for Jenna? Or maybe get one of your sisters to do it?"

"Nope. Mary Grace pinches, and Tess pulls my hair."

Lee accepted the bottle and peered at the hand-lettered label. Aloe ointment. He uncorked it, took a sniff and wrin-

kled his nose. "Smells like turpentine." He tipped it over
and let the thick liquid ooze out onto his forefinger.

"What's turp'tine?"

"Smelly stuff. Turpentine is what they use to clean
things that are oily."

Ruthie tipped her face back and closed her eyes. "I'm
ready for the bad smell, mister. Do it now."

He had to laugh. His sister, Serena, had gotten sunburned once. Hattie had doctored her with baking soda,
and that night she had sneaked into his room and asked
him to wash it off because it smelled funny.

He tilted Ruthie's chin up with one finger and smeared
a thin film of the ointment over her nose and cheeks.

"What's your real name, mister?"

"My name is Robert E. Lee Carver. Why don't you call
me Lee? It's shorter than 'mister.'"

Being named after General Lee was probably one more
reason why people on the train disliked him. Long before
he became a general, Bobby Lee had been a close friend
of his father's.

He recorked the medicine bottle and stood up. "Show
me where Jenna keeps this and I'll put it away."

"In the med'cine box. Inside the wagon."

Lee frowned. "Then you'd better do it. Your sisters don't
like me being anywhere near your wagon."

"What's your horse's name? Is it a boy horse or a girl
horse?"

"His name is Devil. He's a boy horse. They're called
stallions."

"He's real pretty."

He watched the girl clamber up into the wagon and dis-
appear through the bonnet, then started off to check on Sue
and Sunflower grazing in the roped-off infield.

The instant he was out of sight, Ruthie emerged, climbed

down onto the ground and headed straight for the big black horse tied up at the corner of the wagon.

"Why, Jenna," Emma Lincoln exclaimed. "How are you doing?" She gestured at the fire pit behind her, where a blue speckleware coffeepot steamed. "Do sit and have some coffee with us."

"No, thank you, Emma. That is kind of you, but I have come to speak with Sam."

The large, graying man rose from his seat by the campfire and came toward her. "How's your driver working out?"

"I— Well, that's just it, Sam. I came to ask you—"

"I bet I can guess. The girls don't like him."

"Well, no, they don't. Except for Ruthie, and she loves everyone. But—"

"And you don't like him."

"No, I don't."

"Is he rude? Or mean to the girls or you?"

"Well, no."

"Talk too much? Spit tobacco juice? Smoke too many cigarettes? Drink spirits?"

"N-no. It's that he—"

"Shot your husband."

Jenna nodded. "It is difficult to be around him. The girls hate him, and I…well, I don't hate him, exactly. But, well, he *did* kill Mathias."

Sam Lincoln pressed her down onto his vacated seat and squatted in front of her. "You're right, he did kill Mathias. Mathias was stealing his horse. Now, let me say something on Carver's behalf."

Jenna twisted her head away. She didn't want to hear anything Sam had to say; she just wanted Lee Carver off her wagon and as far away from her as he could get.

"Carver's a good man. Stepped right up and asked to make it right with you and yours by driving your wagon on to Oregon. He didn't have to do that. Nobody holds Carver to account for shooting Mathias. It's the risk any horse thief takes."

"But I can't abide…"

"You don't have to like him, Jenna. Fact is, nobody on this train likes him much. He's a Virginian and a Johnny Reb, a Confederate major."

Jenna stared into the fire. "He's the only Confederate soldier on the train. And that horse of his! Did you know he hand-feeds the animal? With oats that I could use to make mush."

"That horse is pure Arabian, worth about a thousand dollars. Carver plans to breed horses for the army. The *Union* army," he added. "Ever since the surrender, Carver's been with our army, fighting the Sioux."

"Oh."

Sam laid a gentle hand on her hunched shoulder. "Anything else botherin' you?"

"Sam, is there no one else who would volunteer to drive our wagon?"

Sam shook his head. "I trust Lee Carver. Might be a Reb, but like I say, he's a good man. There's some on this train that aren't so good. Some I wouldn't trust around you and three young girls. You take my meaning?"

Jenna nodded. Once again she felt helpless, caught at the mercy of a man she didn't know but had to accept.

"You have any trouble, Jenna, you come to me, agreed?"

She bit her lip. Emma stood near the fire, pouring coffee into a ceramic mug. The older woman looked inquiringly at her. It did smell rich and enticing, but Jenna shook her head. She had duties back at her own camp.

Jenna knew that Lee Carver had been a Confederate soldier, as Emma had said. Well, she didn't admire him for that. The South favored slavery, and her father had died opposing it. Besides, she just plain didn't like the man.

She should have asked Sam how far they were from

Oregon, how long she would have to put up with Lee Carver. Months, probably. *Oh, Mathias, I wish...*

No, she acknowledged, she did not wish him back. Not even with the baby coming. The man she had married in such desperate haste back in Roseville had turned out to be no bargain. But now she was stuck traveling in that tiny, cramped wagon with all their earthly goods crammed in among sacks of flour and sides of bacon with the man who...

She folded her hands over the slight swell of her belly and stared at the thick grass under her feet. It was difficult before; it would be intolerable with Mr. Carver. Perhaps...

She raised her head and rounded the corner of the wagon just in time to see Ruthie bounce up beside that huge black stallion and reach out to pat its side. Then she stepped backward, toward the animal's hind legs.

With a gasp Jenna started forward, and in that same instant she heard a shout.

"Ruthie!" Out of nowhere Lee Carver appeared, running hard. He snatched the girl up into his arms and barreled straight into Jenna, who was racing from the opposite direction.

Chapter Four

Lee managed to keep his body underneath Ruthie as he fell, but he knocked Jenna sideways and felt his elbow connect with her cheek. He lay still, catching his breath, while Ruthie clung to his chest, her small head just under his chin.

"Ruthie?" he rasped. "Ruthie, are you all right?"

Her head moved in a nod, and her small voice answered. "I wanted to pet the horse."

Jenna picked herself up off the ground and flew at him, batting his hands away from Ruthie. "You fool!" she screamed. "She might have been killed!"

A red mark bloomed on her cheek where his elbow had clipped her. He sat up slowly, feeling a muscle pull in his shoulder. "It's my fault," he shouted. "I'm sorry. I'm thankful Devil didn't kick her."

"That horse is dangerous! I don't want it anywhere near our wagon."

Lee got to his knees before realizing he must have hit his head on the wagon wheel when he went down. He was so dizzy he felt like vomiting. He rocked back onto his heels and put his head between his knees while Jenna paced around him like a stalking cougar.

"Get rid of that animal," she ordered. "Now. Tonight."

He shook his head to clear it and she gave a little screech. "Did you hear me? I said—"

"I heard you. Stop yelling for a minute and listen."

"Listen! What can you possibly say that will…" Her voice was unsteady. Oh, hell, she was going to cry. He tensed, waiting for the tears.

But she surprised him. She spent the next five minutes calling him names and maligning his horse, and he let her get it all out of her system. But no tears. She was tougher than she looked.

When she began to run down, he got to his feet and stuck his face in front of hers. "You finished?"

She stared at him in mutinous silence. She had eyes that were an odd shade of green, like moss. And her mouth, when she shut it, looked soft and as rosy as ripe raspberries. He hadn't been this close to a pretty woman in over a year, and funny things were happening in his belly.

"That horse," he said quietly, "stays where I can see him, and that means he goes where I go. He stays tied up to the wagon until we get to Oregon."

"I won't allow it."

"If you want me to drive your wagon, you don't have a choice. I'll talk to your daughters about staying safe around him."

She glared at him. Ruthie sidled toward him, and then he became aware of two wide-eyed faces peeking out from the back of the wagon.

"Come on down, you two," he ordered. "I need to talk to you." While they climbed down, he knelt before Ruthie.

"Honey, listen. A horse doesn't understand little girls. When you get close to his hind legs, he thinks you're going to hurt him and he'll kick you."

Ruthie nodded, but she wouldn't look at him. Tess and Mary Grace moved to stand on either side of their sister. He noted that they gave Jenna a wide berth.

"Now," he continued with a glance to include the older

girls, "if you want to pet a horse, you first look him in the eye and talk to him. Keep your voice low and don't make any sudden moves. Then you can lay your hand on his neck. But you don't do any of this unless I'm around."

"What do you say to him?" Ruthie whispered.

Tess gave an unladylike snort. "You say 'how do you do,' I suppose. The whole idea is preposterous."

"No, it's not 'posterous," Ruthie protested. "I want to know."

Tess sniffed. "That just shows how stupid you are."

"She's not stupid," Mary Grace interjected. "She's… well, she's not stupid."

"Huh! That's all you know."

"Girls!" Jenna snapped out the word in a tone Lee had never heard her use. "Hush up and listen to Mr. Carver. Since he insists on keeping that animal, you should know how to act around it." Then she shot him a look that would ignite kindling.

Lee stood up. "That includes you, Mrs. Borland. Don't startle the horse by shouting or screaming when you're near him."

She propped both hands on her hips. "I plan never to be near him, Mr. Carver. I dislike horses. And I dislike—" She snapped her jaw shut. "But since I seem to be stuck with your services, I will do as you say."

Her voice was pure frost. He'd guess Sam Lincoln had refused to replace him, and for the first time since he joined the emigrant train he felt a small amount of acceptance. By Sam maybe, but not by Mary Grace or Tess.

And not by Jenna. Jenna was the only one he really cared about, besides Ruthie. Strange, that the little girl accepted him with an almost adult understanding; she didn't care that he was a Virginian or a Confederate soldier.

"Mrs. Borland, would you have any coffee?"

She twitched her skirt. "Of course. I don't drink it at night as it keeps me awake."

"Mind if I brew some up?" He ran two fingers over a lump swelling above one temple. "I have the beginnings of a headache."

She whirled away to the wagon, rummaged around for a moment, then emerged with a small canvas bag of coffee beans and a small wooden coffee mill. "Tess, poke up the fire and fetch the coffeepot, please. I'll go for water." She snatched up one of the buckets and marched off toward the creek.

While she was gone, Lee ground a handful of coffee beans, and Tess unceremoniously clunked the coffeepot onto the fire. He saw Jenna stagger across the field with the heavy bucket and went to lift it out of her hand. Her grudging "thank you" came out cold as an ice chip.

Lee drew in a long breath. Looked like he was in an enemy camp with just one ally, a little girl less than three feet tall. Well, hell, he'd lived through Gettysburg and Appomattox, and he'd lived through the grinding emptiness of his life after Laurie died; he guessed he'd live through this.

Suddenly everyone disappeared into the wagon, even Ruthie. He brewed up his own coffee and sat alone by the fire gulping it down as hot as he could stand it. Anything to remind him that he was alive, even if he wasn't liked or wanted.

The soft murmur of a woman's voice drifted from the wagon. From the measured cadence of the sounds, he guessed Jenna was reading aloud. Poetry, maybe. That must be why Tess knew a word like *preposterous*. Jenna was obviously well-lettered, and apparently she was educating the girls.

After a time her voice stopped, and she climbed out of the wagon and moved into the firelight. She ignored the coffeepot and perched on a wooden crate across the fire pit from him.

"I heard you reading to the girls," he said. "Poetry?"

"Yes. *Idylls of the King.*"

"I admire your sharing your knowledge, even though they resent you."

"I don't want them to grow up ignorant, Mr. Carver. They will also know how to cook and sew and keep house. An ignorant girl in a wild new country like Oregon is asking for trouble."

"Forgive me, Mrs. Borland, but an ignorant girl anywhere is asking for trouble." He watched her back stiffen and waited a good ten heartbeats before he opened his mouth again.

"On another subject," he began, "is it all right with you if I spread out my bedroll under your wagon?"

She didn't answer.

"I sleep with my rifle next to me. Thought you'd like to know you'll be protected at night."

"Yes, I appreciate that."

"You sleep inside the wagon?"

She waited so long to answer he thought maybe she hadn't heard; then he realized where she'd been sleeping up until last night.

"There is not enough room inside for me," she said at last. "I have been sleeping under the wagon."

That stopped his breath. He'd bet a month's pay she didn't know what to do now. He could make it easy for her, volunteer to sleep outside, next to his horse. But something inside rebelled at that. Maybe it wasn't the gentlemanly thing to do, but he wanted to sleep near her. Couldn't say exactly why except that she was damn pretty and she had a nice voice. When she wasn't yelling at him, that was.

Anyway, she was so mad at him she probably wouldn't speak three words to him.

"Suits me," he said quietly. He noticed she wouldn't look at him.

The situation was awkward. Embarrassing. Never in a month of Sundays would Jenna have imagined lying next to a man who was not her husband. Her mother would have apoplexy if she knew.

She decided to sleep in her dress and petticoat, even though with Mathias she had stripped to her chemise and drawers. She arranged her pallet opposite to what she thought his would be, putting her head where she supposed his feet would be.

She did not like Lee Carver. But for some reason she did not fear him. She lay back on her quilt and closed her eyes until his voice startled her.

"Jenna."

Just her name, spoken so low she might have imagined it.

"Yes?"

"Can the girls in the wagon hear us down here?"

"I don't know. Mathias and I never talked at night."

"Listen, then. You know I mean no harm to your family, or to you."

No harm! She wanted to scream the words at him. *You shot my husband. Your horse could have killed Ruthie.*

She watched him spread out his blanket and prop his saddle at his head. He stretched out fully clothed and folded his arms behind his head. His rifle lay between them.

"Is that loaded?"

"Yes, it is. Did your husband not keep a rifle handy?"

"Mathias did not have a rifle."

"Revolver, then."

"He had no revolver, either."

He sat up. "Good God, how did he plan to protect you?"

Jenna swallowed. "He did not think of it. Mathias did not plan ahead."

She had often thought about it after they joined the emigrant train at Independence. Mathias was the only man other than Reverend Fredericks who went unarmed.

"Your older girls should learn how to fire a weapon, Mrs. Borland."

"They will be proper, educated young ladies in Oregon. Why should they know about firearms?"

"It's a long way to Oregon. Their lives might depend on knowing such things."

She edged her body farther to the right, away from his rifle and away from him. Then she realized with a start that they were facing each other. So much for her head-to-foot plan.

"Tomorrow…" His words halted.

"Tomorrow," she said in as matter-of-fact a tone as she could manage, "I will make coffee and breakfast and you will yoke up the oxen and we will move on toward Oregon. We need not even speak to each other."

"Not quite," he said. He shifted his frame, rolled onto his side and propped himself on one elbow. "You can't shut me out like that. You don't have to like me, Jenna, but you do need me."

She sucked in an angry breath. "I do not need you, Mr. Carver. I will never need you."

He laughed softly. "Yes, you do. You need me to teach your daughters about horses. About how to protect themselves in case…in case something happens to you. Or to me."

A dart of fear stabbed into her chest. "What do you mean? What could possibly happen?"

"God! We've got over a thousand miles to go with two aging oxen. Rivers to ford. Four wooden wheels that could break or get mired in quicksand. Dust storms. Dried-up water holes and God only knows if there's enough flour and beans in your wagon to last. Wolves. Indians."

"I am well aware of the dangers. You need not elaborate unless you are trying to frighten me."

"Hell, yes, I'm trying to frighten you!"

"Well, it's working, so please hush up!"

She heard him chuckle, and then he gave a long, drawn-out sigh and settled back on his blanket. After a while his rhythmic breathing told her he was asleep.

She tried to forget his words, but they swarmed and circled in her brain until she wanted to shout them out of her head.

A thousand miles, he'd said. She wanted to weep.

Oh, no she wouldn't! She might be frightened to death at what was ahead, especially now that she alone was responsible for the Borland girls, but she would not let it show. She would cry when they reached Oregon. By then, she supposed, she would be completely unhinged.

And by then she would be a mother.

Oh, God, she couldn't do it. She couldn't do any of it. Why, *why* had she let Mathias talk her into heading across this rough, uninhabited country?

And why, dear God, why had he taken Lee Carver's horse?

Chapter Five

Lee woke before dawn and looked over at the still form that lay next to him. She was curled up on her side like a young girl, her face resting on her folded hands, and a little fluff of white petticoat peeked out beside her drawn-up knees. Her leather shoes sat off to one side, the coarse stockings stuffed inside. He wondered what kept them up after walking all day.

Her eyelids looked shadowed with fatigue and a purpling bruise bloomed on her cheek. Quietly he drew the rumpled quilt up over her sleeping form and crawled out from under the wagon.

Sue and Sunflower grazed peacefully a few yards away. He fed Devil a handful of oats, then tramped down to the creek to wash and shave using his army kit. He hung the mirror on a low branch, but in the half-light he could barely see the dark stubble on his chin.

The air was so still and balmy it reminded him of spring back in Virginia. And it was quiet, a good time for mentally sorting things out. Jenna, for example.

She bothered him. It was more than her sharp words and obvious dislike of him; something about her didn't make sense. Had she really wanted to come west with three stepchildren? Somehow she didn't seem ready for a journey this arduous. Maybe she'd let her husband do the planning, and right about now she might be realizing that had been a mistake.

It made him angry. Made him want to take her by the shoulders and shake her. On another level it made him want to put his arms around her and hold her.

He hadn't held a woman in a long time. Hadn't wanted to.

Until now. The thought of holding Jenna, maybe kissing her, sent hot prickles all over his body, and he had to laugh. *You damn fool, what about your Never Again resolution?*

Yeah, what about that? He'd sworn he'd never let any woman touch his heart again. It had worked just fine until he'd shot Jenna's husband and ended up with her in the middle of a family he hadn't expected.

He rinsed his straight razor and folded it back into his kit, then filled two buckets of water from the creek and lugged them back to camp. He found the coffeepot, rinsed it out and moved away from the wagon to grind the beans so the noise wouldn't wake anyone. An iron skillet waited beside the fire pit, but the bacon, if there was any, would be in the wagon. He'd rather brave a Sioux ambush than tangle with Tess.

Ruthie popped out through the bonnet and he pantomimed slicing meat. After a long minute she produced a small hunk of not-too-lean bacon and watched in silence as he sliced some off with his pocketknife and laid it in the skillet.

Jenna awoke to the smell of coffee. Coffee? The sun was up and her empty stomach was rumbling. She pulled on her shoes and stockings, folded up her bedding and crawled out from under the wagon. The sight that met her eyes made her blink twice.

Lee Carver stood over a skillet of sizzling bacon, but it was Ruthie who was forking over the strips. Steam puffed out the spout of the coffeepot sitting on a flat rock next to the fire. Without a word, Carver sloshed a mug full and presented it to her.

"Thank you," she managed. It was hot and strong and just what she needed as an antidote to her annoyance with the man. Well, it wasn't annoyance, really, she admitted. It was fear, plain and simple. Not of him, necessarily, but…

She hadn't wanted to leave Roseville, where there were streets and board sidewalks and shops. She'd been completely unprepared to find herself with three stepdaughters, two of whom resented her, and a husband who had not cared about her, not really. Mathias had offered marriage simply to gain a mother for his girls. She had not allowed herself time to think too carefully about his offer because she had no choice, really, considering her situation. She had not dared to tell her mother the truth; instead she had unthinkingly agreed to marry Mathias.

"Any biscuits left over from supper?" he asked.

"In the wagon. Ruthie can get them."

Tess yanked open the canvas bonnet, took one look at Mr. Carver and disappeared back inside with a sniff. But Mary Grace climbed out and marched up to Lee.

"When are you gonna show us about your horse?"

"After breakfast."

"Can I ride him?"

"Not until I say so."

Mary Grace propped her hands on her hips. "You are just plain mean!"

"I am sensible," he replied without looking up from the skillet. "People who don't know what they're doing around a horse get themselves killed trying to ride before they're ready."

"You sure are hard to please," she snapped.

"Maybe."

Tess finally descended from the wagon and sent him a black look. Jenna laid out the leftover biscuits on the warm fire-pit rocks, and after a few minutes they gathered to devour them, along with the crisp bacon. Then, while she heated water to wash the tin plates, Lee marched the girls over to his horse and she could hear his low, patient voice giving instructions.

All at once he appeared at her side. "Now you."

"Now me, what?"

"Horse lesson."

Her heart somersaulted into her stomach. "No."

"Yes. Jenna, you have to know how to behave around a horse."

"Not this horse."

"Any horse. How is it you grew up without knowing anything about horses?"

"I grew up in a town back in Ohio. I walked to school and the mercantile and the dressmaker and my music lessons. I had no need of a horse."

"Well, you do now. This isn't Ohio. Come on."

Tess and Mary Grace drifted near and stood watching, waiting to see what she would do. No doubt they relished her discomfort, and the thought made her grit her teeth.

Carver turned his head toward them. "Mary Grace, would you finish washing up the plates? Maybe Tess could help you."

To Jenna's astonishment, both girls advanced toward the bucket of warm soapy water, and Lee muscled her over to confront the stallion.

Lord, the animal was huge! It looked at her with a giant black eye that clearly held a message: *I hate you.* She flinched away.

Lee caught her arm and pulled her back within touching distance, but Jenna put both hands behind her back. "I can't. I just can't."

"Can't what? I haven't asked you to do anything yet."

"If it's about this horse, I can't do it."

He looked sideways at her. "Jenna, you can do this. You're not a coward. You have plenty of backbone."

"I don't care about backbone."

He gave her arm a little shake. "Are you going to give Tess and Mary Grace more ammunition just because you're afraid of this horse?"

"Yes, I guess I am." She thought that prospect over for a moment. Her relationship with Tess and Mary Grace was bad enough already; she would die before she gave them something else to dislike about her.

"No," she blurted out. "I am not!"

"Good girl. We'll take it slow."

She drew in a careful breath. "I am not a girl, Mr. Carver."

"That, Mrs. Borland, is obvious. Now stand here and just talk to the horse. Keep your voice low."

Jenna stared into the big black eye and opened her mouth. Nothing came out.

"Jenna?"

She tried again. "H-hello, horse."

"Devil," he prompted. "His name is Devil."

"That's ridiculous. Surely he doesn't recognize his name?"

"Try it."

She stiffened her back and looked straight at the animal. "Um… Hello, Devil. What a d-dreadful name you have. It's enough to scare anyone who has any sense at all."

Carver laughed. "Good," he said. "Keep going. Tell him who you are."

Jenna shut her eyes. If she lived through the next ten minutes she would put hot pepper in Lee Carver's coffee the first chance she got. She peered again at the big black horse.

"My name is Jenna West—Jenna Borland."

Carver sent her a puzzled glance. Behind him she saw Tess and Mary Grace watching her with avid interest. She squared her shoulders.

"You're doing fine, Jenna. You want to pet his nose?"

"No," she said quickly. "I do not."

He ignored her, took her hand in his and lifted it to the stallion's shiny nose. She tried to jerk away, but he held her fingers firmly under his. His hand, warm and insistent, pressed hers into the animal's smooth skin.

"Let go of me," she whispered.

"No. Just relax. He won't bite you." He kept her hand pinned under his.

"Please, Mr. Carver."

"My name is Lee."

"Lee, please. I am truly afraid. Surely he, I mean Devil, senses that?"

"He won't hurt you if you don't startle him, or yell at him, or hurt him. He's just like a human being. If you mistreat a man, he will strike out."

"Is—is that a warning?"

"About the horse? Yes. About me? No."

"I don't believe you."

He grinned suddenly. "I know you don't."

She could not think of one single thing to say. She just stood there with her hand captured under his and her heart fluttering like a frightened bird.

And then he bent toward her and whispered in her ear.

Chapter Six

Jenna jerked away from Lee so fast he thought something had bitten her. "What? How dare you say something like that to me!"

The truth was he didn't know how he dared. First off, she was carrying another man's child. And second, after his wife died he'd sworn never again to think twice about any woman. But Jenna wasn't just "any woman." All he knew was that even after a day under the broiling sun and a night sleeping in all her clothes without even a spit bath, Jenna Borland smelled good, like something flowery.

So he told her so.

"You," she said, her blue-green eyes accusing, "smell like a horse. A smoky, bacon-y horse. A…sweaty horse."

He laughed aloud. "That's because I've been working around the oxen and frying bacon over a campfire and haven't taken a bath in a while."

"I must pack up the breakfast things," she said quickly.

"Get Tess and Mary Grace to pack up. I want you to watch how I yoke up the oxen."

She knew better than to argue, because she walked with him into the center area where the animals were grazing and watched in silence while he drove Sue and Sunflower to the wagon and wrestled the harnesses and the wooden yoke into position.

"Slide the hoop under the yoke, like this," he instructed as he worked. "Then attach it to the tongue, here. Next, put a lead rope through the nose ring, see? Be sure not to tangle those lines there."

Jenna nodded. She stared at the two animals. Hour after hour, day after day, they plodded patiently along the wheel-rutted trail, hauling their wagon loaded with everything they owned.

Some days she'd felt just like those two oxen, as if she were pulling a crushing weight with no respite, with no encouragement from Mathias or from the girls, working until her back ached and her hands were chapped and her nose sunburned.

Lee sent her a swift look. "Think you could manage this if you had to?"

"You wouldn't force me to, would you? As you did with your horse?"

He shook his head and bent toward her. "Just look over yonder at Tess and Mary Grace," he intoned.

Both girls stood transfixed at the sight of Jenna scratching behind Sunflower's ear. At least she assumed that's what they were staring at. Or perhaps her petticoat had come unsnapped, or her drawers…

But no. The instant the traces were attached, both girls lost interest. It wasn't *her* they watched; it was the oxen. And Lee Carver.

Lee offered to show her how to drive the wagon, but after the horse, she couldn't face another challenge. The man made her nervous; he asked things of her she wasn't ready for.

He climbed up onto the driver's bench and looked at her expectantly. She didn't want to sit next to him, even with Ruthie between them. Maybe it was the way he smelled.

But you like his smell. Admit it. Mathias never smelled

like anything except, well, hair oil and strong spirits. Imagine, dousing oneself with hair oil on an emigrant train. There were some things about Mathias she had never understood.

One by one the wagons rolled into a long, ragged line, and the day's journey began. Mary Grace and Tess walked on the side of the wagon opposite Jenna, occasionally stopping to pick wildflowers or collect buffalo chips in their aprons.

The route skirted the south fork of the Platte River. Lee said they would have to ford it ten miles farther on.

But after their nooning, the sky darkened and it began to rain. At first it felt refreshing. Tess and Mary Grace yanked off their poke bonnets and turned their faces up into it, but then the sky opened up and fat drops pelted down. Ten minutes later both girls were soaking wet and took shelter inside the wagon.

Lee dragged his rain poncho out of his saddlebag and sheltered Ruthie underneath it. She insisted on riding on the box with him, but Jenna gave herself up to the cleansing downpour, unbraided her thick, dark hair and let the rain wash through the dark strands. Then she shook the dust out of her skirt and held it out so the water soaked through it. If only she dared, she would strip off her dress and let the downpour cleanse her body, but when she saw Lee watching her, she gave up the idea and dropped back to the rear of the wagon.

"Tess? Mary Grace? Come on out! The water isn't cold, and it feels wonderfully refreshing."

Silence.

Mathias's daughters had no sense of adventure. Well, why should they? Mathias himself had had little sense of adventure. Then why had he insisted they travel to Oregon?

"Jenna!" Lee yelled over the rumble of thunder. "Climb up here under the poncho."

She shook her head, feeling the wind slap wet tendrils

of hair across her face. "No," she called. "I like the rain. It's like taking a bath!"

He slowed the oxen. "There may be lightning," he shouted. "Don't get caught in the open."

She nodded, then stretched out both arms and turned lazy circles in the wet. A jagged bolt of blinding white lightning cracked across the black sky, and she bolted for the wagon. Lee pulled to a stop and reached his hand down to her. She climbed up and took Ruthie on her lap, and he draped his poncho over them both.

Water sluiced off the wide brim of his hat. Jenna reached out and tugged it lower on his face, but he brushed it back with an impatient gesture. "I have to see," he yelled. She nodded, but he didn't turn away. Instead he stared at her for a good half minute.

Goodness, she must look a sight!

Finally he refocused his gaze on the muddy trail ahead, an odd smile playing about his mouth. Well! He'd look messy, too, if he was as wet as she was.

An hour passed, then another, and the oxen kept lumbering forward. Then Sam Lincoln rode up on his bay mare and signaled to Lee.

"River's dead ahead," he shouted. "Hurry it up. With this much rain there might be a flash flood."

"Can't," Lee yelled back. "Oxen can only go so fast."

Sam frowned and rode off toward the Zaberskie wagon.

When the wagons drew up along the riverbank, Lee heaved out a long sigh. "Flooding" was an understatement. Muddy brown water rushed past, swelling what had been a series of shallow rivulets and sandbars into a wide, slow-moving sea. He pulled the oxen to a halt and studied the situation until Sam reappeared.

"The rest of the men feel it's worth a try to ford now, before it gets any worse. What do you think?"

"No," Lee said. "Too risky."

Sam rode off again, returning within a quarter of an hour. "We're going across. Yours will be the last wagon over."

It was midafternoon before all the wagons but theirs had lumbered across the swollen river, and then the rain-bedraggled wagon master returned one last time. "Hurry it up, Lee," Sam yelled over the roaring water.

Lee clamped his teeth together. "I'll take the girls and Jenna over on horseback first. Then I'll drive the wagon across."

Sam nodded and was gone.

"Jenna, get the girls dressed in warm clothes. You, too. It can get cold in the middle of a river."

She climbed down and reached up for Ruthie. When they disappeared into the wagon, he wrapped the leather reins around the brake handle and dropped to the ground to untie Devil and throw on a harness and bridle.

"I'll take Tess across first," he announced to Jenna. "Then I'll come back for Ruthie and Mary Grace."

The rain-soaked girls nodded, biting their lips. Mary Grace began to whimper.

"Hush up," Tess snapped. "It's just water. Besides, I'm going first."

"Tess, I want you to catch your dress up between your legs, like a split riding skirt," Lee instructed. When she was ready, he lifted her onto Devil's broad, wet back and swung up behind her. Then he walked the horse to the riverbank, now shelving off under the onslaught of rain, wrapped an arm around Tess's middle and turned the animal into the water.

"Hold on to his mane," he shouted. "Dig your fingers in deep."

The current sucked at them, swirled up around his boots. He kicked Devil hard and they lurched forward. Tess was trembling, but she kept a death grip on Devil's thick mane. He put his face near her ear. "Don't let go, no matter what."

Her head tipped down in a nod, and the next thing he

knew Devil stepped into a rampaging freshet up to his belly. Tess yelped.

"Hold on!" he shouted.

Water flooded up to the girl's knees, then her thighs, but she didn't let go. Ahead of him Lee saw the other wagons lined up on the opposite bank.

The horse started to swim but was swept downstream a hundred yards. Sam Lincoln and another man rode along the bank, keeping pace with Devil as he struggled through the raging water.

At last Lee felt the stallion's hooves hit solid ground and he dug his heels into the animal's sides. The bank was a slurry of mud, slippery as molasses. Twice the horse tried to heave its body up onto dry land, and twice he floundered.

Tess began to gulp noisy sobs. On the third try, Devil lurched up onto the bank, and Sam and someone else, Ted Zaberskie, standing ankle-deep in mud, reached to grab Tess. She tumbled off into Sam's arms.

"Wait!" Sam shouted to him. "Lee, don't go back across."

Lee shook his head. "Jenna and the young ones are back there, plus the wagon." He reined back into the river without looking back.

The return trip was easier. He mounted Ruthie tight against him, then snugged Mary Grace in front and wrapped his arms around them both. Jenna gave the two girls a wobbly smile and stood back, her arms clasped across her waist, to watch them go. Her face was white with fear, and suddenly Lee wanted to kiss her. Instead, he started back across the river.

This time the river seemed less wild, or maybe he was just getting used to it. Mary Grace cried all the way across, but Ruthie maintained a stoic calm until they reached Sam and Zaberskie on the other side. Sam lifted Mary Grace off the horse and slogged up to where Tess stood, wringing her hands; Ruthie threw her little arms around Ted Zaberskie's neck and wouldn't let go.

The downpour increased. Hell, if the river rose any higher, the wagon would never make it. He swam the stallion back across to Jenna, who stood with the rain pounding down on her head and shoulders, calling something up to him.

"Wagon!"

"No," he shouted. "You next."

She pointed to herself, then cupped her hands and yelled back. "Go with wagon. You drive. Devil swim across."

That was one smart woman, he thought. She was right. If he didn't get the wagon across now, they would be stranded on this side with no shelter and no food.

He dismounted and slapped Devil's rump, hard. The animal trotted down the bank and splashed into the river; with a knot in his gut, Lee watched him start to swim.

He couldn't afford to lose that horse. But right now he had other things to worry about. He grabbed Jenna around the waist, pushed her up onto the driver's box and climbed up after her. While she covered them both with his rain poncho, he unwound the reins and flapped them over the oxen.

Jenna slipped one arm around his middle, and he had to laugh. Did she think she could keep him from floating off the box? He shook the traces, and then they were rattling down the bank into the rain-swollen water.

Almost immediately the wagon hit deep water and started to lift off the bottom. Still, Sue and Sunflower plowed inexorably forward until they were chest-high in muddy river water.

Jenna's arm tightened around him. It would feel great if he had time to relish the moment. But he didn't.

Ahead of them he watched Devil's dark neck drifting downriver.

"Got a whip?" he shouted.

She shook her head.

Well, hell. He needed something to urge the team on, a

stick, a goad, anything. Should have thought to cut some willow switches. He yanked off his hat and swatted at their broad rumps, letting loose with some swearwords he hadn't realized he knew.

And then the current caught them broadside and swept the wagon downriver.

Chapter Seven

The wagon slewed sideways, and Jenna bit back a scream. A surge of terror rolled through her. The weight pulled the oxen off balance, and no matter how much Lee shouted and slapped at them with his sodden hat, the animals had to struggle to keep their footing.

Suddenly he ripped off the poncho and slapped the thick leather reins into her hands. "Hold them tight," he yelled.

He jumped down off the box into the river and fought his way through waist-deep water until he reached the oxen. He gripped the side of Sue's wooden yoke and half pushed, half pulled the animal toward the riverbank.

The reins jerked and bucked in Jenna's hands, but she resolved she would not let go. With Lee urging them on, Sue and Sunflower stumbled forward to a place where the bank flattened out and the exhausted animals heaved their heavy bodies up onto level land. The wagon splashed up behind them and ground to a stop just as Sam stepped forward to grip the harnesses.

Inexplicably Jenna thought of the flour barrel. Had it gotten wet? Was their bedding dry? She sat with her head down, unable to move, until she heard a voice at her side.

"You can let go now, Jenna." Lee reached up and pried her fingers off the reins. Shaking, she inched across the driver's box and put one foot on the iron step. Her knees turned to mush. She grabbed for the brake handle, then felt strong arms scoop her up.

At that moment the sun broke through. Rainbows arched in the distance, beautiful wide bands of color shimmering through the mist. Lee set her down in front of Emma Lincoln, who handed her a tin cup of something. "Drink it up, dearie. You earned it."

Jenna gulped down a swallow and choked as something fiery slid past her throat. "Whiskey," the older woman explained. "Warms your cockles."

It certainly warmed something. After two more gulps she decided she liked the effect.

"The girls are drying off in our wagon, Jenna. Sam says as soon as you're rested we'll continue on for another hour and make camp early." As she spoke, Sam stepped forward and settled his large hand on her shoulder.

"Lucky day for you, I'd say. That Virginian's got sand, all right."

"Sand?"

"You know, grit. Courage. Smarts, too. Good man, like I said." He gave Jenna's shoulder a fatherly pat and moved away.

They *were* lucky, she acknowledged. She glanced back at the wagon. Under the sun's rays, steam rose from the canvas covering. She still wore Lee's rain poncho and it, too, began to steam.

Lee collected his horse from Sam and stood scratching the animal's ear and talking to him. Then he tied him to the wagon and swung up onto the driver's box. Jenna set the cup of whiskey on the bench and climbed up beside him. She lifted the poncho over her head and spread it out over her knees to dry.

Lee looked pointedly at the tin cup. "You all right?" Without a word she offered him what was left. He kept his gray eyes on her and emptied the cup in one gulp.

"Didn't know you drank, Mrs. Borland."

"I didn't know you had such a…colorful vocabulary, Mr. Carver. You have names for Sue and Sunflower I've never heard before."

"Made your ears burn, I'll wager."

"And my eyes and my nose and everything else. Where did you learn such words?"

"In the War."

After a short rest, the wagons once more began to roll along the now-muddy trail. Sue and Sunflower stepped sure-footedly over the slippery tracks ahead of them as if the day had not been the least unusual. For a split second Jenna envied them. Nothing seemed to bother them. They had no worries, really; all they had to do was follow orders and trust that the driver knew what he—or she—was doing.

An hour later the wagon master called a halt. Jenna climbed into the wagon bed and checked over everything— food barrels, bedding, even the canvas sacks of beans and cornmeal. Amazingly, everything was dry except for Ruthie's yellow poke bonnet, which had fallen onto the wet floor. Jenna laid it outside in the fading sun to dry.

Evening fell. The air smelled sweet and fresh until smoke from the campfires drifted into a gray haze. Emma and Sam invited the girls to take supper with them, and all at once Jenna realized she was alone with Lee. She studied his tall form as he stood brushing his horse and drying off the saddle he stored in the rope rigging underneath the wagon.

He would expect her to cook something. Pancakes, that was it. Rolled up, with blackberry jelly, if she could unearth the jar from inside the wagon. And coffee. Nothing could keep her awake tonight; she was so tired she ached all over.

Lee brought water from the stream, poured some into a bowl for Devil and dipped enough into the coffeepot to half fill it, then set the bucket near the rock fireplace he had cobbled together. He had not spoken one word.

After all that yelling and swearing in the river, it was strange he was so quiet in camp. He sat on the sturdy apple crate they used for a chair, whittling on something with his pocketknife, saying nothing, while she stirred up the pancake batter and clanked the skillet over the fire.

They ate their supper in complete silence, and after a time Jenna's nerves were stretched so thin she fancied she could hear them humming inside her head. They had just been through a horrifying experience. Why did he say nothing about it?

Finally she couldn't stand it one more minute. "I'm going for a walk," she announced.

"No, you're not," he said, his gaze on the block of wood in his hands.

"Don't tell me what I can and cannot do. Why shouldn't I go for a walk?"

"Because my horse is twitchy tonight, and when he gets that way there's usually something afoot."

"What kind of something?"

"Coyotes, maybe."

"I may be afraid of horses, but I am not afraid of coyotes." She moved past him.

"Or a wolf."

That stopped her cold. "Wolf? There are wolves out here?"

"And renegade Indians."

"Indians!" She stared at him, her heart pounding.

"This is Sioux country."

"Oh." For a long time she stood uncertainly at the edge of camp, twisting her skirt in her hands and pondering what to do. Then Tess and Mary Grace and Ruthie trooped over from the Lincoln's wagon and with no urging whatsoever, all three climbed up into the wagon.

"Are your dresses dry?" Jenna called.

"All dry," came Ruthie's voice. "But my dolly got all wet."

"Are you gonna read some more about King Arthur tonight?" Mary Grace queried. "If you are, hurry up, 'cuz I'm sleepy."

An hour later, Jenna closed the leather-bound book, gathered up her two quilts and crawled under the wagon. A single candle burned next to Lee's discarded boots. She found he had spread his poncho flat to serve as a ground cover and rolled his pallet out on top, and he gestured for her to do the same.

But the poncho wasn't large enough to reach under them both.

"Come closer," Lee said. "After all, there's a loaded rifle between us." His voice sounded tired and his eyes were already closed.

The proposition jarred her, and she had to think it over. For one thing, being that close to him made her uneasy. It was almost harder, now that she was beginning to see the kind of man he was. But no one would know if she did as he suggested. And what if they did?

She removed her shoes and stockings and puffed out the candle flame.

"My mother used to wear stockings like that," he said. "Before the War."

"You were watching me!" she accused.

"Hard not to." He went on as if she hadn't spoken. "After the War, none of our women had stockings."

She floundered for something to say. "My mother was never without proper stockings," she said at last.

"Yeah?"

"Yes. My mother was never without proper anything. She wanted me to be proper, too, but she certainly failed in that."

Why was she telling him this? She never talked about her mother, not even to Mathias. Besides, why would he care? Mama was a Yankee through and through, starched so stiff her spine crackled. Lee Carver was a Confederate, a Virginian, from a slow, genteel life she could scarcely imagine.

Water and oil, that's what she and Lee Carver were. Oh, well, it was only for another thousand miles or so. Then he'd ride off to raise his horses on a ranch somewhere and…

She caught her breath. And she would have her baby. And she would have it in Oregon, in a nice, civilized, safe town.

A town where no one could ever find her.

Chapter Eight

Lee was close to exhaustion, but for some reason he still couldn't sleep. Lying on his pallet under the Borlands' wagon, hours dragged by as he listened to Jenna's soft breathing beside him and the night sounds around the camp. Crickets. An owl in the ash trees at the edge of camp. The rustle inside the wagon when one of the girls rolled over under her blanket.

Sure was an odd family, he thought for the hundredth time, a young woman expecting a baby and two older step-daughters who obviously resented her. But he'd watched the youngest, five-year-old Ruthie, gently pat Jenna's shoulder as if she were the adult and Jenna the child.

He puzzled over it until a new sound drifted to him, a long, mournful cry coming across the far-off plain. Tied to the wagon, Devil gave a muffled whicker; the horse had heard it, too.

He listened for a while, his arms folded behind his head, wondering exactly where the animal was. Then another cry answered, and the first one, now longer and more drawn out, grew more intense.

"Lee?" Jenna whispered beside him. "What is that sound?"

"Wolf," he answered. "Not close, just noisy."

"There are two of them," she said after a moment. "They sound so forlorn."

"Hungry, probably. And lonely."

She was silent, but he could sense her listening in the dark. He hadn't thought about being lonely since the War, but the howling from the hills sure as hell crawled under his skin.

"Are they going to find each other?" she asked.

The question sliced into his brain clean as a razor. "Yeah, they will. Probably going to mate."

He heard her breath suck in. She must be pretty ladified if the word *mate* brought that reaction. Made him wonder even more about her.

"You said your mother was 'proper,'" he ventured. "How come she let you join an emigrant train?"

"She didn't have a choice, really. I mean *I* didn't have a choice. Mama had to let me marry Mathias and join the train."

"How come she let you marry a horse thief in the first place?" He held his breath, expecting an explosion of anger. No woman wanted to hear her husband called a horse thief.

She stayed quiet for a good two minutes while he waited.

"Again, Mama felt she had no choice."

"Your father still alive?"

"No. He was killed in the War. At Antietam."

"Too bad. It's hard on a woman alone. She never re-married?"

"Mr. Carver, you ask far too many questions."

"Maybe. Some might say I don't ask nearly enough."

"Well," she huffed, "I would not be one of them. I thought Southern people, refined people from the state of Virginia, were too polite to probe into others' affairs."

"We are, usually. No law says we can't be curious, though. And we're out here in the West, Mrs. Borland. Not in Virginia. We're in Yankee country, and Yankees, I've observed, are often ill-mannered."

"That is insulting!" Her voice held more than a bit of frost. "Surely you, a supposedly genteel Southerner, recognize bad manners?"

Lee exhaled a long sigh. "I'm less Johnny Reb now than I was a few years back. Maybe now I'm more like your bluecoats. Your husband, for instance."

"You are nothing like my husband," she countered, punching out the words. "Nothing at all."

He laughed quietly. "I'll take that as a compliment, if you don't mind. I didn't like your husband."

"I do mind," she retorted. "You didn't even know my husband."

Lee chose his next words with care. "I knew him enough to see some things."

"What things?" Her tone went from frosty to cold, stinging sleet in sixty seconds.

"For one, he had no business bringing his family on a wagon train with as little preparation as he'd made."

"What do you mean?" Her voice rose. "Mathias prepared for this trip."

"Then I'd have to say he didn't have much experience. And for another thing, looks to me like you're gonna run out of food before you get halfway to Oregon. Your man didn't plan far enough ahead."

Her voice turned to steel. "I'll thank you to shut your mouth, Mr. Carver."

Again he laughed. "You know, whenever you're mad, it's 'Mr. Carver.' And when you're learning something, or scared, it's 'Lee.'"

"I cannot make up my mind about you, *Mr. Carver*." She bit his name out in hard, clearly enunciated syllables.

"You might want to hurry that up a little, *Mrs. Borland*. We're going to be in each other's back pockets for another two months."

That seemed to shut her up. He closed his eyes, listening to her uneven breathing. He knew she wasn't asleep because she kept twitching under her quilt.

The wolves were crooning loud and long by now. Lee let himself listen and thought about Jenna, about what she'd sound like if... Ah, hell. That wasn't any way to get to sleep.

But he couldn't help thinking about it. He smiled up at the shadowy underside of the wagon and closed his eyes.

Odious man. He was laughing at her, and if there was one thing Jenna hated it was being laughed at. Who did he think he was, anyway? She would never last another two months in the company of this man with his outspoken ways and his subtle goading.

The South had lost the War, hadn't it? Mathias always said the Confederate soldiers should have slunk back to their ruined plantations and done some honest work. At the moment she half agreed with him.

On the other hand, some of the things Mathias said, which he'd expressed often and crudely, were things she could not agree with. Now that he was gone, she could try to erase some of the hateful poison he'd spewed into the minds of his daughters. It hadn't all been about her; mostly it was about how worthless other people were. How they owed him something. How he was better than they were.

"Jenna."

"Oh, what is it?" she said sharply. She clamped her jaw shut. At least he hadn't called her "Mrs. Borland."

"I owe you an apology. I had no right to question you in that manner."

"Oh." Instantly her annoyance began to fade, but she couldn't resist one last jab. "Tit for tat, Mr. Carver. The next time we converse it will be *my* turn to pry."

He chuckled. "I will look forward to it, Jenna. Good night."

She debated making a retort until she heard him roll

over on his pallet. "Good night," she said at last. After a long pause, she added, "Lee."

His soft laugh made her grit her teeth. Why, *why* was it that he got under her skin? Tomorrow, when he least expected it, she would find some way to make him squirm. She could hardly wait.

Chapter Nine

Ruthie gazed up at Lee with round blue eyes. "Mister, I heard funny noises last night."

Lee snapped his pocketknife closed. "Noises like what?"

"Like something crying."

"Do you know what a wolf is?"

The girl shook her head. "Tell me 'bout a woof."

"A wolf is like a dog, honey. In fact, a long, long time ago, dogs *were* wolves."

"What happened to them?"

"I guess they grew up. Some of them got to be dogs, and others stayed wild."

"I want one," Ruthie announced. "A big one."

Lee swallowed a smile. "Would you like a new doll instead?" From his shirt pocket he produced the small figure he'd been carving.

Her eyes grew larger. "A dolly? For me?" She reached out her small hand and touched it with one finger. "Is it a boy doll or a girl doll?"

"A girl doll, I think. See, she has on a dress." From the corner of his eye he saw Jenna watching them, her hands propped at her waist. But her eyes looked soft and kind of shiny.

Ruthie flung her arms around his neck and smacked

a kiss onto his stubbly cheek. "Gosh, mister, you're all scratchy."

"Yeah. Guess I'd better shave, huh?"

"Oh, goody. Can I watch?"

Over the girl's blond curls he saw Jenna shake her head.

"Maybe another time," he said. "What will you name your doll?"

"I'm gonna call her Lee."

"What? Lee is a boy's name. *My* name is Lee."

"You're not a boy, mister. You're a man."

At Jenna's burst of laughter he felt a rush of relief. From the moment she rolled out of bed at dawn, she had been glowering at him, all through their breakfast of cornmeal mush, right up to the moment Ruthie had interrupted his wood carving. Didn't take a genius to see Jenna had something stuck in her craw.

He rose, pressed "Lee" into Ruthie's hands and strode off to the creek to shave. As he scraped away at his chin he thought about Tess and Mary Grace and what he had planned for them this morning.

And Jenna. That is, if he could he persuade her to do it.

"Not on your life," Jenna announced an hour later. "No. No. No. Never."

"Listen," he said, his voice oozing patience. "The girls will learn, and that will make your presence out here on the plains a good deal safer."

"I understand that," she said. "But you don't need extra hands for firearms we don't have. We have only your three weapons."

He shook his head. She knew what he was thinking, that Mathias had not taken proper steps to protect his family. In that, perhaps, the Virginian was correct.

She watched him walk Tess and Mary Grace off some fifty yards away from the wagons, nail a scrap of white cloth to a tree stump for a target and direct the girls' attention to his revolver.

With a sniff, Jenna turned back to the fire pit where the kettle of beans sat soaking.

A single gunshot cracked into the quiet, and she looked across the plain to see Tess standing with Lee's Colt gripped in both long-fingered hands. Lee was bending to show her how to reload.

He was right about their need to protect themselves. It was foolish to depend solely on him. What if he fell ill, or was injured? Yesterday he'd risked his life getting their wagon across the Platte River. What if he had lost his footing and drowned?

Another shot sounded. This time it was Mary Grace, whose two-handed grip wobbled with the revolver's weight. She had managed to nick the target, and Jenna felt a surge of admiration for the eleven-year-old's accomplishment. And, she thought grudgingly, for Lee's skill at instruction.

The rifle lesson was next, she gathered from the difference in the sound. She tried not to listen. In an hour, the target practice session drew to a close, and Jenna grew edgy. Lee had insisted on showing her how to yoke up the oxen and touch that precious horse of his. She prayed he would draw the line at handling firearms.

Probably not. Once this man made up his mind about something, he was stubborn about it. Sam said Lee had "sand." Right now, she wished he had a good deal less of it.

"Ruthie," she called into the wagon. "Let's walk down to the stream and take a bath, shall we?"

"Don't want a bath, Jenna."

"Why not?"

"I want to do it with Mister Lee."

Jenna stuffed down a chortle of laughter. "You can't do that, honey. Boys and girls don't bathe together."

Ruthie pushed out her lower lip. "He's not a boy, Jenna. He's a man."

Oh, my. How could she explain the difference? Before she could come up with anything remotely proper, Tess and Mary Grace flitted back into camp.

"Did you see us, Jenna?" Mary Grace chirped. "I hit the target twice. Tess didn't even come close."

"Show-off," Tess muttered. "Who wants to hit a dumb old tree stump?"

"I do!" Mary Grace challenged. "Lee says it's important."

"And it is," his low voice announced behind her. "Now, Jenna…"

She spun to face him. "No."

His dark eyebrows rose. "No what? I haven't asked you anything yet."

"Whatever it is, the answer is no."

He looked at her steadily with crinkles growing in the corners of his gray eyes. "I was going to say that I'm going to take a bath before supper. All right with you?"

"As long as I don't have to—"

His snort of laughter told her he'd read the thought she had squelched. Still chuckling, he strode off toward the stream, his canvas shaving kit dangling from his hand.

"All right, girls," Jenna said when he was out of sight. "Let's find us a private spot and do the same."

Lee hung his shaving mirror over a huckleberry branch and lathered up his chin with the bar of soap he'd extricated from his kit. He finished stropping his razor and had just bent to peer into the mirror when a pair of blue eyes showed in the reflection.

"Ruthie! What are you doing here?"

"Wanted to watch."

"Does Jenna know you're here?"

"Nope. She's takin' a bath."

His blade jerked. "Really?"

"Yes. Tess an' Mary Grace are finished already. Jenna's real slow."

Jupiter! A picture rose in his imagination of Jenna emerging from the stream wearing nothing but her... Wearing nothing. He tried to keep his mind on shaving and his hand steady as he scraped away at his whiskers. Ruthie watched in total absorption, and for that he was grateful. It forced him to pay attention and keep his mind off other things. Like Jenna, all wet and...

He nicked his chin.

When Ruthie scampered off to play with her new doll, Lee tucked his shirt into his jeans, packed up his shaving things and headed back to camp. He was three yards from the creek when he heard a soft splash and a female voice humming a tune. "Polly Wolly Doodle." A damn Yankee song if there ever was one, but it drew him like a magnet.

He walked eight steps past the huckleberry bush and there she was, thigh-deep in the water, with her back to him. Her dark hair tumbled around her shoulders in wild disarray, and water glistened on her skin. His groin tightened. She was too damn beautiful.

And then she turned, and he saw the slight curve of her belly where the baby swelled under her heart.

His fists clenched. She was carrying a child, he reminded himself. Another man's child. He could want her, even ache for her, but he could never have her. She belonged to that unborn child. Not to her husband, the man he had killed, but to a being she could not even see yet. From the moment of conception until she reached Oregon and was finally delivered of her burden, she would belong only to that child.

Jenna Borland needed him only to yoke up her oxen and drive her wagon across the Great Plains and the Rockies to a new life. He didn't belong here, with her. Once again he was the outsider. He and Jenna Borland were in two different worlds, heading toward two completely different lives.

With a groan he acknowledged he was headed straight for another wrenching loss at the end of another long, hard campaign. He wished he'd never laid eyes on her, especially as she was now, naked and singing to herself as she dried the moisture from her hair and that silky-looking body and pulled on her clothes.

When he strode back into camp, Sam Lincoln was waiting for him. The man nodded a greeting, then took a closer look at him.

"Anything wrong, Lee? You look like you've just seen a ghost."

Lee shook his head and waited for the wagon master to continue.

"Ted Zaberskie and the Gumpert boy brought down a deer this afternoon. Thought you might like a share of the meat."

"Sure, Sam. Thanks."

Sam made no move to leave. Instead he kept his gaze on Ruthie and Mary Grace, playing with their dolls in the shade of the wagon. After a long moment the wagon master stepped closer and spoke in an undertone.

"While the men were out hunting, they caught sight of three Indians. Mounted. Too far away to tell what nation, but I thought I ought to warn you."

"Thanks, Sam. I'll keep my eyes open. Don't tell Jenna. If it looks like trouble, she'll—"

"No, she won't, Lee. From what I've seen, that girl isn't the least bit fainthearted."

"I've got two Colt revolvers and a Winchester rifle. Tess and Mary Grace can handle them, so that makes three guns if they're needed."

"Let's pray it won't come to that," Sam growled. He tipped his leather hat and tramped off past the fire pit just as Jenna returned from her bath.

Lee found he couldn't look at her. Even now, he could feel his groin swell, and she was covered in blue gingham from her neck to her ankles.

"I'm going for a walk," he announced.

"No, you're not," she said, her voice quiet.

He stopped short. "You telling me what I can and can't do? Sounds like the conversation we had last night."

She leveled a long look at him, her blue-green eyes challenging. "I wouldn't presume to tell you any such thing, Mr. Carver. It's just that, well, I need your help with something."

"Can it wait?"

"No, it cannot."

Well, damn. He needed to be away from her, not standing around being helpful, so close to her he could smell her hair.

"In the wagon," she said. She gestured toward the curtained opening.

He climbed in after her and she pointed to a large barrel of flour. "Move that over…" she paused, one finger tapping her chin "…over there, behind that sack of cornmeal."

First he had to wrestle the cornmeal away from the curved wooden bow overhead, then shove the flour barrel into the space she indicated.

"No, that won't work," she said when he finished. "Put it back."

Lee clenched his teeth. Without comment he reversed the position of the barrel and the cornmeal sack, but before he could get the flour back in place, he heard her voice.

"No, I don't think that will work," she murmured. "Put the molasses crock over there, by the…" She stopped. "No, over there, in back of the cornmeal but in front of the flour barrel."

He bent to lift the ceramic container, then changed his mind and straightened. "Jenna, why are you moving all this stuff around?"

"To make room, of course."

"Room for what?"

"For me," she said, her tone cool. "From now on I will be sleeping inside the wagon."

Lee surveyed the cramped interior where they stood, crammed with barrels and jars and burlap sacks of sugar and cornmeal, a side of bacon, a carved bureau and what looked like a piano stool, and the three girls' pallets rolled up and stacked on top of the square wooden pantry box.

"You think there's enough room?" he asked.

"I will make room."

"You mean *I* will make room. *I'm* the one shoving your supplies back and forth." He worked the sack of cornmeal out a few feet and placed the molasses crock behind it.

Jenna paced across the few feet of space, her lips pursed. "That's not going to work, either. Move the crock back over behind the pantry box."

He rolled his eyes but obliged, then waited, sweating in the midday heat while she studied the space. He could see there wasn't enough room for one more sleeper inside the wagon; in fact, there wasn't really room enough for the three girls. He figured that's why Jenna and her husband had slept underneath the wagon in the first place.

He opened his mouth to point this out, then decided not to tangle with the mama bear. She had her mind made up. He knew that all four of them scrunched in here together at night would swelter in the late summer heat. He swallowed a chuckle, enjoying a ripple of secret satisfaction. *You can lead a horse to water...*

He waited while she eyed the new arrangement. Finally she blew out an exasperated breath. "Could you move that sack—?"

"Jenna?" Emma Lincoln's voice called from outside the wagon.

Jenna moved to the curtained opening. "Yes? I'm coming." She climbed down from the wagon, but Lee stayed where he was. The minute he decided she was done shifting things around he figured she'd come up with another idea. So he waited, listening to Emma and Jenna talk outside.

"We're having a social tonight after supper, Jenna. You'll come and bring the girls, won't you?"

"Oh, Emma, I don't think—"

"Your young-uns need other people," the wagon master's wife continued. "It's not good for them to be so isolated, 'specially now that Mathias is gone."

A long silence fell. Lee would give a nickel to see Jenna's face. She was probably torn with indecision since he guessed that when Borland was alive he hadn't been too friendly with the other emigrants. That was a hard thing for young girls. Maybe for Jenna, too. Jenna didn't mix much with the other emigrants except for Hulda Gumpert, who stopped by occasionally with a quart jar of milk and another of cream from the cow tied to their wagon.

Silently Lee willed Jenna to say yes for the girls' sake. But she didn't. "I… That is, I don't enjoy—"

"Well, glory be, Jenna, you should!" Emma urged. "I know you've suffered a great loss, dearie, but life must go on. Especially for your daughters. Think about it, won't you?"

The woman's footsteps scraped past the wagon, and then he heard Mary Grace's hesitant voice. "Please, Jenna, couldn't we go? Just for a little while? There'll be music and maybe even dancing. Oh, please?"

Another long silence. He could almost see the stubborn tilt to Jenna's chin. Quietly he moved to the back of the wagon and peeked out the bonnet. The three girls stood in front of their stepmother, their faces upturned.

"Tess, Mary Grace, do you two even know how to dance?" Jenna asked.

"No, but…"

"I do!" Ruthie piped up.

"Huh!" Tess scoffed. "Where'd you ever learn to dance?"

"Didn't hafta learn," Ruthie returned. "It's just somethin' I do when I feel like it." She spread her arms wide and twirled in a circle.

"That's not dancing," Tess sniped. "Dancing is *with* someone."

"It is so dancing!" Ruthie challenged.

"Is not!"

"Girls!" Jenna's voice sounded tight. "We are not going to attend the social, so stop arguing."

Against his better judgment Lee stepped forward. "For God's sake, Jenna, why not let them have a little fun?"

She turned hard green eyes on the back end of the wagon where he stood. "I do not recall that anyone asked for your opinion, Mr. Carver."

He stepped through the canvas bonnet and jumped down to the ground. "You're right, no one did. Still, what's the harm in a bit of music and dancing?"

"For a young, impressionable girl?" She tipped her head sideways to indicate Tess. "There can be immense harm."

Aha. Another piece in the puzzle that was Jenna Borland slipped into place. "My family back in Virginia used to vote on things we didn't agree on," Lee said.

"No doubt that is why your family back in Virginia lost the War," Jenna retorted.

"That's not fair," Mary Grace shot back. "Let's *us* vote on it!"

Jenna's lips thinned.

"I think," Lee hazarded, "you are already outvoted, Jenna."

She stared at him for so long he thought he might have a blob of shaving soap on his nose. "Very well," she said, her tone resigned. "We will attend for a little while."

"A *long* while!" Ruthie shouted. "Let's vote on *that*, too."

Jenna frowned, but she said nothing. Instead she caught his gaze and shook her head. He couldn't fathom what that meant, but it was a triumph for the Borland girls. Later maybe he'd ask her what she had against socials and dancing. Maybe he'd even ask her why she was so... Oh, the hell with it. Maybe he didn't want to know.

All through their supper of molasses-baked beans and corn bread, Tess, Mary Grace and Ruthie chattered with excitement. Jenna felt nothing but trepidation. The worst part was that Lee had persuaded the girls to his way of thinking. She bit her lip. Attending a social might be good for them, but it would certainly *not* be good for her. She had no wish to mingle with these people, especially since Mathias's death. Being a widow made her feel...exposed.

She washed up the dishes with an unusual amount of careless clatter, and even when Lee got out the coffee mill and ground the beans for her, she wasn't inclined to soften her anger. They had all ganged up on her, even him. *Mostly* him. Her jaw ached from gritting her teeth.

After an endless round of brushing each other's hair and trying on different ribbons, the girls stood expectantly at the edge of camp. Already fiddle music floated on the soft night air.

Tess eyed the bubbling coffeepot and Lee's waiting coffee mug. "Can't you hurry up?"

"Just one cup, all right, Tess? Gives a man courage."

Inside the wagon, Jenna gave one last swipe at her tangled hair with her mother's silver-backed brush and wound her hair into a bun at her nape. Then she splashed water on her overwarm, perspiring face, shook the dust out of her skirt and emerged just as Tess flounced off.

She noted that Lee now wore a fresh blue flannel shirt and his hair was neatly combed. Cleaned up like that, she had to acknowledge he was extraordinarily good-looking. Why on earth would a man this handsome need courage to attend a social? He'd have women sticking to him like cockleburs.

"Very well," she announced. "I am ready."

The three girls dashed off toward the Lincoln wagon. Lee set his coffee mug on a flat rock and moved, rather reluctantly she noted, to her side.

"What is the matter, Mr. Carver? You don't enjoy socials?" She heard the sniping tone in her voice and instantly regretted her words. Jenna had not been raised to be spiteful. Mama was proper, but she was never mean. Mama just didn't like most people.

He hesitated. "I used to enjoy them, before the War," he said in a low voice. "Out here on the trail, I feel like I don't belong."

"I find that hard to believe. Sam tells me that after the War, you served with the Federal Army. As a widow, *I* am the one who feels like an outsider."

Lee stopped dead, took hold of her arm and jerked her around to face him. "You know something, Jenna? The world doesn't dance to your tune. Don't you ever wonder how other people feel about things?"

Her face turned pasty for a moment, then a rosy color flared over her cheeks. "Of course I do! However, most of what these people on the wagon train feel doesn't concern me."

"You know what? You have a chip on your shoulder as big as a wagon wheel."

She propped her hands on her hips. "Oh, I do, do I?"

"Yeah, you do. Maybe it's because you've lost your husband. Maybe because you've been saddled with two squabbling, rebellious stepdaughters and one who's too young to talk back to you, but sometimes you are hard to be around for any length of time."

He expected her to slap him, or scream at him. Instead she just stared at him, her eyes slowly filling with big fat tears. He wanted to call back his words, but it was too late. Instead he gave her arm a little shake and turned her toward the sound of fiddles.

Chapter Ten

Jenna didn't utter a single word until they reached the camp gathering, where "She'll Be Coming 'Round the Mountain" pulsed from a fiddle, a squeezebox and two exuberantly played banjos.

"Emma, where is Ruthie?" she asked.

"Over with the Zaberskies."

Jenna quick-marched toward the Zaberskie wagon.

Lee hesitated. He hated the feeling that he didn't belong here. It hadn't bothered him so much when he'd been on patrol, fighting the Sioux, but it sure did now. To these people on the emigrant train, all of them Northerners, he was still the enemy, even though his family and everyone he knew had been wiped out during the War. It didn't seem to matter. In the eyes of these folks, he'd always be a Johnny Reb.

Well, shoot. He was attending this shindig only to accompany Jenna and keep an eye on the girls. He guessed he'd been through worse campaigns than this one, so maybe he should try to make the best of it for their sake.

With a hard look, Jenna stalked off toward Sophia Zaberskie, seated on the sidelines. Tess and Mary Grace were holding hands and bobbing together to the music, imitating what other couples were doing. It made him wonder what their upbringing had been like. Didn't they have barn dances in Ohio? Or maybe they hadn't been allowed to attend?

Ruthie bounced up beside him. "Wanna see me dance?" She spread out her arms to demonstrate, but Lee stepped forward and lifted her up into his arms. "How about we dance together, all right?"

She grinned, and when she clasped her small hands about his neck, he circled around and around in the cleared space among the wagons while she squealed with delight. He spotted Jenna on the sidelines chatting with Mrs. Zaberskie and surreptitiously watching Ruthie, who was crowing happily in his arms. He wondered what Jenna was thinking.

When he'd danced Ruthie into quiet, he set her down on the ground. Immediately she made a beeline for Jenna and climbed onto her lap. "Why don'tcha come and dance, Jenna?"

Jenna bent forward and said something inaudible, but Sophia Zaberskie laughed. "You are not either too old. You go on, Jenna."

Jenna spoke some more words that Lee couldn't make out, and suddenly he found himself striding toward her. He didn't know what he planned to say; he just knew he wanted her in his arms.

The music changed to a waltz: "Beautiful Dreamer." He nodded at Mrs. Zaberskie and bent toward Jenna. "Dance with me."

Jenna hesitated. Then, with a little half-frozen smile, she stood up and stepped forward. He led her off a few paces, turned and took her left hand in his. He carried it to his shoulder, lifted her other hand and without speaking slipped his arm around her waist.

Despite her pregnancy, she was still slim, her waist curving in above the flare of her hips. Her body felt warm under his fingers and he noticed a tiny tremor in the hand he held in his. She smelled good, like soap and something spicy.

Suddenly he wanted to undo that bun at her neck and thread his fingers into her dark hair.

The violin sobbed out the melody and Lee found himself remembering other dances, another woman in his arms. Laurie. *Oh, God, Laurie*. He closed his eyes.

When Jenna began to hum he thought his heart would walk right out of his chest. *Beautiful dreamer, wake unto me…*

Her voice stopped. "Lee?" she murmured.

"Yeah?" His throat felt thick and hot, and he didn't feel like talking.

"Am I really self-centered?"

He sucked in a gulp of air. "You want me to be honest?"

"Yes. I think so."

"The answer is yes. Sometimes you act like you're the only one who matters."

"I guess I am…protecting myself."

He released her hand and nudged her chin up with his forefinger until her gaze met his.

"It's not Borland's child, is it, Jenna?"

Her lashes swept down to cover her eyes and she shook her head. "How did you guess?"

He couldn't answer that. "Is that why you married him?"

"Yes."

"That's why you worry about Tess, isn't it?"

She nodded. "She is young. And mistakes are easy to make."

"Jenna, how old are you?"

"Twenty-four. Almost."

He laughed. "Tess is fourteen, almost. Mary Grace is twelve, almost. Girls sure want to grow up as fast as possible, don't they? My sister, Serena, did, too. She was eleven. Almost."

"What happened to her?"

"I told you before, Jenna, she was killed," he said shortly. "By a Yankee lieutenant."

"And your wife?" she asked softly. "What happened to her?"

Again Lee closed his eyes. "She died having my child. I found out later it was the day the Yankees marched through our plantation. The baby died, as well."

Jenna said nothing for a long time, just gazed up at him with a stricken look on her face. "How clumsy of me!" she whispered finally. "I had no idea. How can you stand to be around us? Yankees, I mean."

"I try not to think about it."

But telling her had sure cooled him off. "I've never told anyone about Laurie before. Or about my sister, Serena. The men at Fort Kearney called me Sobersides, I guess because I didn't join in the revelry at the fort. Or smile much."

But he noticed he did smile around Jenna. A lot. Maybe because he was trying hard to get along with this prickly woman and her odd-lot family. Except for little Ruthie, he'd like to dunk them all in a cold river. Tess he'd like to dunk twice.

At the thought of Ruthie, he lifted his head to check on her whereabouts. Jenna's eyes followed his. "She is over there, with Tess and Mary Grace."

She stiffened. "Oh, dear, Tess is attracting the attention of the Gumpert boy. I must go and—"

"Let her alone, Jenna. As long as the girls are together they can't get into much trouble. Anyway, young Jimmy Gumpert is tongue-tied around females."

"Just like his father," Jenna said with a laugh. "Hulda Gumpert tells me Emil never says more than three words to her at a time."

"He must have chosen the right three words, because they did have young Jimmy!" He waited for the implication to sink in. He knew the exact moment it did, because that rosy flush was back on her cheeks. She bit her lower lip until it was the color of strawberries, and he wished he'd never mentioned Emil Gumpert's three words.

"Tell me about your stepdaughters," he said to get his mind off where it was drifting. "How old were they when you married their father?"

"The same age they are now. Mathias and I had been married only a short time before we started for Oregon."

Lee noticed that the music had stopped, but even without it he and Jenna kept moving. Then the fiddle player launched into a reel, and Tess and Mary Grace were the first couple to line up.

"Are you up to dancing a Virginia reel?"

Jenna nodded. "The baby's not due for another four months. Dr. Engelman says I should keep active."

He led her into place, and when the other couples assembled he found himself standing next to Tess. The girl sent him an unbelieving look that clearly said *why would an old man like you want to dance a reel?* Then and there he decided to show her how an "old man" danced.

When the music started he paced forward toward Jenna, bowed and retreated, stepped back to her again to swing her, and then turned to his right to swing a rigid Tess.

"Loosen up," he said as he grasped her waist. "And hold on tight!"

He double-stepped the girl around and around in a tight circle, chuckling at the dumbfounded expression on her long, narrow face. Then he had to laugh aloud at the way Jenna was looking at him, all wide green eyes and pink cheeks. But when he lifted her hands in his to form the bridge under which the other couples ducked, he noted she was no longer smiling.

"What's wrong?" he shouted over the thump of the music.

"Short of breath," she gasped.

When the reel ended, she was panting hard. He escorted her to the nearest wagon, where she leaned against the sideboard, catching her breath. Mary Grace and Tess whirled past in an awkward version of a Texas two-step.

Jenna's gaze followed her stepdaughters and she frowned again.

"How come you don't like your two older girls?" Lee asked.

"You have it wrong. *They* don't like *me*."

"Did you ever look at it from their standpoint? Must be hard for them, having a new mother who's young and pretty."

"I don't see why it should be hard. I take good care of them."

"Maybe there's more to being a good mother than taking good care of them. Maybe they want *you* to like *them*?"

She didn't answer, and then she surprised him with a question of her own. "You don't like me much, do you, Lee?"

He hesitated. "I like parts of you, Jenna. The part I dislike I already told you about."

She gnawed more color into her lips.

Lee tipped his head toward her. "Tomorrow you're probably gonna fill Sam Lincoln's ear with more complaints about me and ask him again for somebody else to drive your wagon."

"Well, what if I did?"

He shifted his weight against the wagon. "In one way I'd be relieved. I don't fancy traveling another thousand miles squabbling with you."

"Oh? What else don't you fancy?" she retorted. "You might as well say it all and get it over with."

He pushed away from the wagon. "I'd be worried."

"Worried? Whatever for? Someone else can drive my wagon."

"Jenna, if you'd open your eyes you might see what's staring you in the face. You have no protection. Even if Tess and Mary Grace turn out to be sharpshooters, you have no weapons. You can't drive the oxen yourself. You don't even know how to yoke them up properly."

"I'll get someone else to yoke them up," she said in a chilly tone. "And drive my team."

"Make sure it's someone you trust around your girls. And," he added with a growl, "around yourself."

"I am sure there are some gentlemen on this train who—"

"Jenna, why don't you face it? I'm your best bet. From the men I've encountered on this train, maybe I'm your *only* bet."

She stomped off four steps, then spun back toward him and opened her mouth to reply. But instead of the tongue-lashing he expected, she snapped her jaw shut, pivoted and marched away four more steps.

Lee caught up to her, grasped her shoulders and stood at her back, anger churning in his gut. "It's plain as biscuits we rub each other the wrong way," he growled.

"We most certainly do!"

"And maybe there's no way around it. But…"

"But?" Under his hands he felt her shoulders begin to tremble. "I don't… I can't…" Her voice broke.

"But I can," he said slowly. "Let me tell you something, Jenna." He filled his lungs gradually, then let the air out. "I don't know how to say this, but I need to know you're willing to listen. Are you?"Jenna waited for Lee to speak, holding back the sobs that bubbled up from her throat as best she could. She hated to cry in front of anyone, especially in front of the girls. Even more she hated to cry in front of Lee Carver.

She knew whatever it was he wanted to say would hurt her feelings all over again, and she was tired, tired, *tired* of being disapproved of. Being disliked.

"Well, say something!" she snapped.

"Give me a minute," he said. "I've got to think how to say this right."

Chapter Eleven

Jenna waited, twisting her hands in her skirt. She tried to step forward, away from him, but he held her shoulders so firmly she couldn't move.

"Let me go, Lee."

"Not yet. Not until I've said everything I want to say." She heard him suck in a long breath and slowly let it out.

Something in his voice set a flock of birds flitting about in her stomach. What more could he possibly have to say to her? She already knew he didn't like her. Why should that matter a whit to her, since she didn't like him, either?

But you do like him, a tiny voice nagged. And for some crazy reason she wanted him to like her.

But the man was annoying. Intimidating, even. He said things she didn't want to hear, things about herself. He wasn't mean about it, the way Mathias had been. And the girls. Lee wasn't spiteful. He just said what he believed.

I like that. I respect that. And I respect him, as well.

He cleared his throat and went on in a low voice. "It's true I said I dislike a part of you, the part that is…"

He paused and drew in another breath. "There's no easy way to say it, so I'm going to be blunt. I dislike the part of you that is self-centered."

A shard of pain lodged under her breastbone. How his words hurt!

Was she really self-centered? She didn't want to be, truly she didn't. It was just that now with Mathias gone she was frightened to death of what the future held. She had to think about getting to Oregon with her quarrelsome stepdaughters, about not having enough food, about all the things she didn't know how to do. She had to think about being strong for the girls. She had to think about her unborn child.

The truth was she was frightened to death about what the future held.

He cleared his throat and then she heard his low voice close to her ear.

"I like parts of you, Jenna. Many parts. Maybe too many. You're courageous and hardworking and sensible and resilient and practical and..." He stopped.

"And?"

"And you're beautiful."

A kernel of warmth crept into her chest. Beautiful? He thought she was beautiful? Five months pregnant and he thought she was...*beautiful*?

"You might as well hear all of it, I guess," he murmured. "I'm a man who hasn't said this to many women, but I'm saying it to you now. I want you. Not just because you're beautiful, but because when you look into my eyes I feel you understand. You move me, Jenna."

Her heart squeezed into a fist-sized lump. She couldn't speak.

"So..." He cleared his throat again. "So, I'd like to be the man who drives you to Oregon. I like being around you."

He bent his head, pressed his lips to her bare neck and then released her.

Blindly she stumbled back to the Zaberskie camp. She felt torn in two. What Lee had done frightened her in a way she didn't understand. He made her feel shaky inside. Hungry for something.

But she didn't want to feel anything at all for this man. For any man. Certainly not for Lee Carver, who was merely putting up with her and the girls until they reached Oregon.

"Why, Jenna," Sophia said. "You haf been crying! What iss wrong?"

"N-nothing, Sophia. Just…" Her throat closed.

Sophia's soft brown eyes filled with tears. "I know, my friend. You are missing your husband."

A sudden urge to laugh overtook her. She sank onto a folding stool and buried her face in her skirt. *Mathias?* It was not Mathias she missed at this moment. It was the feel of Lee Carver's hands on her, the pressure of his lips on her skin.

Lee's voice spoke from the shadows. "She's just had a shock. She'll be fine in a minute or two. Would you have any coffee, Mrs. Zaberskie? Or some tea?"

"Ah, I haf good tea," Sophia said. "You wait here, I bring."

Sophia disappeared into her wagon and Jenna lifted her head. Lee was nowhere to be seen, but in his place stood Tess and Mary Grace, looking flushed and happy. Instinctively she knew Lee had sent them, and she remembered his words. *Maybe they want* you *to like* them.

Very well, she would try. She would try to understand how the Borland girls might feel about the unknowns facing them now that their father was gone and they were left alone with a stepmother they detested.

Ruthie tagged along behind the girls, sidled to Jenna's side and patted her arm. Jenna took her small hand in her own. "Did you have a good time at the social?"

"Yes! An' so did Mary Grace and Tess. They danced lots, and I danced, too."

Jenna listening to the girls chatter about dancing the Virginia reel and flirting with the Gumpert boy while she gulped down the hot, flavorful tea Sophia brewed. Even when they returned to their wagon, the girls were so excited they continued to laugh and giggle until Jenna climbed through the bonnet opening.

Instantly a heavy silence fell.

Ruthie gazed up at her with wide, unsleepy blue eyes. "Where you gonna sleep tonight, Jenna?"

"Why, I…" She surveyed the jumble of blankets and quilts in the wagon bed. The girls' bedrolls filled up the entire space, leaving not an inch for herself and her own two quilts.

"Do you suppose you could…?" With her hands she gestured moving closer to each other.

"There isn't enough room," Tess announced flatly. Mary Grace nodded. "We can't crowd any more, Jenna. Ruthie's elbow is already poking me in the face and—"

"Besides," Tess interrupted. "You're bigger than all of us. 'Specially now." She glared at Jenna's belly.

"Girls, listen to me. It is not proper for a woman to sleep next to a strange man."

"Why not?" Tess spit out. "You're not married to Papa anymore."

Jenna stared at her angry face. Oh, what did it matter? She'd never really felt married to Mathias anyway. His daughters wanted to exclude her and she had no way to fight it. But it hurt.

She had never been excluded from anything before, by anyone. Growing up in Roseville she had known everyone in town, had been invited to birthday parties and teas and picnics ever since she could remember. She had never been disliked by anyone.

Lee was wrong about the girls wanting her to like them. They did not want her to like them any more than they wanted her to make a new home for them in Oregon. They wanted to punish her for coming into their lives, for coming between them and their father. Only little Ruthie tolerated her.

Abruptly Tess leaned forward and puffed out the small

lantern. "There is no room for you here, Jenna," the girl said into the dark.

The next thing Jenna knew a bundle of her rolled-up quilts hit her shoulder, accompanied by Mary Grace's words. "There will never be room for you."

Tears stung into her eyes. She blinked them back, groped for the thrown bedroll and found her way out through the bonnet opening. She could sleep out in the open, but where? It was too dark to see even as far as the next wagon. What if wolves were out there?

She shuddered, then dropped to her knees and peered beneath the wagon. Lee wasn't there. Her heart kicked, then froze. She would be completely alone. In all her life she had never been alone at night. Her mother's bedroom had been just down the hallway, and after she and Mathias were married, he had been there, next to her, snoring loudly.

She couldn't force herself back inside the wagon. She also couldn't steel her nerves to crawl underneath and sleep there all by herself. But she had to do one or the other.

Gritting her teeth, she felt her way under the wagon, rolled out her quilts and unbuttoned her shoes. Whoever was it who had said "nothing ventured, nothing gained"? At this moment she'd like to strangle them.

She closed her eyes and tried to shut out all the strange noises that were suddenly very loud. Insects scraped. Something rustled in the grass near the animals' enclosure. Oh, Lord, was it a snake? An owl *hoo-hooed* overhead. That darned horse of Lee's whuffled and stamped its hooves nearby. Someone in another wagon shushed a crying child and began to sing. "Hush, little baby, don't you cry…"

There! She heard a coyote bark. Or, God, was it a wolf?

She wished she had a weapon to lay beside her, as Lee did. But she didn't know how to fire a revolver or a rifle, or load it, or even how to aim it. She hated feeling helpless.

Well, what did you expect? She realized suddenly that

she had been helpless all her life, had expected to be taken care of. Her face grew hot. She had been foolish ten times over.

She woke with a gasp when a new sound pricked her ears. Someone was breathing next to her!

Lee. *Oh, thank God.*

Her next thought was *Damn the man.* She jolted upright and cracked her head on the under-springs.

"Easy," he murmured. "Hurt yourself?"

"No." She ran her fingers over her scalp and felt something sticky. "Y-yes."

He fumbled around for a moment, then pressed a piece of cloth into her hand—his handkerchief, she guessed. "Hold this against it. Hard. I'll look at it in the morning."

"Thank you." She lay staring up at nothing.

"How come you're sleeping under here, anyway?" he said. "I thought you moved all those things around in the wagon so that—"

"There wasn't enough room." She bit down on her lip. "The girls didn't want me."

Lee shoved his rifle aside and rolled toward her. "Well, I do, Jenna. I'm glad you're here." Gently he laid his arm across her waist. "Go to sleep."

He could tell she was crying from her ragged breathing. Part of him wanted to grin at her ordering him to shove barrels and sacks around in the wagon and then discovering there still wasn't enough room for her. Part of him wanted to gather her close and let her sob it all out of her system.

But all of him realized that, whether Jenna admitted it or not, she needed him. And after tonight, he was afraid he was beginning to need her, as well.

"Lee?" she whispered.

"Yeah?"

"Tomorrow I want you to show me how to shoot your revolver."

He was glad she couldn't see his face because he felt his smile widen into a grin. "Sure. Sam says we'll lay over here another day. Plenty of time to teach you anything you want."

He swallowed hard. He wasn't exactly sure what he'd really meant by that remark, but one thing he knew for certain; he wanted to teach her a helluva lot more than marksmanship.

But he'd have to watch his step. In another month she'd be so big with child he wouldn't be able to get close enough to her to brush a speck of soot off her nose.

After breakfast the next morning, Lee took Ruthie over to Sophia Zaberskie's wagon, then walked Jenna a few hundred yards away from the camp and taught her to fire his revolver. And how to reload it and clean it.

She learned fast, and while she still couldn't hit a target smaller than a cow, he felt better about their safety in case something happened to him. He had an extra revolver stowed in his saddlebag; when they returned to camp he showed it to Jenna.

"I keep it loaded, so don't let the girls know where it is." He stuffed the weapon back up under the wagon springs. "It's safer here, out of the way."

She nodded her thanks and he grinned at her. "Now, are you ready to ride Devil?"

She turned white as chalk. Chuckling, he patted her shoulder. "Maybe tomorrow."

The look she sent him made him laugh out loud.

Chapter Twelve

The next morning Lee threaded his way among the wagons down to the creek to shave. He hadn't slept much, kept thinking about holding Jenna in his arms, dancing with her. He felt on edge. Couldn't say why exactly; maybe it was the envious looks he got from the other men on the train. He didn't want any of them within a hundred feet of her.

At the creek bank he hung his shaving mirror on a cottonwood limb and was stropping his razor when a voice behind him broke the silence.

"Hey, Reb. Seen you dancin' last night with the widow Borland," Mick McKernan taunted. He stroked meaty fingers through his thick russet beard.

Lee's nerves went on alert, but he adjusted the shaving mirror and went on pulling his blade back and forth across the leather.

"Thought we warned you off our women, Reb," the stocky Irishman persisted. Lee gritted his teeth. It wasn't the first time one of the McKernan brothers had shot off his mouth about Lee's Confederate heritage, and he supposed it wouldn't be the last.

Now in the mirror's reflection he saw another, shorter man slouched beside Mick. Arn, the younger McKernan brother. He'd gotten into it with Arn not four days ago over something involving his Confederate military service. Ever since he'd shot Mathias Borland off his horse, the jibes about his Virginia roots had gotten more pointed.

Mick took a step closer. "Lotta trouble to go to, killin' a man, just to dance with his wife."

"Yessir," Arn echoed. "She's plenty good-lookin', even if she is in the family way. I'd drive her wagon any day."

Carefully Lee set his razor aside. "Mrs. Borland already has a driver."

McKernan elbowed his way past his younger brother. "Yah. I also hear you're sleepin' with—"

Lee slammed his right fist into Mick's jaw, snapping his head back. The man staggered, and when he came at him, Lee drove his left fist into the Irishman's overstuffed belly. Groaning, the man gripped his protruding stomach and bent double. "Damned Reb," he muttered.

"You can say things about me," Lee said, his voice low and even. "But you keep Mrs. Borland's name out of your mouth. You hear me?"

Mick nodded and backed away, his thick arms crossed tight over his torso.

Lee swung his gaze to the Irishman's brother. "Arn?"

"Oh, sure, Carver. No harm meant." He edged away, and the two men headed back to camp.

Lee managed to lather up the bar of soap and spread the suds over his chin, but he couldn't hold the razor steady enough to scrape off any whiskers. *Should have used my left fist, not my right.*

When he finished shaving he bathed his aching hand in the cold stream. He hoped McKernan had sense enough to keep quiet about the incident and keep Jenna's name out of his filthy mouth.

When he returned to camp, Jenna was frying bacon over the fire. She gave him an odd look. "What did you do to Mr. McKernan?" she asked, forking over a thick slice.

"Settled him down," Lee said shortly. "Why?"

"The man barreled past here as if the devil were after him."

"His brother, Arn, with him?"

"Yes, now that you ask. What happened?"

Lee ignored her question. "They been with the train long?"

Jenna turned over another strip of bacon. "They started out with us in Independence. Arn is a blacksmith. Sam Lincoln thought he'd be a good addition. His older brother is a farrier."

Lee turned away to stow his kit in his saddlebag and feed Devil a handful of oats. He resolved he'd never let Mick McKernan get within shoeing distance of his horse.

"The girls up yet?"

"Any minute. Tess is braiding her hair."

"I thought I'd give her a riding lesson after breakfast."

Jenna propped both hands on her hips. "After taking her across the river half-frozen with fear I doubt you'll get her back on a horse anytime soon."

"Want to bet?"

Tess and Mary Grace scrambled out of the wagon with Ruthie at their heels, and his question hung unanswered.

"Wash up, girls," Jenna said.

"Aw, do we have to?" Tess moaned.

"I'm so clean my skin squeaks," Mary Grace added.

Ruthie followed her sisters over to the fire pit and the sizzling skillet of bacon. "My skin doesn't say anything!"

"Huh!" Tess shot. "Your skin is red as an Indian's."

Jenna pointed her fork in the direction of the creek. "Go." None of the girls made a move.

Lee cocked his head. "First one washed up and back here gets to ride Devil this—"

Before he could finish, Mary Grace streaked off, Ruthie at her heels. Tess ambled sullenly after them.

"Yes, I will bet," Jenna said with a stiff smile. "Tess will kick and scream before she gets back on that horse. I think Mary Grace may be your most eager student."

"What about you?"

She sent him a sharp look. "What *about* me?"

"Riding Devil."

She whirled back to the skillet without answering. "Sam Lincoln stopped by. Our wagon is being rotated to the front this morning."

"Good. Kinda dusty at the end of the line."

They ate biscuits and bacon around the fire, and before Jenna and Tess had finished drying the tin plates, Mary Grace tugged Lee over to Devil for a riding lesson.

Ruthie threw her arms around Jenna's knees. "When do I get to ride the horse?"

"What a stupid question," Tess snapped, shoving her younger sister's shoulder. "Who wants to ride a horse, anyway?"

"Tess, let her alone," Jenna said. She bent down to Ruthie's level. "When you're bigger, honey, then you can ride."

"Tomorrow?"

"Not tomorrow. You'll have to grow much taller."

"How tall?"

"You must ask Mr. Carver that question, Ruthie. I think you have to be able to reach the stirrups, and your legs aren't long enough yet."

"What about Tess? Her legs are real long."

"I don't want to ride your old horse," Tess said, a sneer in her tone. "It's big and smelly."

Ruthie danced in front of her. "You're scared!" she crowed.

"I am not."

Ruthie clasped her small hands together and glared up at Tess. "*I'm* not one bit scared."

Tess gave her another shove. "You haven't got the brains of an ant or you'd be scared, too. Even Jenna's scared, aren't you, Jenna?" She sent Jenna a mocking smile.

Jenna straightened. "Yes, I admit I am apprehensive about riding. I have never liked large animals."

"See?" Tess stuck her tongue out at her sister and flounced away toward the wagon.

Jenna bit back her angry words. Tess was stuck between being a petulant child and being a young woman, noticing things like Virginia reels and Jimmy Gumpert. If she had had more time to establish herself as the girls' stepmother before she married Mathias, it would be easier to curb their meanness toward each other and guide their behavior. As it was, she had her hands full just getting them to be civil.

Especially to her. When they joined the wagon train to Oregon, Jenna had expected Mathias to discipline his daughters, particularly when it came to their treatment of her. Now she realized that nothing was going to change unless she herself took on the disciplining, and Lord knew she didn't want that role.

She reached for the bucket of dirty dishwater, intending to dump it out, but instead she bowed her head over it and closed her eyes. She could not imagine life in Oregon alone with bickering stepdaughters and a new baby.

Behind her she heard Ruthie scramble into the wagon, and in the next moment the quarrelsome voices rose again.

"I did not!"

"You did, too! I saw you."

Jenna clenched her hands under her apron. She felt like screaming. Even riding a horse would be easier than stopping this constant warfare. At least riding would get her away from the girls' incessant squabbling.

She looked up to see Mary Grace coming across the camp mounted on Devil, her dress rucked up in front. Lee walked beside her. He directed the girl to bring the horse to a stop, steady it and dismount by herself.

"You're not done yet," he said to the grinning girl. "Remember what I told you?"

"Rubhimdownandgivehimsomeoats," Mary Grace rattled off. "Do I have to?"

"Yeah, you do. Currycomb and brush are in my saddlebag."

Jenna jerked to attention. "Lee," she cried softly. "Your revolver. It's in your—"

"No, it isn't. I stowed it somewhere else."

"Where?"

He turned questioning eyes on her. "Why? You planning to shoot me?"

She couldn't tell if that was a half smile on his lips or a scowl, but it nettled her. She sent him a sour look and he stepped closer, glancing at the bucket of dishwater still sitting on the fire.

"What's wrong?" he asked.

"Nothing, I guess. I'm just tired."

"Physically tired? Or fed up?"

A spurt of laughter erupted. "However did you guess?"

"It wasn't hard. You look like you could chew nails."

"I might prefer nails over having words with Tess. I am…well, I am failing at being a stepmother. The girls need guidance, especially Tess, and I am the last person she will listen to. It's draining away any good spirits I may have had when we started out last May."

Lee watched Mary Grace's progress with the currycomb and tipped his head toward the girl. "She likes riding. She's going to be good at it."

Jenna nodded and bit her lip.

"Riding would be good for Tess, too," he went on. "Give her something to think about besides herself."

"I wouldn't get my hopes up about that."

He lowered his voice. "Did you two have words this morning?"

"Tess has words with everyone. Except you."

"Yeah. I'm not a threat to her, the way you are."

"How am I a threat? Besides marrying their father, I mean."

He hefted the bucket of dirty water, strode off a few yards and splashed it out onto a patch of grass. When he returned he closed her fingers around the handle and spoke in a low voice.

"For one thing, you know how to dance. For another you're a grown-up woman, and pretty, and that's what both Tess and Mary Grace want to be. They'd like admirers, too. All women want admirers, don't they?"

"I did not when I was their age. That came later."

"Then you up and married their father, and everything went to hell, huh?"

"Yes. I've often wondered if…if I should have married Mathias."

"Too late now," he observed. He signaled to Mary Grace, and the girl put aside the brush and stood patting Devil's nose. Again he rested his gaze on Jenna.

"Do my thoughts make sense to you?" he asked.

"How would you know anything about raising girls to be young ladies?"

Lee let that pass in favor of a more pertinent question. "What do you plan to do when you reach Oregon?"

Her face changed. "Mathias had some idea about running a store."

"But now you don't have Mathias. What is it that *you*, *Jenna*, plan to do?"

She twisted her mouth and passed the empty bucket into her other hand. "The girls must go to school, of course. And I want… Oh, I don't know anymore. Well, yes, I do know. I want my baby to be born safely. I want to not feel on the outside all the time. Disapproved of. Excluded. I want to start a new life in Oregon."

"What happened to the girls' mother, Mathias's first wife?"

She studied the empty wash bucket, then the patch of

damp ground where he'd tossed the contents. "Mathias said she ran off with another man. Later he received word that she'd been killed in a stagecoach accident."

She eyed him over the bucket. "Since we're asking personal questions, why didn't you go back to the South after the War? To Virginia?"

"I did." He gazed out at the grassy enclosure between the wagons. "I found my land ruined, my wife and baby son dead. I couldn't stay. The only thing I could salvage was my horse. Now Devil's the most important thing in my life. In Oregon I plan to start a horse ranch. Breed horses for the army."

It was a way for him to start over, build something he could believe in. Something he would never lose, unlike a wife or a child. He'd never remarry; it was too damn risky. Loving someone meant he could be emotionally destroyed all over again.

He strode off to yoke up the oxen and insisted that Mary Grace watch. A grumbling Tess stood by. "How come we have to learn this?"

"Because," Lee said evenly, "I want you to be able to do it if you have to."

"But why would we have to? You'll be here, won't you?"

"I don't like the prospect of having men like…" He stopped himself. He was going to say the McKernan brothers, but thought better of it. "Men that might muscle their way in too close to the Borland women under the guise of being helpful."

"Like you?" Tess's hazel eyes were hard.

"I'm not muscling in."

"What makes you different?" she challenged.

Lee straightened and took a step toward her. To her credit, she didn't back up and he hid a smile. "I'm just different."

He'd be damned if he'd explain to a spoiled thirteen-year-old how protective he felt toward Jenna.

"It's because you feel bad 'cuz you killed our pa, isn't it?" Tess sniped.

"Some." Hell and damn, the girl's tongue was sharp enough to slice jerky. He looked straight into her hostile eyes and let her have it.

"You want to know something, Tess? About getting a boy to like you? Maybe someone like, say, Jimmy Gumpert?"

She tried to hide it, but her eyes took on an avid interest.

"Then listen up. First off, you're nice to him. Second, you let him see that you're nice to other people, too. Like your sisters. And Jenna. No man likes a shrew."

Ruthie popped up behind her sister. "What's a shrew?"

Lee blew out a breath. "A shrew is a female who says mean things."

Tess's face tightened, but she said nothing.

He finished yoking the oxen and climbed up onto the driver's box. Ruthie clambered up next to him and he drove the team up to the front of the line. Mary Grace and Tess and Jenna walked alongside.

"How come we're not last anymore?" Ruthie questioned.

"Because the wagons rotate."

"What's 'rotate'?"

"It means to trade places so no one has to be last in line longer than a couple of days. This wagon has been dead last for three days. Now it's someone else's turn."

He pulled in just behind the leader, Sam Lincoln, and climbed down to check on Devil, roped to the right rear corner. He nodded to Emma Lincoln as he passed, glanced at the next wagon in line and stopped short. Directly behind the Borland wagon sat Mick McKernan, jiggling the reins of his four-horse team. The Irishman fingered his jaw and sent him a black look.

Lee bit back a groan. He'd known men like Mick before. There was only one thing on their minds, and it didn't involve getting to Oregon. He waited until Sam signaled the start, then climbed back onto the bench and motioned to Jenna.

"Don't fall behind when you're walking. Make sure you and the girls keep with this wagon."

"What difference will it make?" she asked. "We often walk beside other wagons."

"Look behind you." He waited as she peered past him. He knew the instant she saw McKernan because she pressed her lips into a thin line.

"Oh."

"If you or the girls can't keep pace, I'll stop so you can climb inside. Understood?"

"Yes, I understand." Then, after a long pause, she looked up at him. "Thank you, Lee."

She tried to smile and his gut clenched. Jenna Borland wasn't cut out for this journey. Probably wasn't cut out for life on the Oregon frontier, either. But she was trying to do the best she could, and that counted for a lot in his book.

The next time he talked to Tess about what men liked about women, he'd make sure to mention courage.

Chapter Thirteen

The long line of wagons rolled across endless miles of knee-high grass punctuated with patches of yellow and orange wildflowers. The girls wore holes in their shoes from trudging beside the wagon, and then the leather uppers began to disintegrate. Ruthie preferred going barefoot, but both Jenna and Tess suffered with blisters because the loose, stretched leather of their shoes rubbed their heels raw.

The Borland team of oxen pulled up long, gradual hills and rattled down the other side, and then the wheels rolled on, crunching rhythmically over the prairie. The warm air smelled of sage and animal dung dropped by the cattle, mules and horses in the train.

Mary Grace spent more hours riding Devil than walking beside the wagon with her sisters, but both the older girls still refused to walk next to Jenna.

As the endless days dragged by, wagons broke down and were repaired, horses were reshod, suppers cooked over campfires were devoured by hungry men and exhausted women. Jenna noticed their food supplies were beginning to run low, especially cornmeal and coffee. Lee gave up his morning cup of hot coffee and Jenna accepted Sophia

Zaberskie's offer of a canister of tea instead, but she found that tea no longer agreed with her.

Gradually the thick groves of ash and elm trees started to thin out, and Sam ordered the nooning stops in the small clusters of cottonwoods that appeared near the occasional stream.

Then the streams began to dry up. Now the emigrants struggled not only with heat from the blazing sun and dust kicked up by the wind and the rolling wagons themselves but agonizing thirst.

Lee tried to talk Jenna into riding with him on the driver's bench, but she said Dr. Engelman had advised her to avoid the bumping and jostling of the wagon in her condition and to walk instead. Also, she insisted she wanted to keep an eye on the girls, and she couldn't see them sitting next to Lee on the driver's bench. He wondered if it was more than that. She'd been skittish ever since that night at the social when he'd said things he probably shouldn't have.

He felt pulled in two directions. Ripped apart was more like it. Part of him wanted to protect Jenna, keep her and the girls safe. Another part of him, the part he was trying hard to ignore, wanted to hold her in his arms and make her his.

He slapped the reins and called out to the ox team. "Ho, there, Sunflower. Come on, girl, pull!"

Jenna still shied away from learning to drive the team. He knew the physician warned her to stay clear of the oxen in her condition, but he also knew that, deep down, she was afraid of the animals. He was pushing her to overcome her fear of Devil, but he was learning that when Jenna made up her mind to something, she was plenty hard to budge.

He admired her stubbornness in a way. She had backbone. She shouldered her responsibilities without buckling when the going got rough, but she could be as immovable as a brick wall when it came to some things.

Him, for instance.

She tolerated him. She was even polite to him now, after

nearly a month of traveling together. But he sensed she was afraid of him. Maybe he'd never understand her, but that sure didn't stop him from wanting to touch her. Sleeping next to her at night was tearing him up inside.

During the long, scorching August days Jimmy Gumpert began walking beside Tess, and in the evenings the boy often wandered into their camp after supper and serenaded her with songs badly played on his guitar.

"Interesting development," Lee intoned to Jenna one night, listening to Jimmy's halting efforts at "Barbara Allen."

"Oh? Why is it interesting?"

"For weeks, Tess has been unfriendly," Lee said carefully. "Sometimes she acts downright mean to the boy."

"Yes, some girls can be that way," Jenna said. "Tess can be extremely unpleasant and tart in her speech."

Lee looked sideways at her. "Well, now she's being halfway civil to the boy. Maybe a male is a good influence on a female."

Jenna concentrated on the glowing coals in the fire pit.

"The right male, perhaps. I know nothing about the Gumpert boy."

"I do. Jimmy's more scared of Tess than predatory."

"Why on earth would he be scared of her? He's bigger than she is and about six inches taller."

Lee fished the last tin plate out of the bucket of wash water and dried it. "It isn't a matter of size. Maybe he doesn't want to get his heart broken."

"Of course," she sniffed. "Tess could always have *her* heart broken."

"Or," he said, shooting her a quick glance, "they could end up being friends. Close friends."

"Oh." All at once Jenna didn't know where to look. "I never considered that."

"Did your mother and father like each other?" he asked.

"Why, of course. They were husband and wife." She

laid his damp dish towel on a rock near the fire. "They *loved* each other."

"They were fortunate, then. Lots of couples don't love each other. Most couples don't even like each other. Take you and Mathias, for example. I'd bet a stack of silver dollars you did not love Mr. Borland."

"Well, you would lose!" she said sharply.

"Would I?" he said at her back.

She clamped her lips shut. "I refuse to answer such a question. My marriage to Mathias is none of your business."

"Yeah, I know. Just wanted to poke at that soap bubble you're living in."

Jenna spun to face him. "If I am not mistaken, Mr. Carver, you have your own bubble."

He swallowed and slowly withdrew his pocketknife from his jeans. "Yeah, I do. I thought it didn't show."

"It doesn't show, really," Jenna said, her voice softening. "I was guessing."

He tossed his knife into the air and caught it. "A man hates to show his vulnerability. Especially to a woman."

She faced him, her cheeks hot, and jabbed her forefinger into his chest. "How do you think a woman feels?"

He laughed. "If I knew that, Mrs. Borland, I'd be a rich man."

In a huff, Jenna shooed him off to talk with Sam Lincoln. When he'd gone, she insisted the girls take spit baths using a single bucket of precious water she'd saved from their reservoir barrel. When they were finished, she stripped to her waist and sponged off her sticky skin, then brushed and rebraided her hair.

The girls went to bed and she crawled under the wagon and lay staring up at the underside. She was still awake when Lee came back into camp. She watched him move to the wash bucket she'd left heating and strip off his shirt.

He was a fine-looking man, lean and long-limbed,

his back ropey with muscles, his arms and hands deeply tanned.

Suddenly he dropped his trousers.

"Oh, my!" she gasped. He wore no drawers! His buttocks… Oh! He turned sideways, and she forced her eyes shut. Her face burned, and the heat washing over her had nothing to do with the scorching day or the sultry evening air. A delicious tingly sensation lodged below her belly.

She swallowed and concentrated on keeping her eyes closed until she heard him splash the water out onto the grass, hang the bucket on the hook on the wagon box and step toward where she lay. When he crawled underneath onto his pallet she pretended to be asleep.

"You awake?" he murmured.

She almost blurted out no, then she remembered to lie still and say nothing.

He chuckled. "Were you watching?" he whispered.

Oh! She would die of mortification. Then she sucked in her breath. "Yes, I was."

Suddenly she wondered if *he* had been watching *her* when she took her spit bath.

"Yes," he said, as if he'd heard her unspoken question. "I was watching."

Oh, for mercy's sake! The man was reprehensible. He reached over and patted her tense shoulder. "Night, Jenna."

She struggled to keep her mouth shut. After a few minutes she heard his breathing even out and deepen. It infuriated her that he could sleep while she found she could not. She lay staring up at the wagon springs, trying to calm her tumbling thoughts.

Face it, Jenna. Lee Carver makes you nervous. And that was because…well, she didn't really know why. She knew only that he got under her skin and she couldn't make him go away.

But you don't really want him to go away, do you?

With an exasperated sigh she flopped onto her side and shut her eyes tight.

She *did* want him to go away.

But at the same time, she didn't. She liked the way he made her feel when he touched her. At odd hours of the day and— Oh, heavens! At night, she found herself remembering the feel of his lips pressed near her ear, the sound of his voice, low and sure. *I want you.*

She shivered and tried to force her thoughts elsewhere.

Tonight she heard no coyotes or wolves or whatever they were, and that was a mercy. Their mournful, lonesome howling made her insides feel funny. But after some hours she heard something else. Beside the wagon, where Lee hobbled the stallion each night, Devil shuffled and stomped his hooves. Could the horse have worked itself free?

A hand covered her mouth. "Don't scream," Lee muttered in her ear. "Lie still."

She turned her head toward him without making a sound. "What is it?" she whispered.

"Someone's after my horse." He lifted his hand away, levered his body across hers and slid noiselessly out from under the wagon.

Before she could count to ten, he was back.

"Who was it?"

"Indian."

With a cry she jerked upright and once again banged her forehead on the undercarriage. "An Indian? Where is he? Oh, the girls!" She scrambled out from under her quilt.

He grabbed the back of her skirt. "He's long gone."

"How do you know it was an Indian?"

"Because whoever it was left no tracks. Indians won't attack at night, but they will steal horses."

He settled beside her, drew in a heavy breath and was instantly asleep. Jenna could not close her eyes until the sky turned pink.

In the morning Lee went off to confer with Sam Lincoln. When he returned he reported to Jenna that he and Sam would keep a sharp eye out at night but they would not alarm the train.

"Why not let the others know? Surely people deserve to know there are Indians about? Besides, the men could help keep watch."

"Think about it, Jenna. A whole train of trigger-happy men might dig us into a hole we wouldn't be able to get out of alive. Better to lie low and wait it out."

She wrapped both arms across her midriff. "I get the shivers just thinking about it."

"Then don't think about it." He squeezed her shoulder and turned away.

After a breakfast of hot corn cakes and bacon, Lee hitched up the oxen, with Tess's grudging help, and they rolled into the line of wagons. Today they were third in line after the wagon master.

Ruthie rode next to him on the driver's bench; he confided to Jenna that with Indians around he didn't want the girl out of his sight.

Tess and Mary Grace walked beside the wagon. Jenna started off on foot on the opposite side. Lee had cautioned her not to mention last night's Indian visitor, but she could not help scanning the horizon for the dust cloud that would indicate a rider. Or riders.

All morning she marched resolutely forward, putting one foot in front of the other even when the dust kicked up by the animals and wagons was so thick she could scarcely breathe. She squinted against the harsh sunlight and prayed for courage. *I can do this. Others have done it, and I can do it, too. I must do it!*

Her blistered heels rubbed raw. Her parched skin pulled tight across her cheeks, and even under her floppy sun hat her cheeks began to sunburn. She kept her back straight and her head up, hoping a show of defiance would give her strength and the will to survive. *If I have to, I will walk all the way to Oregon.*

She trudged on hour after hour until her head pounded and her ears buzzed. Despite the handkerchief tied over her nose and mouth, dust choked every breath she drew. Mile after mile she concentrated on the creaking of the wagon wheels and tried to think.

She was many miles from everything she had ever known, and with each step she was moving farther away. Every bone in her body ached and her throat screamed for water.

But there was no water. The wagons crossed two dried-up streams, and not even when the men dug down through the cracked mud surface had a drop of moisture appeared. The oxen and cattle lowed their distress. Jenna knew if they didn't find water soon, the animals would begin to die. And after that...

She couldn't think about it. She focused her eyes on Sue and Sunflower, doggedly plodding forward mile after un-complaining mile, and felt a surge of admiration for the patient, hardworking team. She moved forward to pat Sue's head and heard a squeak from Ruthie on the driver's bench, an odd little hiccup of distress that made Jenna glance up at the girl.

Ruthie was staring at something off to the left. Jenna turned her head to look, and her heart stuttered to a stop. *Indians.*

A tall, savage-looking Indian wearing a magnificent feather headdress, his face painted black and yellow, sat his horse with five or six half-naked men on horseback ranged behind him. The taller man in the center held his rifle across his knees. As she watched, he stepped his mount forward and drove a lance into the ground in front of him. Then all of them sat silent, waiting.

The wagon jerked to a stop, and then the entire train

halted. Lee came off the driver's bench with Ruthie clasped in his arms.

"Get in the wagon," he ordered.

The Gumpert boy was already herding Tess and Mary Grace through the bonnet. Jenna grabbed Ruthie and shoved her through the opening, then climbed in after her.

She and the girls and Jimmy huddled together in the stifling heat. Ruthie didn't make a sound, but Tess sat sniveling with her back against the flour barrel. Minutes dragged by. Finally Jenna couldn't stand not knowing what was happening, and she peered out the front to see Lee striding off to confer with Sam Lincoln.

In a few moments he was back, motioning to her. "Sam's pulling the wagons into a circle. He knows I speak some Sioux, so he wants me to talk to them. Shouldn't take long. I don't know that many words."

He retrieved his saddlebag from underneath the wagon, then walked to the back of the wagon, his rifle in his hands.

"Mary Grace?"

"Y-yes?"

"Take my Winchester." He handed it up to her. "I hate to ask you to back me up, but Sam's busy getting the wagons into position."

"I can do it, Mr. Carver. You said I was a good shot."

"Sight on the man with all the feathers. He's the chief. If anything happens to me, you shoot him, you hear me?"

"I hear you, Mr. Carver. But—"

"If they're hostiles, they'll kill one of us. Probably me. If that happens, killing their chief will stop them, at least for a while. Understand?"

"Y-yes," the girl said, her voice unsteady.

"Aim for his chest, dead center."

He stepped away from the wagon, and Jenna watched in growing horror as he moved away from the train and walked straight toward the group of silent Indians. As he went he slowly and deliberately unbuckled his gun belt, making sure the chief noticed his gesture, and let it drop to the ground.

Jenna gasped. *They will kill him.*

Lee advanced until he faced the chief with only a few yards separating them. Frozen, Jenna watched, clenching and unclenching her hands. Beside her, Jimmy pressed Tess and Ruthie to the floor of the wagon, and Mary Grace raised the rifle and sighted down the barrel.

Chapter Fourteen

Lee watched the chief as he approached. Sioux, he figured from the face markings and the calf-high deerskin moccasins. His small black eyes looked hard and unyielding as flint chips, and the six braves flanking him had war party written all over them.

He kept moving forward, lifting his right hand in a traditional greeting. The tall Indian sat his horse without moving until Lee was within three yards of him. If he'd wanted to kill him, he'd have raised his rifle by now, but the man's expression gave no indication that was his intent.

Sweat slicked the back of Lee's neck. Finally, the Indian raised one arm, and Lee halted. He spoke the only Sioux word he could remember from his army days; it was a greeting, but he couldn't recall if the word carried a hostile or peaceful meaning. Peaceful, he prayed.

The chief stepped his horse forward and returned the greeting. Lee waited, listening to the cicadas hum in the hot silence and wondering if that was the last thing he'd hear on this earth. Off to the right, a hawk made lazy circles in the cobalt sky.

The six braves smoothed their hands over their rifle stocks. Lee wondered if a hundred more Sioux warriors were already surrounding the wagons behind him, but he didn't dare break eye contact to look. He could feel sweat roll down his face, but he waited without moving.

At last the chief spoke. "I recognize you, White Eyes. You rode with the soldiers, the ones who attacked our people at Coyote Creek."

At the mention of the name, the braves behind him stiffened, and one raised his weapon. The chief barked a word and the scowling man lowered his rifle. But Lee noted that he kept his finger curled over the trigger.

"I know of Coyote Creek," Lee said.

"Then you know our squaws and many children were killed that day." Lee tried to read what was in the older man's dark eyes. Pain? Revenge?

"It was a shameful day," he said. "It should not have happened."

The chief's mouth tightened into an unsmiling line. "You were there with the soldiers?"

"I was not there." *Thank God for that, or I'd be a dead man.*

The Indian waved a weathered hand at the wagons. "Where do you travel?"

"We travel west, to Oregon. Many miles from this place." He drew in a deep breath and decided to risk a question of his own. "Where do the Sioux travel?"

"We seek the Crow," the chief replied. "We make war on our enemy, take many horses, many prisoners."

And scalps, Lee thought. Lordy, the wagon train had blundered into the middle of an Indian war. He wanted to ask where they fought, but wasn't sure he wanted an answer.

"We do not seek war," Lee said. "We seek water."

The chief grunted and spoke to his braves in their own language. "I will take you to water. But," he added, "there is a price."

Lee's neck prickled. "What price?"

"Two of your fat cows and that fine black horse." He

gestured toward Devil. "Without water, your people will die. Without food, our people will die."

"You are welcome to the cows. The horse belongs to me. He is not for trade."

The old chief laughed soundlessly. "The Crow will steal it from you. Better you give to us."

"The Crow have tried to steal it. They were not successful."

The chief's black eyebrows went up. "The Crow have been here?"

Lee nodded. "Last night."

"Many?"

"I do not know how many." He waited a moment. "We will trade two cows if you take us to water."

The chief spoke rapidly to his braves, but they began to mutter and gesture with their rifles. Lee felt the hair on his bare forearms lift. He hoped Mary Grace had the Winchester trained on the chief's red-shirted chest.

Again the Indian grunted. "Come. We take you to water." They wheeled their horses and trotted off a few yards, then reassembled, their narrowed eyes on the wagons.

Lee made a sign to the chief, pivoted and strode to scoop up his gun belt from where he'd dropped it. Then he headed straight for Sam's wagon.

The men of the company had gathered in a tight knot around the wagon master, and Lee knew they had all watched his exchange with the Sioux chief.

"They want two cows," Lee said as he came up. "In exchange they will lead us to water."

Sam nodded, but Mick McKernan raised his voice. "I wouldn't trust an Injun," he shouted. "How do ya know they won't slaughter us and take *all* our cows? And our horses and our women, too."

"These Indians are Sioux," Lee said evenly. "I know this tribe. They are more trustworthy than some whites."

"Wouldn't trust a Johnny Reb Injun lover, either," Mick snarled.

"Looks like you'll have to, McKernan," Lee said, his voice level. "We don't have water enough for another day, and the Crow are already sniffing around our wagons at night."

"An' just how d'ya know that, Reb?"

"I heard them last night. The way I figure it, dying of thirst is about the same as dying from a Sioux bullet or a Crow arrow. We need water. They need food. We have to accept their terms."

Mick planted his thick body in Lee's path. "Says who?"

Sam stepped between them. "Carver's right. He knows the Sioux from his army service."

"I'll just bet he does," the Irishman blustered. "Prob'ly got an Injun squaw hidden away somewheres."

Lee shoved past Sam, but Mick ducked away. "Button it, McKernan!" Sam snapped. He caught Lee's eye and nodded. "Mount up, everybody. Let's get rolling."

Lee made his way back to Jenna's wagon, walking past a few proffered handshakes and one quietly spoken "Thanks, Carver," from Ted Zaberskie.

At the wagon he found a shaking Mary Grace inside, his Winchester across her knees. He patted her hunched shoulder. "Thanks for backing me up," he said.

"I'm so g-glad to see you," the girl stammered. "I was afraid I'd have to f-fire at that feathered man, and I'd miss and shoot you in the back."

"Wouldn't be the first time," Lee muttered. "Load up, now. We're moving on to water. Jimmy, you think your pa would let you drive the wagon with me? When those oxen catch the scent of water, they'll be hard to hold back. I could use a strong arm."

The boy grinned. "Sure, Mr. Carver." He bolted off to the Gumpert wagon and the girls and Jenna climbed down. Jimmy was back in less than a minute; he stopped near Tess and Mary Grace, and Lee heard the youngster make a hash out of his budding romance with Tess.

"Gosh, Mary Grace, where'd you learn to fire a Winchester? That's pretty neat for a girl."

"Damn fool," Lee remarked, leaning down from the driver's bench. Jenna sent him an amused look, rolled her eyes and shook her head.

"He's just being a male," she observed.

Lee flapped the reins and she turned away, put her head down so her bonnet hid her face and started walking beside the wagon. Tess and Mary Grace took their usual places on the opposite side, but Lee noted the two girls put their noses in the air and kept a good six feet between them. Neither said a word to the other.

He shot Jenna a look. "Just being female, I guess," he said. He heard a choked sound come out of her mouth, and then she turned her back on him and quickly paced ahead.

The train stopped for their nooning in a hot, dusty, shadeless area of grass sered to the color of straw. Buzzards soared like black sails against the cloudless blue sky.

Jenna was so tired she no longer knew where her shoes ended and the ground began. Her arches burned. Her lips burned. Even her eyelids burned. She had allowed herself one swallow of water that morning, but she had begun to wonder how long she could last in this heat without another. She smoothed one hand over her belly.

Tess and Mary Grace were so parched they had stopped arguing about Jimmy Gumpert. Ruthie lay on a pallet in the back of the wagon, a dampened cloth over her flushed face.

Lee climbed down from the bench and walked up to the head of the line of wagons where the Sioux warriors had now regathered. He raised his right hand and addressed the feather-bedecked chief.

"How much farther to water?"

"Two day," the Indian replied. "Maybe three."

Lee stared at him. They could not last three more days without water. Two, maybe, but the animals were already suffering. If the oxen collapsed…

He couldn't let himself think about it. When he returned to camp and relayed the news to Jenna, she shook her head in disbelief. "Can we manage for two more days?"

"Maybe. How much is left in the water barrel?"

"Only about two cups. I have been very careful with it, Lee, but there are five of us, counting you. We are all thirsty, and the oxen are, too. And I know your horse needs water."

"Try to ration it out, a swallow for each of us in the morning and another at night. That might get us through the next two days. After that we better pray for a thunder-shower."

"I have been praying," she said, her voice dull.

"Keep it up. It's all we can do."

They ate leftover biscuits for their meal, though no one was hungry and their throats were so dry swallowing was difficult. They rested for an hour, and then once more wagons rolled off across the prairie.

The Sioux led the way, riding slowly some yards ahead of the wagon master. Lee said they had no choice but to trust the Indians to lead the train to water, but her spine prickled all the same. She trusted Lee's judgment, but after all the horrible stories she'd heard, she didn't trust Indians.

Sue and Sunflower plodded forward, and the girls and Jenna tried hard to keep up. Jimmy Gumpert walked between Tess and Mary Grace, but Jenna could not hear their conversation, if there was any, over the noise of the wheels. Her own throat was so dry it was difficult to talk, and she imagined the three youngsters were no better off.

Surreptitiously she watched Lee on the driver's bench, looking into the sun, his wide-brimmed gray hat pulled low. Ruthie perched beside him, her floppy yellow sun hat covering her face. Usually she chattered away to him, but today she was uncharacteristically silent. The child was thirsty. God knew they were all thirsty.

Ruthie leaned her head against Lee's side, and he curved one arm around her so she wouldn't tumble off if she fell asleep. He kept his gaze on the oxen he was driving, his mouth pressed into a straight line, his jaw muscle working.

He was a good man, Jenna thought. She knew he was distrusted, even disliked, by others in the train, but he steadfastly did what he thought was right. Even her two contentious older girls were beginning to like him. Sam had been right about him.

That night at supper she opened the last jar of peaches and portioned out the juice. At least it was liquid, she thought as she gulped down her share. The girls were so exhausted they went to bed before it was fully dark without a single objection and no request for another chapter about King Arthur.

Jenna wiped the last of the tin plates, pulled her gingham apron off over her head and prepared to crawl under the wagon, but Lee stopped her with a hand on her arm.

"Give me your quilt, Jenna."

"My quilt? But why?"

"I want to try something we did in the army."

Too tired to question him, she handed it over. On the dry grass a few feet away from the wagon he spread out his own blanket next to her quilt and stood studying them for a long minute. Then he turned away and motioned for her to crawl under the wagon.

She rolled herself up in her remaining quilt, curled her body over her expanding belly and was asleep in an instant. All night she dreamed of sparkling waterfalls, springs that bubbled into cool flowing streams, and sarsaparilla sodas at the candy shop back in Roseville.

Before dawn, Lee jostled her awake. "Wake the girls. The blankets I spread out are covered with dew."

Her tongue was so swollen she could scarcely speak,

but she did as he asked. Lee dragged the wet blankets into camp, and they squeezed enough moisture from the wet wool to add another half-mouthful each to their morning ration of water. He gave what was left over to the oxen and wrapped the damp quilt around Devil's muzzle.

They ate a scanty breakfast of cold corn bread and then set off to face another day of God knew what following the Sioux braves riding ahead of the train. As she walked, she did some hard praying. *Surely God must be weary of the word* water.

By midmorning she was dizzy, and with every step her temples pounded as if a blacksmith's hammer were beating at them. Just when she thought she could not walk one step farther, Lee pulled the team to a stop. Behind them, Mick McKernan shook his fist and shouted.

"Get a move on, Carver. Yer holdin' up the line!"

Lee ignored him, climbed off the bench and scooped Jenna up in his arms. "Sit beside me or lie in the wagon—what'll it be?"

"I am all right," she whispered. "I can walk. Besides, Dr. Engelman said—"

"You cannot walk," he rasped. "Not in this heat. You're staggering like a drunken…" he shot a look at the McKernan wagon close behind "…Irishman."

"Maybe one of the girls should ride?"

He shook his head. "Neither of them is carrying a baby, Jenna. Choose. Me or the wagon."

She looked at the wagon and then back to him. "You."

He set her on her feet, climbed back up onto the bench and reached down to lift her up next to Ruthie. With a soft cry the child tipped over onto her lap.

A whip cracked behind them. Lee considered descending once more to confront McKernan, then decided against it. He hadn't strength enough for a fight. They would all die if they didn't reach water soon. Every minute counted. He'd save his business with Mick for later.

He lifted the traces, and the wagon rolled forward. He concentrated on the sound of the wheels crunching over the dry grass, trying not to think about Jenna's unborn baby's need for water. He knew Jenna was thinking about the same thing; the expression in her eyes was distant. Unfocused. Idly she combed her fingers through Ruthie's blond curls.

Suddenly Sue and then Sunflower raised their heads and Devil gave a soft whuffle. Had they smelled water?

Unaccountably the oxen picked up their pace, and Lee began to notice the grass, still bent over but now more gray than brown. The team tugged hard against the reins, and before another two miles passed the grass began to turn yellow green. He craned his head to see ahead.

Cottonwood trees! Green leaves and even greener grass. "Jenna, look!"

She lifted her drooping head and stared.

"Has to be water," he said. "Can't hold the team back."

She started to cry. "Oh, Lee."

"Hell, Jenna, don't cry."

"I c-can't help it. I am so thankful. I will never again think ill of an Indian."

"Probably more than one tribe knows about this water source. Let's hope we don't run head-on into a war between the Sioux and the Crow."

They wheeled around another curve and there it was, a clear stream fed by water bubbling from a surrounding rock wall. The oxen lunged forward.

The wagon train halted. Men scrambled to unhitch mule teams and let the animals drink, then scooped up containers for their own use. Lee unyoked Sue and Sunflower and led them off to drink, then returned for Devil.

Tess and Jimmy bolted off with buckets in their hands. "It's even cold!" Tess exulted when they staggered back into camp. She dipped up a tin cup for Ruthie, then another for Mary Grace.

Jenna had to find her own cup, but she was so grateful

for the water she gave thanks before she swallowed a drop. After her first cup, she resisted the urge to unbutton her dress and pour the cold liquid down between her breasts.

When Lee returned, she scooped her cup full of cold, clear water and held it out to him. He drained it, threw his head back and closed his eyes.

"And on the seventh day," he pronounced, "God did not rest. He created water!"

The girls joined hands and did an odd bouncy dance around the camp. Lee brought his hands to Jenna's expanding waist and swung her around and around in a tight circle.

"Do you have any whiskey?" he asked.

Giddy with relief, she laughed aloud. "Yes, I do have whiskey. Medicinal, of course."

"Whiskey is whiskey. I'll buy you another bottle when we reach Fort Caspar."

By suppertime the Sioux warriors had ridden off with two of Ted Zaberskie's fattest cows, and Jenna was half-intoxicated on her medicinal whiskey. Tess finished cutting up the potatoes and dried venison for the stew, and Mary Grace rolled out the biscuits following Jenna's instructions.

Lee watched her from across the campfire. Ruthie was perched on his knee, playing with the doll he'd whittled for her. Sam walked into camp to announce that the wagons would hold over an extra day so the women could bathe and do laundry.

Lee had his own idea about tomorrow. He planned to teach Tess to ride Devil. He'd come up with a plan that made him smile.

After supper he had another shot of Jenna's whiskey while she and Mary Grace washed up the tin plates. He couldn't wait for darkness when he could crawl onto his pallet under the wagon and lie next to Jenna.

Chapter Fifteen

Jenna took a towel and some soap and carefully walked down to a sequestered part of the stream for a quick bath. The girls could bathe in the morning, but she could not stand herself one more minute; her skin was sweat-sticky and caked with dust and grime, and her hair—mercy! It was stiff with dirt. Quickly she unbraided the fancy French twist she hadn't brushed out in three days and dunked her head under the water.

She soaped and rinsed her hair twice, then waded out to the deepest part of the stream and dove in. As she dried off, she studied her discarded garments. Tomorrow she would wash everything, the girls' pinafores and under-clothes and her own blue homespun dress and petticoat. But tonight she could not stand to put on her filthy dress again. She would sleep in just her camisole and petticoat. Lee would never know; as exhausted as he was, and with a good deal of whiskey inside him, he would be asleep before she returned.

Back in camp she scooted quickly under the wagon and pulled the quilt over her body, but immediately felt the covering lift away. She gave a small scream and snatched at it, then heard Lee's soft laugh. He wasn't asleep!

"Damn, you smell good."

"You would, too, if you'd had a bath."

"Matter of fact I did," he said. "Not as long as yours, maybe, but I bet I'm just as clean."

"You left the girls in camp alone?" she accused.

"Just long enough to bring a bucket of water from the stream and—"

"You watched me!"

"No, I did not. I wanted to, but like you say, I couldn't leave the girls in camp alone."

She flounced over onto her side and snugged the quilt up to her chin. Again he tugged it away, snaked his arm around her middle and pulled her back against his chest.

She didn't move. She liked the feel of his hard, warm body at her back.

"Definitely not." He pushed her loose hair aside and pressed his lips just behind her ear. A jolt of something hot and sweet shimmered all the way down her spine to her bare toes.

She opened her mouth to protest but just then someone started playing a guitar. Oh, Lord, it was Jimmy Gumpert, serenading the girls. Jenna recognized the song. "Down in the Valley." A young, uncertain male voice began to sing.

"Down in the valley, valley so low…"

Lee gently kissed her neck. "Looks like the Gumpert boy has come courting. Poor lovesick kid," he murmured.

Jenna smiled into the dark. "Is he singing to Mary Grace or Tess, I wonder?"

"Could be he's not sure."

"What? How could he not know?"

"Young men often don't know their own minds. Or," he continued, his voice slow and lazy-sounding, "maybe he's waiting for some sign of encouragement. A man can get discouraged."

"Encouragement? What kind of encouragement?"

"A smile once in a while. Or a soft word. Or…"

"He must not even think of kissing Tess or Mary Grace," she said quickly. "Lee, you have to talk to the boy."

"He's thinking about it already," he said with a chuckle. "He's probably been thinking about it for days." He rolled her over to face him, then laid his hand on her shoulder.

"Lee..." She pushed at him.

"Don't stop me, Jenna. Not tonight." He leaned toward her until his mouth grazed hers. "Tonight I'm feeling that life is good. We have water. And food. A good wagon and strong oxen. And we have this."

He kissed her again, a long, lingering kiss that had her heart thundering beneath her camisole.

"There is something happening between us, Jenna. Let's not waste it."

"Lee, stop."

"I will if you really want me to. I don't think you do."

Jenna drew in a shaky breath. "I—I don't know what I want."

He drew her into his arms and pressed her head against his shoulder. "I think you want me, Jenna."

"Lee, be sensible. I am five months pregnant. Almost six." She pushed forward so her belly touched his middle.

He smoothed his hand over the swelling. His touch sent a shiver through her.

"I know you're pregnant, Jenna. It makes no difference."

"Oh, it must make a difference. I know what I look like. Why would a man want a swollen, misshapen woman who is carrying someone else's child?"

He waited a long moment before answering. "Because it isn't your body that's pulling me." He settled his mouth on hers, and when she gave a little moan he rimmed her lips with his tongue and deepened the kiss.

Her heart kicked. She had never been kissed like this! Certainly not by Mathias, and not even when she was younger, before she married. His lips moved over hers, and her breathing slowed. Her nipples swelled and felt hot and tingly.

His tongue slipped into her mouth. Without conscious thought she slid one hand around his neck and felt his fingers thread through her damp hair and caress the back of her neck.

"Jenna?" he said, his voice rough. "Jenna, why are you crying?"

"Am I? I hadn't realized I was. I think… I think it's because, oh, this is crazy."

"What is? What do you think is crazy?"

"The fact that I'm crying, and it's because I like kissing you."

"And that makes you cry?" he murmured. He brushed tears off her cheeks with his thumbs. "Why?"

"Because." She sucked in a gulp of air. "It shows me how much I have missed." She buried her face against his neck while he lightly rubbed his hand in large circles on her back.

"I have never felt so foolish," she confessed. "I'm acting like a girl who is no more grown-up than Tess." She lifted her head as a thought struck her. "Oh, I do hope someday she will like being kissed."

"But not yet," Lee said. He settled beside her, pressed her head against his shoulder and laid his hand over the mound of her belly. Something rippled under his palm and he shot upright.

"The baby," Jenna explained with a laugh. "He likes to dance at night."

Gingerly Lee replaced his hand. Goodness, a Virginia reel was fluttering under his fingers. He resisted the urge to touch the area with his lips.

"Do you think kissing gets him excited?" he asked softly.

"Probably. Remember after the dance at the Zaberskies'? When you touched me? He jumped around so much that night I scarcely slept."

"Tonight might be worse," he said with a gentle laugh. "We could keep your baby dancing right up to the day you deliver."

"Mmmm-hmmmm," she murmured sleepily.

"Is that a yes or a no?"

She didn't respond, so he answered his own question. It didn't matter if it was a no. He drove her wagon every day. She slept beside him every night. After the War, he'd lost everything, including his faith, but only an idiot would not give thanks for this.

After breakfast, Lee drew Tess aside and proposed his idea. "How would you like to pop Jimmy Gumpert's eyes out?"

"Huh?" she scoffed. "How am I gonna do that? I'm scared of guns."

"It's not a gun I have in mind to impress young Jimmy. It's a horse."

Her hazel eyes went wide. "Oh, no, not Devil. Why would I want to get anywhere near that big mean animal?" Nervously she slapped the dish towel at the water bucket.

"I'll tell you why. A man admires a pretty girl on a horse."

Her mouth formed a big O. "You think I'm pretty? Really?"

"You are when you smile," Lee said carefully. "Seated on a handsome horse, you could knock Jimmy's socks off."

"His socks? Why would I want his socks?"

Lee hid a smile. "It's just an expression, Tess, for when you impress someone. Jimmy, for instance."

Now he had her attention. He almost laughed at the eager look on her face.

"All right," she said slowly. "What do I have to do?"

"Ride Devil. I'll teach you how to mount and sit that horse like a queen. Maybe even canter around the inside of the wagon circle. How about it?"

She bit her lip. "I can't. I have to help Jenna do the laundry."

He glanced over at the fire where a bucket of water sat heating balanced on two flat stones. "How about a lesson right now, before her wash water gets hot?"

"Well…"

"A man sure notices a girl who can master a horse."

"Ummmm." Her gaze darted to Devil, grazing on the other side of the wagon. "What if I fall off?"

"If you're smart you won't fall off, unless Jimmy is there to pick you up. And I know you're smart, Tess. It's time you put your brain to good use."

"Well…" He could see her hesitation, but both she and Mary Grace should know how to ride, not to impress the Gumpert boy but because the girls needed to know how to handle a horse. On a long journey like this, you never knew what you might run into.

Tess tossed the dish towel onto the wagon wheel, snatched it up again, folded it deliberately and laid it back down. "All right, teach me."

Lee showed her how to climb up on Devil's back using a fallen log as a mounting block; then he led the horse around in a circle and finally let her ride on her own. He'd never seen a smile that wide on Tess's usually sour face.

When they walked back into camp, Jenna looked up from her washboard. "Where have you two been?" she demanded.

"Working," Lee said quickly.

"Working?" She eyed Tess with suspicion. "At what?"

Lee stepped in close to her. "Leave her be, Jenna," he said in a quiet voice. "She's learning to ride. I think it might sweeten her up a bit."

Jenna's dark eyebrows went up. "Oh?"

"I'll help with the laundry," Tess volunteered.

Jenna's eyebrows rose even farther. "Thank you, Tess. I

could use some help. Perhaps Mr. Carver will help, as well."
She waited, letting a little smile play around her mouth.

"Uh, well, sure. What do you need?"

"Your trousers," she announced. "And your shirt and your under—" She stopped. Lee wore no drawers, she recalled.

"And your socks," Tess added with a sly smile. Jenna stared at her stepdaughter. She had never seen Tess say anything remotely teasing. Was it possible the girl was softening?

She and Tess took turns scrubbing dresses and camisoles and petticoats and Lee's jeans and shirts over the corrugated tin washboard until their knuckles were red and raw. Tess didn't say a word while they worked, but Jenna noted that she didn't snipe or complain, either. Maybe Lee had wrought some sort of miracle.

Lee lugged the bucket of wet garments down to the stream to rinse and Mary Grace helped wring out the clothes and drape them over huckleberry bushes and low tree limbs.

Late in the afternoon, Jenna returned to gather up the dry garments, loading them into her arms until she could scarcely see over the pile of clean clothes. She took care to avoid tripping over rocks and hillocks of grass. The load wasn't heavy, but her body was growing ungainly, her movements awkward.

Keeping her eyes on the ground ahead of her she finally stumbled into camp.

Lee stopped repairing a frayed rope and went to lift the garments out of her arms, but she halted abruptly, her gaze focused on something behind him. Her face went white and with a cry she backed away.

"Randall!" she said, her voice shrill. "What are you doing here?"

"Looking for you," a male voice grated from behind Lee. "And I've had a devil of a time finding you."

"But…but why? You know I don't want—"

"I've been halfway to hell and back, searching every wagon train out of Independence."

Jenna's mouth snapped shut and her lips tightened. Her face became a mask.

Before Lee could react, the stranger strode past him and gripped her shoulders. He was tall, very lean, with a hawk-like face under his black Stetson. He wore dark dust-covered trousers and a tooled leather vest over his shirt.

And a holstered .45 revolver under his coat. Instantly Lee quietly backed up two steps and slipped under the wagon, where he'd hidden his rifle.

Jenna's voice came to him over the pounding in his ears. "Randall, I cannot believe you are acting as if you had a right to—"

"I have a right, Jenna. You're carrying my—"

"No! You mustn't think that."

"Don't lie to me."

Lee heard her gasp and her voice hardened. "Randall, let me go."

"No. I'm never letting you go, you hear me? Never."

Lee eased out from under the wagon, stood upright and lifted his Winchester. "Take your hands off her, mister."

The man froze but didn't move. "Yeah? Who says so?"

"I do. Name's Carver. I said take your hands off her."

The tall man lifted his hands from Jenna's shoulders and pivoted to face Lee, his right hand resting on his holstered revolver.

Lee gestured with his rifle. "Don't even think about it." He watched the stranger hesitate. "Just who are you?" he demanded.

"Randall Morgan. This woman belongs to me."

"Like hell she does. This woman belongs to no one but her husband. Where's your horse?"

"Behind the lead wagon, but I'm not leaving."

Lee raised his rifle. "You're leaving, all right. Do it slow, with your hand off your weapon."

Morgan said nothing, but he lifted his hand away from the revolver.

"Move!" Lee barked. Morgan moved away a few feet, then turned his head and spoke over his shoulder. "You haven't seen the last of me, Jenna."

"Oh, yes she has, mister. You come back here and I'll kill you."

"Just go away, Randall," she cried. "Please."

He said nothing, just gave her a long look, touched his hat brim and stalked past Lee without looking at him.

Lee followed him to his horse, keeping his rifle trained on his back. Behind the lead wagon, Morgan mounted a tired-looking roan gelding with bulging, worn saddlebags and stepped it away, then suddenly twisted in the saddle and sent Lee a long, hard look. Then he kicked the horse into a trot and rode off.

Lee watched until he was out of sight, then lowered the rifle and went to find Sam. How the hell had the wagon master allowed a stranger to search among the emigrants for Jenna?

Chapter Sixteen

When Lee returned, the camp was deserted, the pile of laundry Jenna had gathered nowhere in sight. He unloaded the rifle, stowed the weapon in its hiding place under the wagon carriage, then checked the interior.

The clean clothes had been sorted into piles. His mind churning, he lifted his neatly folded jeans and shirts and stuffed them into his saddlebag, trying not to think about Jenna and the look on her face when she saw Morgan.

His fists clenched. Deliberately he flexed his fingers, extracted his pocketknife, and went in search of something to whittle on. Deep inside lurked a yawning uneasiness. He didn't like seeing Jenna frightened. In spite of all the hardships and uncertainties she'd endured, he'd never before seen her genuinely frightened.

He worked away at the block of cedar in his grasp until Jimmy Gumpert appeared. "Golly, where is everybody?"

"You mean Tess?"

"Yeah, I guess so. Where is she?"

Lee shrugged. "Don't know, exactly. Maybe down at the creek."

"Nope. Been there. You know somethin', Mr. Carver?"

"What?"

"Girls can drive you crazy."

Lee gave a harsh laugh. "Women can drive you crazy, too."

"Well, whaddya do about it? I mean, how are you s'posed to act around them?"

"Damned if I know, son. Why not ask your pa?"

"Heck, no! Pa's never even figured out my ma. You'd think he would have by now, huh? They've been married for fifteen years."

"Jimmy, I gather you want Tess to like you."

"Yessir. You got any ideas?"

Lee suppressed a groan. "If I had any ideas about how to get a female to like me, I'd be a rich man and a lot happier."

"Yeah, me, too."

"Actually, Jim, I do have one idea."

"Whazzat?"

"Just stick close to her. Don't have to say much, just be there. Don't push her. Maybe play your guitar."

"Don't see how that's gonna help. I can't play it too good yet."

Lee sighed. "You don't have to, son. Just be there."

All through supper he tried to follow his own advice. Jenna spoke to him as she always did, direct and polite, but there was no warmth. No humor.

And no smile, not even a single hint of one. She wouldn't meet his eyes, either. The air between them was thick with something dark and turbulent; it made his gut feel like knives were slicing into it, cutting deep and twisting in his vitals. She'd retreated someplace far away from him.

He'd lost her.

Jenna hated feeling this way. Randall had destroyed her once, and she would not, could not, allow it to happen again. Thank the Lord the girls had spent the afternoon with Sophia Zaberskie; she could never explain Randall Morgan to them.

Or to Lee. *Oh, God, Lee.* She couldn't bear to look at him and see the accusation in his eyes. She wanted to talk to him, wanted to watch his eyes follow her around camp and darken when her gaze met his the way they usually did. But she could not utter a word. Randall had caught up with her, and now nothing, *nothing* would ever be right.

She couldn't lie next to Lee under the wagon tonight; she just couldn't. Instead she would take a blanket from the wagon and go…where? Could she sleep by herself down by the stream? Or maybe among the animals inside the wagon circle? She hesitated. A restless ox or a cow could trample her, and Dr. Engelman had warned about being extra-careful.

She decided she would wait until she was positive Lee was asleep and then edge under the wagon and lay out her quilt as far away from him as she could get.

She sat by the fire until the last coals turned to ash and her head was lolling toward her chest, then gathered the blanket around her and crept quietly to the wagon.

Lee's deep, even breathing told her he was sleeping. Very quietly she took off her shoes, worked her way under the wagon and rolled herself up in the quilt. Then she closed her eyes and let the tears come, stuffing her fist against her mouth to stifle the sobs racking her body.

She had made a terrible mistake. Two mistakes. Marrying Mathias had been wrong. As clumsy and thoughtless as he'd been, he had not deserved a wife who did not care for him, a wife who carried another man's child.

She hated herself. She had ruined her life, and it was all her own fault. She had been headstrong and stubborn and prideful. She had sinned with Randall just once, but it had been enough to snare her in a web of her own weaving.

She wept until her head ached and her eyes and nose were so swollen she could scarcely breathe. Tears rolled across her temple, across her cheeks and on down her neck. She closed her eyes.

Dear God, help me. Please, please, help me.

A hand touched her, lifted her head and pulled her blanket-wrapped body next to one that was hard and warm. Lee's arms came around her and a hand pushed her head down against his shoulder.

And all the time he said nothing. Not one word. No accusation, no anger, no disapproval. Nothing. She didn't understand, but she was grateful beyond measure.

In the morning Tess stood at the fire pit beside Lee, stabbing a fork at the bacon sizzling in the iron skillet. "How come Jenna's not cooking breakfast?" she said, her tone petulant. "She's supposed to take care of us, not you."

Lee faked surprise. "You think I can't cook?" he joked. "I cooked breakfast the first morning I joined your wagon, remember?"

"You're not supposed to cook for us. You're supposed to drive our wagon. Where is Jenna, anyway?"

"Jenna is asleep. She had a bad night, didn't get to sleep until almost dawn."

"Is she sick?"

"Not exactly. She's...upset."

"What about? We already know she's gonna have a baby." Tess scowled down at the curling bacon strips. "It's too late to be upset about that."

Lee nodded. "Yeah, maybe."

And maybe not. Jenna was wrestling with something else, something brought on by Morgan's appearance yesterday. Her nerves were strung up tight, and he knew she wouldn't want the girls to see her like that. She probably thought it would undermine her authority with her stepdaughters. Given Tess's reaction this morning, maybe she was right.

Sam Lincoln stopped by. "We'll be pulling out today after breakfast," the wagon master said. He shook his head at Lee's offer of coffee. "We'll pick up the trail and press on to Fort Caspar."

Sam made no mention of Morgan. Lee had already questioned him and discovered that apparently Morgan had sneaked past the wagon master to search for Jenna on his own. Damned snake had probably followed every wagon train out of Independence.

Mary Grace and Ruthie appeared, their faces wet and shiny from washing up at the stream, gobbled down the bacon and leftover biscuits from last night's supper, then helped Tess wash up the tin plates.

Lee filled the water barrel and yoked up the oxen while Mary Grace fed a double handful of oats to Devil; then he sent the girls to ask Jimmy Gumpert to walk beside the wagon with them when they got under way.

When the girls had left camp, he crawled under the wagon, rolled up his pallet and shook Jenna awake. "You're riding inside today," he announced.

She'd cried enough last night to give her one helluva headache, and she was so groggy she just nodded. He lifted her into his arms, quilt and all, walked to the back of the wagon and loaded her through the bonnet as gently as he could.

"You want some coffee?" he asked.

"No," she rasped. "It would make me sick." She spoke with her eyes closed, and Lee noted that her lids were red and swollen.

"Where are the girls?"

"I sent them to the Gumpert wagon to get Jimmy."

"Did they eat any breakfast?"

"They did. Tess cooked it."

Her eyebrows rose and then she nodded, but her eyes looked funny. Distant, the way soldiers looked after a battle. She was retreating into herself. He had to keep her talking.

"Tess is growing up fast," he said as conversationally

as he could manage. "She's learning to ride, did she tell you that?"

Jenna shook her head.

"Girls can be surprising," he said. "Don't give up on Tess."

She said nothing.

"Don't give up on yourself, either, Jenna."

He saw her tears well up again. He reached out to touch her shoulder, but the sound of the girls' chatter outside stopped him, and he backed out of the wagon.

"Is Jenna in there?" Mary Grace asked.

"She is. She's not feeling well this morning, so she's going to ride inside today. Ruthie, you come up on the bench with me."

He nodded to Jimmy Gumpert. "Jim, you watch over the girls, will you?"

"Yessir, I sure will."

Lee took Ruthie's hand and walked to the front of the wagon where the yoked oxen waited, hoisted the girl onto the bench and climbed up beside her. When he lifted the reins, he heard choking sobs from inside the wagon, and his gut tightened.

One by one the wagons fell into a long line that snaked along a meandering stream. Today the Borland wagon dropped back one position, but that still left Mick McKernan behind them.

Lee had a bad feeling about McKernan, which was one reason he wanted Jimmy to walk with the girls. He'd cautioned the boy to keep up, but he hadn't told him why.

At their noon stop near a grove of cottonwoods, Jenna emerged from the wagon and walked unsteadily out of camp to splash cold water on her swollen face. Her eyes ached and her temples throbbed.

Tess and Mary Grace made sandwiches of biscuits and bacon, and Lee boiled some coffee. When Jenna returned, he handed her a cup without a word and sat her down on the apple crate.

She shook her head at Mary Grace's offer of a biscuit sandwich, and when Jimmy and Mary Grace went off with Ruthie to sit in the shade of an alder tree, she tried to swallow some of the coffee.

Tess stomped around camp with short, jerky motions, obviously resentful about something. Maybe having to help out.

Lee took his cup of coffee and left camp. Just as well, Jenna thought. It wasn't anger she felt radiating from him; it was something far more somber, something thick and heavy, and it frightened her. Or it would, if she let herself feel anything. She prayed the numbness she felt would never wear off. Lee returned, but she still couldn't look at him, and she couldn't bear to talk about anything with the girls, not even Ruthie. All that afternoon she rode curled up on a quilt inside the wagon, trying not to think.

The trail turned rough, and the jolting brought back her headache. The pain was insignificant compared to the searing ache in her heart.

Late in the afternoon the wagon train slowed and rumbled to a stop at Fort Caspar. Lee climbed down and sent Ruthie off with Jimmy and the girls to inspect the few buildings at the fort. Then he busied himself building a cook fire and waited for Jenna to come back to life.

Chapter Seventeen

At dusk, Jenna finally climbed down from the wagon, her motions so slow Lee wondered if she had downed more of the medicinal whiskey. He couldn't blame her, but it would sure make it harder to find out what he wanted to know. He focused on the half-carved horse he was whittling.

"You ready to talk?"

She did not look at him. "That is the very last thing I want to do," she said in a flat voice. "Where are the girls?"

"They went off to explore the fort."

She studied the fire crackling in the pit he'd dug. "I should see to supper."

"Jenna." He folded up his pocketknife and stood up.

"I'm not ready to talk," she said quickly.

"I don't care if you're ready or not. There are things I need to know."

She ignored him. Keeping her head down, she turned back to the wagon, reached inside for the skillet and the coffeepot, and set them on the apple crate.

"Jenna," he said again.

"Not now, Lee." She climbed back through the bonnet, and this time when she emerged she had a tinned can in each hand.

"Corn and tomatoes," she said. "Succotash."

He lifted them out of her grasp. "Forget the succotash."

"I could make biscuits."

"Forget the biscuits, too. I need—"

Before he could get the words out, Mary Grace flew into camp, breathing hard. "We got invited to supper. Mrs. Lincoln asked one of the soldiers from the fort, and she sent me to see if—"

"You girls may stay to supper," Jenna said. "And Mr. Carver, too. I am...not hungry."

"Mr. Carver is staying here," Lee said.

"Oh, but...Lee, I know you would enjoy Emma's cooking."

"I'm staying here," he repeated.

Jenna frowned at him, then at her stepdaughter. "Go on, then, Mary Grace. Be sure to wash up first, and don't stay too late. And tell Mrs. Lincoln thank you."

The girl raced off, and Jenna stood staring after her.

"Come on," Lee said. "We're going for a walk."

"Oh, I don't think—"

"I didn't ask you what you think. Don't argue." He banked the fire and took her arm. After half a dozen steps she pulled free.

"I don't need help."

He closed his hand around her arm again. "Yes, you do. You're unsteady on your feet."

A strangled laugh escaped her. "Lee, I am expecting a baby. I am learning that women in the family way do not have very good balance."

"We're still going for a walk, Jenna." He guided her away from the cluster of wagons and out onto the smooth parade ground. "It's still light enough to see where we're going," he offered. "And the moon will be rising soon."

"You will be hungry before then," she said.

"I don't think so. Right now I don't feel much like eating."

The air smelled of dry grass and wood smoke from numerous campfires. They walked in silence for a good ten minutes while a song sparrow twittered from a clump of ash trees.

"Jenna, that fellow Morgan is someone you knew back in Ohio, isn't he?"

She hesitated so long he thought she was going to ignore his question. "Yes," she said finally. "He is—was— my mother's attorney."

"And a friend of yours."

Another long silence fell. "Yes, he was a friend."

"A close friend, I gather."

"Lee, for heaven's sake, that must be obvious to you. Why do you keep asking these things?"

Because I'm going to kill him if he comes near you again. "A close friend?" he repeated.

"Yes," she said sharply.

"Are you sorry I ran him off?"

She stopped short, then walked on a few steps. "No. I am glad you did."

"You didn't want to see him, am I right?"

She barked out a harsh laugh. "You sound like an attorney yourself."

"I don't like what he did to you. Upsetting you, I mean."

"I admit it was a shock to see Randall. I never expected to see him again. But I... I will be all right."

"Provided he doesn't come back," Lee said drily.

She came to a dead stop. "Oh! You don't think he would, do you?"

"You don't remember what he said?"

"To be honest, it's all a blur. I only remember his face when he saw that I was..."

He took her arm again, turning her toward the grove of trees. "If he shows up again I might have to shoot him. That all right with you?"

She chewed on her lower lip. "Yes, that is all right with me. I thought I was in love with him once," she said in an unsteady voice. "And then I discovered that…" her voice choked off "…that he already had a wife."

So that was it. Damned bastard.

"You like succotash?" he asked to change the subject.

"What?" She huffed out a laugh. "Do I like succotash? No, actually, I don't like succotash. I do like biscuits, though."

Lee hid a smile. "Your biscuits are good, Jenna."

She stopped walking. "Lee, you say the most unexpected things."

His eyebrows went up. "What, that I like your biscuits? You're pretty easy to surprise."

"As a matter of fact I am not at all easy to surprise. Except when Randall—" She broke off and bit her lip.

"I'll bet back in Ohio he had to work hard to get you to even smile at him."

"Well, yes, as a matter of fact, he did."

"To say nothing about, uh, dancing with him. Or—"

"Don't you dare say it!"

"Making biscuits for him," he finished.

This time Jenna laughed wholeheartedly, and he turned her to face him. Bending forward, he touched his forehead to hers.

"You know something, Jenna? I like you. And it has nothing to do with your biscuits." He lifted his head and tipped her chin up with his thumb.

She caught her breath. "Don't, Lee. Please. If you do anything nice, I'll start to cry again."

He stared at her. She'd cry? Well, hell, that sure took his mind off kissing her.

"Jenna?" a young voice called out. "Mr. Carver? Where are you?"

"Over here," Lee shouted.

"Hurry!"

Lee clamped his jaw tight and ran for the camp. When he got close he saw not only the girls but the figure of a man, and his stomach turned over. He turned back toward Jenna. "Wait here," he yelled.

Mary Grace grabbed his hand. "Look who we brought, Mr. Carver," she sang.

The man turned, his face illuminated by the firelight. Not Morgan, thank God. This man was solidly built, with graying hair and a trim beard, and he was wearing a military jacket. He extended his hand as Lee approached.

"Lee. Good to see you, Major."

"Colonel Owens? I didn't recognize you, sir."

"Wasn't expecting me, either, I'd guess. Your girls told me you were traveling with their wagon. I hope I'm not intruding?"

"Not at all. Just a minute and I'll introduce you to their mother." He walked Jenna back into camp and presented her to the colonel.

"I am honored, Mrs. Borland." Then he surprised Lee with a question. "Would you happen to have some coffee brewed? Mrs. Lincoln served only tea after supper."

Lee grabbed the coffeepot, filled it from the water barrel hung at the side of the wagon and waited while Mary Grace ground up some beans.

Tess bobbed at Jenna's elbow. "Guess what, Jenna? They're having a ball tomorrow night, at the officers' quarters. Can we go? Please?"

Mary Grace tugged at Jenna's skirt. "Oh, could we? I'll watch after Ruthie, I promise."

Colonel Owens spoke up. "I hope you will attend as well, Mrs. Borland."

"Oh, no, I couldn't." She was misshapen and clumsy and she must look positively dreadful.

"We'll be there," Lee countered. He avoided Jenna's angry glare and instead set the coffeepot on the fire.

"Lee," the colonel said in an undertone. "Could I speak to you in private?"

The two men stepped away from camp, and Colonel

Owens cleared his throat. "A man rode into Fort Caspar a couple of days ago, asking after Mrs. Borland. Name of Morgan. You know him?"

"I know him. What did you tell him?"

"Nothing. I had no idea where her wagon might be. Or that you'd be with her. Didn't like the look of him, though. Thought you'd want to know."

"Thanks, Colonel. Don't mention it to Jenna."

"Figured as much. As I said, Morgan didn't impress me. Matter of fact, Lee, something about the man made my skin crawl."

Chapter Eighteen

"Just think," Tess whispered the next night in the wagon. "A ball! Jenna, will you show me how to braid my hair like yours?"

Jenna stared at her stepdaughter. *Tess is asking for my help?* After all the months of obvious dislike and disrespect, she could scarcely believe it.

"Me, too!" Mary Grace exclaimed.

"Your hair isn't long enough to braid," Tess sniped.

"Is too!"

"Is not!"

Jenna laid her hairbrush in her lap and studied the curved wooden wagon staves over her head. "If you two behave like this tonight, everyone will know you are not grown-up enough to attend a ball."

"I behave nice," Ruthie said. "I'm old enough for the ball, aren't I, Jenna?"

Jenna opened her mouth to reply but Tess cut her off. "I apologize, Mary Grace. I shouldn't have said that."

Mary Grace's hazel eyes widened. She and Jenna stared at each other, then both turned their gazes on Tess.

"I accept your apology, sister," the younger girl said primly.

Where on earth had the girls learned this? As far as she

knew since the day they'd laid eyes on her, the girls had never paid the slightest bit of attention to anything she'd said about good manners or social graces, to say nothing about being kind to each other.

She picked up Tess's comb and motioned her to turn around, then combed and braided, gradually feeding in more strands as she went along until a perfect crown of braided dark hair wound around the older girl's head. She handed Tess the hand mirror.

"Oh, it's just beautiful! Thank you, Jenna."

Jenna blinked in astonishment. *Thank you, Jenna?* She must be dreaming.

Both girls scrambled into clean gingham dresses, one blue and one pink, rubbed their dusty shoes with spit and clambered out of the wagon bed. Jimmy Gumpert waited outside to escort all three of them to the officers' quarters.

Lee and Jenna followed, walking side by side in uneasy silence. Jenna was still smarting from their exchange the night before when Lee had refused to tell her what Colonel Owens had said to him in private.

"Not important," he had insisted.

"Of course it's important," she'd flared. "Otherwise the colonel would have said it in my presence."

"Go to sleep, Jenna."

That had made her so mad she'd punched his shoulder. He'd grabbed her wrist and pinned it, then told her to mind her own business.

What on earth was the matter with the man? This *was* her business. This was *her* wagon, after all. *Her* family.

But when she'd pointed this out, he had laid his hand over her mouth and told her to shut up and go to sleep.

All day today something simmered between them. She didn't know how she felt about the man, and trying to puzzle it out just made her head ache. She resolved that tonight, at the officers' ball, she would talk with Emma

Lincoln and Sophia Zaberskie and the officers' wives and ignore Lee Carver completely.

The officers' quarters consisted of a trim, white-painted, two-story building with a wide veranda running along the front. The first floor, where the ball would be held, was a large room with polished plank floors; the second floor was where the men bunked.

Music drifted through the open double doors, and lamplight glowed from the tall windows. The girls dashed up the wide steps and disappeared inside, but Jenna hung back, an odd premonition tickling her spine. For some reason she felt apprehensive.

Ever since Randall had found her she'd felt angry and frightened. It was hard to face up to the mistakes she had made, but it was equally hard to feel that she didn't deserve to suffer for her pride. She hadn't listened to anyone about Randall, her mother least of all. She had been young and foolish, and remembering her stupidity made her cringe.

Never again would she let herself believe anything a man said. She would not, *would not*, be gulled by a man, no matter how attractive or persuasive. Or needy, like Mathias.

She would have to stay as far away from Lee Carver as possible. If she did not, she might admit to herself how much she liked him, how much she was drawn to him. Considering how foolish and headstrong she'd been in the past, that would be dangerous.

Two uniformed soldiers flanked the doorway, and a red-headed youth clicked his heels and bowed. "Good evening, ma'am. Welcome to Fort Caspar."

Just inside the warm, flower-scented room Jenna spied gray-bunned Emma Lincoln and headed for the sidelines to sit with the older woman.

Four earnest young soldiers sat in the far corner, sawing away on fiddles and strumming guitars, their faces flushed with perspiration. Ladies' perfume and bouquets of wild roses scented the air.

Jenna sank down beside Emma and let the music pour over her, then felt the older woman's calloused hand press hers.

"How are you feeling, my dear?"

"Quite well, thank you, Emma." Oh, how glibly she could lie! Not just to Emma, but to herself, as well.

"You look upset. Is something wrong?"

"I am…concerned about the girls. They have never attended a ball, and I do hope they behave."

Emma gestured across the spacious room. "The Gumpert boy is looking after them. Relax and enjoy yourself, Jenna."

She would give her right arm to be able to relax. "Emma, does a woman's worrying over her children, or even her stepchildren, ever end?" But even before Emma could answer, she had to admit she was on edge not just about the girls, but about Lee Carver.

"No, it does not, and I've raised three." She scanned the noisy dancers with twinkling blue eyes. "My advice is to stop stewing about your stepdaughters and enjoy yourself."

Jenna pressed her lips together and studied the dance floor, crowded with soldiers in military jackets and sharply creased trousers and their silk-gowned partners, as well as the emigrants and their less elegantly dressed wives and daughters.

Mick McKernan sidled up to within a yard of where she sat, but she angled her body away from him and pretended to wave at someone. When she looked back, the Irishman was gone.

"You don't like Mr. McKernan, do you?" Emma observed.

"No. I'm afraid I cannot hide my distaste for the man. From the day the train rolled out of Independence, he has leered at me, and it has grown worse since Mathias's death."

"I would think having Lee Carver driving your wagon would discourage Mick."

"Well, it has and it hasn't, Emma. Mr. McKernan behaves himself when Lee is around. It's when he's not that Mick is a problem."

"Then I'd stay close to Mr. Carver."

"But that's the problem, Emma, I—"

"Look." Emma tipped her head toward Sophia Zaberskie, whirling past in the arms of her husband. "That woman has had more than her share of heartbreak, losing two sons in as many years. Tonight she looks almost happy."

"It must take years to recover from losing one's children."

"Ted is a great help," Emma said.

"Funny, her husband doesn't look the least bit heroic, does he?"

Emma laughed. "Not with that shock of red hair and his potbelly."

"Yes," Jenna said, her tone thoughtful. "I am beginning to think heroism is often a quiet matter, not something flamboyant. I think your husband, Sam, is heroic, Emma. You are fortunate."

"I am that." Emma leaned in close and spoke in an undertone. "However, I must confess that Sam feels so much responsibility for getting this train through to Oregon he... well, he hasn't much time for anything else. Me, for instance," she said with a self-conscious laugh.

Jenna opened her mouth to reply, then snapped it shut. What did she know about a relationship with a man? She had made a hash of it both times, first with Randall and then with Mathias. She hated herself for both lapses, for letting Randall bully her into...

She caught her breath and ran one hand over her hard belly. And she hated herself for agreeing to marry Mathias.

Was there something about her that invited men to pressure her into things? Both her older stepdaughters were insolent; if she let them, they would walk all over her. And now, with her advancing pregnancy, she was growing more tired each day. Soon she might not manage to haul water and cook and air bedding and wash clothes and…

What will I do when the baby comes?

"Emma, I wonder if—" She broke off as a shadow fell over her.

Colonel Owens bowed before them. "Ladies."

Emma smiled. "Good evening, Colonel."

The colonel turned to Jenna. "Mrs. Borland, would you honor me with a dance?"

Jenna hesitated. "Oh, I didn't think I would dance tonight, Colonel. I will just enjoy the music."

"Then perhaps you would indulge me a few moments of your time?"

She rose and accepted the colonel's proffered arm. He escorted her through the crowd to the entrance, where the two soldiers on duty snapped salutes and swung the door open before them. Outside, Jenna breathed in fresh, cool air and allowed Colonel Owens to guide her along the veranda.

He halted at the far end and faced her. "Mrs. Borland, I wanted to speak to you in private."

"Certainly, Colonel." She prayed he was going to tell her what he and Lee had talked about last night.

"First," the colonel began, "I want to express my sympathy for your husband's death."

Jenna looked past him onto the shadowy parade ground where she and Lee had walked yesterday evening. She rarely thought of Mathias these days. "Thank you, Colonel."

"I understand it was Major Carver who was responsible."

Jenna said nothing.

"And," he continued, "for that reason I want to tell you something about Lee Carver."

Instantly her instincts went on alert. "What about him?"

"My dear, allow me to be blunt. I've known Major Carver ever since the War Between the States ended and he came west to serve with the Federal Army. We campaigned together out of Fort Kearney, fighting the Sioux and the Cheyenne."

Jenna nodded. "Mr. Carver said once that he joined the army after the War because there was nothing left for him in Virginia."

"Yes, I know. When Lee served under me he was as close to a broken man as I've ever seen. But as the months went by, I observed some things. I'd like to tell you about them, if I may."

Jenna looked up at the older man and tried to smile. "Yes, go on. I am listening."

"First, Mrs. Borland, the major is no philanderer. I say that because far too many soldiers are, especially when separated from their wives and sweethearts."

Jenna felt her face flush.

"Second," the colonel continued, "Lee Carver is a good man. The best. He is also somewhat… How should I put it? Somewhat vulnerable."

"Why are you telling me this?"

Colonel Owens stood looking down at her, then took her hand in his. "Because, Mrs. Borland, I would not want to see this man hurt."

Without another word he walked Jenna back inside and conducted her to the sidelines where Emma sat with Sophia Zaberskie. She listened idly to the conversation between the two women, her gaze darting around the room as they chatted, but in her mind she kept hearing Colonel Owens's words. *I would not want to see this man hurt.*

And then Sophia said something that caught her attention.

"I…well, I t'ink I be, you know, in the family way." Sophia's smooth, round face was pink with happiness, and she kept surreptitiously inspecting Jenna's expanding waistline.

"Why, Sophia, that is wonderful news!" Emma exclaimed. "Have you told Ted?"

The younger woman worked her handkerchief over and under her long fingers. "Oh, no. I wait until I am sure. He suffered much when…"

Jenna reached over and squeezed the young woman's hand. If Sophia Zaberskie could reach once more for happiness after losing two sons, she herself could certainly do her best after losing Mathias. She blinked back tears and gazed out at the dance floor.

The officers' wives looked like colorful butterflies in their gowns of emerald and rose and blue silk. A number of them were obviously expecting; she wondered if they were as frightened as she was at the prospect of giving birth in this harsh, untamed land.

Lee was dancing with one of them, an officer's daughter, she guessed. The girl was no more than seventeen, and she was gazing up at him with adoring blue eyes. She had very yellow hair, not French-braided as hers was, but curled into tight corkscrews that bounced when she tossed her head. Which, Jenna noted, she did often. The girl was slim and quite pretty.

Deliberately Jenna looked away and swallowed hard. When she risked another look, Lee was circling around and around with an ecstatic Ruthie clasped in his arms. Next he danced a reel with Mary Grace as his partner.

During the next set, Jenna watched Jimmy Gumpert determinedly guide Tess back and forth across the floor in a halting two-step, apparently unaware that the music was in waltz-time. And then a tall, gangly young soldier who looked no more than sixteen cut in and spirited Tess away in a flutter of blue gingham ruffles.

"Well, now, isn't that nice," Emma remarked with a smile.

"Oh, dear," Jenna whispered. "Tess will be puffed up for days."

"Jimmy Gumpert certainly won't be," Emma said with a laugh.

Jenna started to reply, but a man's warm hand took hers and pulled her to her feet. The next thing she knew Lee Carver had folded her into his arms.

Chapter Nineteen

Without a word Lee drew her into a waltz. Silence stretched between them, but she didn't mind. Instead, she found herself listening to what his body said as it moved with hers. It said, among other things, that he valued her. He held her so carefully, so gently, it was as if she were made of glass.

When the dance ended, he did not release her. A slow two-step followed, then another waltz, and now he held her close, so close her breasts brushed the front of his white linen shirt, and her long calico skirt kept getting tangled between his legs. His warm hand spread across her back, pressing her into his lean, hard frame.

She felt a bit drunk being so near him, moving with him as if they were one being. She had never danced with a man like this. Randall had always been busy at night, when the Roseville socials were held. She saw him only in the daytime, when she brought documents her mother had signed to his law office.

Lee's chin grazed her temple. She closed her eyes and inhaled the scent of pine soap and tobacco smoke and the faint salty tang of perspiration. His breathing was uneven, as if he had been running.

Her own breathing grew ragged. *This should not be*

happening. Never again did she wish to be the object of a
man's desire.

Over his shoulder she glimpsed Mick McKernan circling
at the edge of the floor, obviously waiting for a chance to
cut in. She stiffened, and Lee's arm tightened about her
waist. Adroitly he kept turning them so his back was always facing Mick, shielding her, and finally the Irishman
stomped off with a scowl on his flushed face.

Lee began gently circling his hand on her back, caress-
ing each bone of her spine under her shirtwaist. Then he
slid his hand lower, to her waist, and then lower still to a
place that sent a shiver through her frame. It was scandal-
ous where he was touching her! But everyone else was
dancing, and no one seemed to notice.

But *she* noticed! And she didn't want to notice. Physi-
cal attraction between herself and Mathias had not been
part of their bargain, but Lee was different. Being close
to him was different. She felt warm and safe and cared
about. This was nothing like Randall's hurried protesta-
tions of devotion and his hot, breathy kisses against the
closed door of his office.

With Lee's body so close to hers she felt something she'd
never felt before, a kind of yearning. She didn't want to
like it. But she did.

You like Lee. You like being near him. She didn't have
to trust him to like being near him, did she?

A sweet, hot ache began below her belly. He folded his
fingers around her hand and after a moment drew it in and
pressed it against his chest. She could feel his heart thump-
ing under her palm.

She forgot all about Mick McKernan, and the girls, and
Colonel Owens. She even forgot about Randall Morgan.
She was aware only of Lee, how he made her feel when
she was close to him. The throbbing, insistent ache building inside her was something she had never experienced.

It sent a jolt of hunger though her that was so heady and demanding it frightened her.

They danced without speaking until midnight, which was just as well because Jenna could think of nothing to say. She couldn't even think clearly. She imagined she was floating high above the dancers on a soft blue cloud, and she seemed unable to stop smiling.

At midnight, the junior officers laid a late supper along a long trestle table, and the musicians stopped playing. Lee released her, loaded up a single plate and stuck two forks into his shirt pocket. Then he walked her out onto the veranda where they ate cold sliced ham and potato salad and shared a thick slice of blackberry pie.

An odd thought struck her. It wasn't intimacy she had with Lee. It was not really friendship, either. It was something between, something rich and unspoken. Something she valued.

Still they said nothing to each other. It was almost as if words were not needed, but that idea was so preposterous she choked on a bite of pie. Words were *always* needed between human beings. She and Lee were different people, from such different backgrounds. They had been brought together only by chance and forced into proximity. And yet she felt no need to make even polite conversation with this man, and that made her wonder. There should be all sorts of things they needed to communicate to each other.

A slow wave of heat surged from her toes to her hairline, prompting a deeper question. Why did she feel no threat from Lee, the way she had with Randall? Randall had always wanted more than she was comfortable giving, but Lee...

Lee asked nothing. He simply let her know what he was feeling, and waited. It was all such a puzzle! She did know one thing, however; the war between her thoughts and her feelings was tearing her in two.

The evening drew to a close with a slow rendition of

"Red River Valley." Lee pulled her close, holding her as if she were made of flower petals. She didn't want this to end. She wanted to keep her eyes closed and keep moving in Lee's arms.

But of course it had to end. She was acting like a silly, addlepated girl, and she would never be that young again. She was wiser now. She knew better than to let herself become involved with a man. It never turned out the way you thought it would.

The musicians began to pack up their instruments, and the crowd thinned and then began to disperse. Lee kept her hand in his and they started back to the wagons. The girls trailed behind them, their chatter and laughter filling the silence that stretched between them. How very odd this was. From the moment he had drawn her into his arms, they had not spoken a single word to each other.

Ruthie skipped beside Jenna, clinging to her other hand.

"That gray man with the beard danced me, too," she chirped. "Did you see me, Jenna? Did you?"

"I saw you dancing with Mr. Carver, Ruthie."

"No, it was that old man, the cern'l," Ruthie insisted.

"You mean Colonel Owens?"

Ruthie giggled. "Am I all growed up yet? I wanna braid my hair like Tess."

They reached the camp, and the girls immediately climbed through the bonnet and into the wagon. Lee went to check the oxen and Devil, picketed some yards away. When he returned, he gave a final look around camp, shucked his boots, unbuckled his belt and stripped off his shirt. Then he crawled onto his pallet and waited for Jenna, who was inside the wagon, reading to the girls.

She was taking so long Lee gritted his teeth. They had not spoken to each other all evening, had not needed to. But there were things that had to be said out loud, and it was by God going to be tonight.

Finally she appeared, scooted under the wagon to lay out

her two quilts and removed her shoes. She began to unbraid her hair, finger-combing the tangle of dark waves, and Lee breathed in the spicy-sweet scent. Roses, maybe. Or lilacs. He propped himself on one elbow and closed his eyes.

"Jenna."

Her motions stilled. "Lee, this is the first time all evening you have said a single word to me."

He kept his eyes shut. "Not true. I've been talking to you all evening." He reached one hand up to her neck and pulled her face down to his until he felt her warm breath against his lips. "Couldn't you tell? I've been wanting to do this for hours."

He raised his head slightly and touched his mouth to hers, gently at first, then more deeply. With his other hand he cupped the back of her head and ran his tongue over her lips, urging her mouth open. She tasted of mint.

He kissed her until his groin ached. Finally he broke free and buried his face in her hair. "Do you have feelings for Randall Morgan?" he whispered.

"No, I don't. Why are you asking me about him?"

He opened his eyes and looked directly into hers. "Because I don't want him to touch you. I meant what I said before—if he comes after you again, I'm going to kill him."

Her head moved up and down in a nod. "Yes," she murmured. "I understand."

He wove his fingers into her hair, pulled her close and kissed her closed eyelids. Then he brought his fingers to the top button of her dress and slipped it free. He heard her breath hitch in, but she didn't move away. He undid three more buttons, and she laid her hand on his.

"Where is your rifle?" she asked. "You usually sleep with your rifle next to you."

"I'm not sleeping with my rifle tonight. I'm sleeping with you."

To his relief she said nothing.

"Jenna," he whispered. "Take off your dress."

He saw her hesitate, biting her lower lip and looking at him with widened green eyes. Then she slipped the buttons free all the way down to her waist. Her fingers trembled. She sat up and slid the calico off her shoulders to free her arms. Lee reached around her to undo the skirt fastening, and she tugged the garment off.

"Now the rest." He untied the ribbon at the neck of her camisole and bent to press his lips against her bare skin.

"Lee, you cannot want this. Me. I am pregnant…big and swollen and…pregnant."

"I know." He pushed her shoulder strap over her shoulder. "Take this off."

"Lee…"

He smiled. "You want me to do it?"

Jenna stared at him in disbelief, not at his suggestion, but at her unspoken response. Yes, she did want him to do it. With a little sigh she lifted her arms, and he pulled the soft muslin over her head. The warm night air washed over her, and her breasts tingled.

He smoothed his hand over her skin, slowly brushing her nipples with his thumbs, moved away, then brushed them again. Her flesh swelled and began to throb, and she blinked in surprise.

"Nothing has ever felt like this before," she whispered.

He raised his head and looked into her eyes. "How do you mean? I thought—"

"Randall never touched me like this," she said quietly. "He just, well, lifted up my skirt and…"

Lee made a noise low in his throat. "Damn fool."

"I thought I wanted him," she said in a low voice. "Now I know that I didn't, not really. Now I know what wanting a man really feels like."

His hand stopped moving. "Yeah?"

"I want you, Lee. You."

Chapter Twenty

Hell, Lee thought, he was as scared as she was. She didn't know what to do, and all at once he felt humbled. It made him wonder about himself, trying to pretend this didn't matter. He chuckled under his breath.

"Why are you laughing?" she whispered. "I know how I look. My belly is all swollen and…" She dropped her face into her hands.

God, she was crying! "Jenna. *Jenna*." He pried her fingers away from her face. "It doesn't matter."

"Of course it matters." She sniffled and wiped the back of her hand across her nose like a child. The gesture made his chest feel tight.

He sat up and pulled her close. "It *doesn't* matter," he said again. "You think a man thinks of a woman as just a pretty object? That he loses interest when she's carrying a child?"

"Well, doesn't he?"

"Not *this* man. Jenna, you are the most unusual, spirited, beautiful woman I've ever known. Don't you know this about yourself?"

"N-no. Mama always said I was too thin and I had freckles, and Randall—"

"Forget Randall. I don't want to hear his name again."

It came out harsher than he'd intended and she stared at him, her eyes shiny and green as spring grass. Quickly he shed his jeans and reached for her.

"I mean," he amended, "I don't want anyone else in this bed but you and me."

She nodded, but her eyes were still puzzled, and then it hit him. That bastard had taken advantage of her. No preliminaries. Probably no real feeling for her other than lust, since he was already married. He'd probably seduced her, tossed up her skirt like she said, and…

Oh, hell. From the way she kept looking down at her hands instead of his naked body, it was clear she'd never done this the way it should be done.

He was pretty sure she wanted him, but… "Jenna, look at me."

She raised her head to meet his gaze, and her tangled dark hair brushed her bare shoulders. He lifted one strand and brought it to his nose. It smelled like roses. He let it drop and picked up her hand.

"I haven't been with a woman since the War," he said quietly. "Haven't wanted one, until now. But I want you, Jenna."

He lifted her hand to his bare chest. "And now we're lying next to each other, and I want to touch you. Not only that…" He moved her hand. "I want you to touch me."

Hesitantly she spread her fingers across his skin, and he sucked in his breath. "Yeah," he murmured. "Like that."

He smoothed his hand over her belly, circled around her navel, then moved to cup her breast. Her skin was like warm cream. He leaned in to swirl his tongue over her nipple and heard her stop breathing.

But she didn't move her hand away from his chest. Instead, she gently drew one finger down his midriff and back up, did it again, and again. Then she looked up at him and smiled.

His heart missed about four beats. He moved to her other

breast, covered it with his mouth, and curled his tongue across the swelling nub.

She liked that. He could tell because her lips came open and she sighed. He raised his head and found her mouth, then blew gently into her ear. Her entire frame jerked.

"Oh," she whispered. He kissed her throat and again breathed into the shell of her ear.

"You like that?"

"Yes."

"More?"

"No," she whispered. She rose up on one elbow to kiss him, which surprised him. Her mouth opened under his, and as she allowed him entry he realized she was trembling.

"Jenna," he breathed against her lips.

"Don't talk, Lee," she murmured. "Just kiss me. Touch me."

That surprised him even more. He smoothed his palm over her belly, gradually moved lower until his hand touched the silky hair between her thighs.

"Yes," she breathed.

He slid one finger past her folds and stroked slowly back and forth. Her breath caught, and her soft moan told him everything he needed to know.

Oh, God, she felt good. She was hot and slick and so soft it was like touching spun silk. His groin began to ache. He wanted her under him, but he knew he'd have to take it slow.

She made a soft noise and the sound sent a bolt of desire through him. He clenched his jaw.

Jenna felt his body stiffen. But his hand, his finger… He was touching her in such an intimate way it made her gasp. It felt wonderful. Intoxicating. And so delicious she never wanted it to end.

He slipped a finger inside her and her heart stopped. Her body slowed and grew warm, as if a hot light were flooding into her being. She lifted her hips to meet his gentle probing, wanting him closer, deeper.

Again his mouth found hers, his tongue teasing and plunging, then withdrawing. He tasted of coffee and something sweet. Blackberries, she guessed.

He made a sound deep in his throat that spoke of hunger and wanting, and she shivered. Her skin felt as if stars were raining down on her flesh.

She strained to get closer, wanted to crawl inside his skin. He lifted his lips from hers, breathing heavily, and spoke against her mouth, his voice low and gravelly.

"Jenna. Jenna, tell me you want this. Say it. That you want me. Want to be with me. Say it."

She couldn't speak. Instead, she kissed his mouth, his closed eyelids, his throat. She moved to his shoulder, ran her tongue over one nipple, then the other, and heard him groan. She slid her palm over his belly and then lower, touching him. His body was shaking.

He sucked in air and grabbed her hand away. "Don't."

"Why?" she whispered. "I want to touch you." She smoothed her forefinger along his length, and again he lifted her hand away, breathing hard.

"I'm too close." He pressed her hand to his chest and held it there while his breath rasped in and out. He put his mouth on her throat, moved behind her ear, then pressed kisses along the valley between her breasts, all the while circling his finger within her intimate folds.

His finger moved deeper inside her and she cried out. It felt hot and sweet and it made her ache.

"Lee," she murmured. "Don't stop."

Gently he nudged her legs apart with his knee and rose over her. "If you don't want this, tell me now. Later, I won't be able to stop."

She reached her hand up to his shoulders and pulled him down to her. "Don't stop. I want to be with you."

Very slowly he entered her. When he filled her completely, he withdrew and entered her again. She heard him whisper her name, and then he began to move.

"Oh, God, Jenna."

She rose to meet him, her body tightening, reaching. She wanted to cry out, to hold him deep inside her. Tears stung into her eyes. She opened her mouth and suddenly something burst inside her and her body convulsed. Wave after wave of exquisite pleasure rocked through her. Behind her eyelids she saw colors, scarlet stars and silver-white shapes that exploded into fire.

Lee covered her cry with his mouth, and then his body stiffened. He was close, so close. Fighting for control, he tried to think of something else, the wagon, the oxen, Devil. But then she moved under him, and he had no choice but to let it come.

He clamped his lips shut against the shout that erupted, he rode her into oblivion.

A long while later he lifted his head and gazed into Jenna's eyes. He could scarcely believe what had happened. Hell, maybe he was dreaming.

She stirred under him, and he rolled off and gathered her into his arms. Her heart was still racing.

"Lee?" Her voice sounded dazed.

Oh, God, don't spoil it. Just let it be. "Yeah?"

"Does it… I mean, does it always happen like that?"

He swallowed and tried to steel himself. "Like what?"

"Like…everything exploding, like fireworks. Does it?"

He tried very hard not to grin, but her question made him so damn happy he thought he would split. "Well, it depends, I guess."

"On what?"

"On whether you want it. On…" he hesitated "…on whether the other person means something to you."

She said nothing, just lay quietly in his arms. He could almost hear her mind working. He'd bet it had never been like this for her. He felt proud and shaken and grateful and possessive all at once.

She reached one hand to his cheek. "It is a wondrous thing, isn't it?"

"Not always. But some special times it is, yes."

"I might never have known this," she whispered. "I am glad I didn't miss it."

Didn't miss...? He sensed finality behind her words, and he didn't like it. He turned her hand over and pressed his lips into her palm. Her skin tasted sweet and a little salty.

Like her.

Chapter Twenty-One

Jenna awoke at dawn to find the pallet beside her empty. She sighed and smoothed her hand over the blanket, still warm from where his body had lain. She felt languid and a bit dazed, yet her body was exquisitely tuned to every sound and scent, the soft whicker of horses, wood smoke from someone's fire pit, the rich smell of frying bacon...

Bacon! She gasped and bolted upright, and the cool morning air washed over her bare breasts. Her camisole and muslin underdrawers and petticoat lay neatly folded at the foot of her pallet; her calico skirt and shirtwaist had been laid out beside them.

She dressed quickly, fumbling with ties and buttons, until she was decent enough to appear in camp, then braided her hair and bound it at the nape of her neck. When she emerged from under the wagon, Lee was bent over a skillet, turning strips of bacon with a fork. Mary Grace stood next to him, mixing up a bowl of something. She smelled coffee!

Lee turned and her heartbeat kicked up a notch. Two notches. She couldn't look at him.

Mary Grace's stirring spoon halted. "You look all different, Jenna. Your face looks...funny. You've been crying again, haven't you? Didn't you like the ball last night?"

"Yes, I liked it," Jenna managed. "I liked it very much." She knew her cheeks were flushing but there was nothing she could do about it. Maybe Lee wouldn't notice.

But he did notice. His eyes met hers for a long moment, and then he grinned. "Are you hungry this morning?" he asked, his voice bland.

"I— Yes, I am. Ravenous."

He forked up a strip of crisp bacon and held it out to her. "There's coffee, too."

"You must have gotten up very early," she said.

Again his gaze held hers. "Or maybe you slept late."

"Yes, I was tired after…after the ball."

"I wasn't." He poured her a mug of coffee, brought it over to her and pointed at the apple crate. "You'd better sit down, Jenna. You're shaking."

She plopped herself down and sipped the coffee while Lee lifted the bacon slices onto a tin plate and motioned Mary Grace toward the skillet.

"I'm gonna make pancakes," the girl said proudly.

Jenna blinked. *She's going to make pancakes?* Good heavens, Mary Grace was growing up right before her eyes. She could only hope that Tess would follow.

That hope was dashed when Ruthie and Tess climbed out of the wagon.

"I wanna make pancakes, too," Ruthie said.

"You're too little," Tess shot.

"Am not!"

"Are too!"

"Girls!" Jenna stood up. "Last night you behaved like young ladies, and I was proud of you. This morning…" She let her voice trail off.

Tess made a face. "This morning Ruthie is still too little to make—"

Lee turned to face her. "Tess." His tone brought both girls to attention. "You want to eat breakfast?"

"Of course I do. I'm hungry!"

"Instead of teasing Ruthie, you could have helped. You ever consider that?"

An uneasy silence fell. Mary Grace dipped a spoonful of thick batter into the skillet and Jenna drew in a deep breath and looked up at the sky. Maybe she was still dreaming.

Sunlight shone through the aspen leaves, turning them scarlet and gold. It was a beautiful, peaceful morning, with thrushes singing in the trees, cows lowing to be milked, the sounds of people beginning to stir about in their wagons. The last thing she wanted was to spoil the wonder of her night with Lee by arguing with Tess. She closed her eyes and said nothing until a plate of pancakes and bacon slid onto her lap.

"Better eat," Lee said. "Got a long day ahead of us. And," he added in an undertone, "a long night."

She opened her mouth to reply, but he was leaning against the wagon wheel, smiling over his plate of pancakes. She closed her eyes again and tried to calm her breathing.

An hour later, the wagon train rolled away from Fort Caspar and out onto the rutted trail to Oregon. It was a scorching day. No trees grew on the flat, unbroken plain, just spiny-looking gray sagebrush and the occasional sparse stand of cottonwoods near dried-up streambeds. By the time they stopped for their nooning, the girls were so wilted and short-tempered they refused to speak to each other.

Lee climbed down from the driver's box and reached up for Ruthie, who was drooping in the heat. He carried her to the shade of a spreading oak and set her down next to Tess, then mopped his face with his bandanna and sought Jenna's eyes. She looked so exhausted his conscience pricked him.

It was his fault. Neither of them had slept much last night, but God knew he wouldn't trade a single hour with her for a whole day under a shade tree. He stepped close to her.

"You need to rest, Jenna. You've been walking since breakfast."

"I am quite all right. It's Ruthie I am worried about."

"Yeah, I know. We're facing a hundred more miles of this desert."

"And some Indians," she added. "Last night at the ball I heard Colonel Owens warn Sam about Indians."

Lee swore under his breath. He'd have to guard Devil closely at night. He couldn't afford to lose his horse; he'd pinned all his hopes for a future on having a horse ranch in Oregon, and to do that he needed his prize Arabian stallion. If he had to he'd sit up all night with his rifle.

The rest of the afternoon on the trail he studied the horizon for a telltale dust cloud signaling Indian trouble and praying the emigrant train wouldn't stumble into the middle of a war between the Sioux and the Crow. Looking into the sun like that made his eyes ache.

He kept an eye on Jenna, walking on the left side of the rolling wagon. Nothing he could say would persuade her to ride next to him on the box. Stubborn woman. Tess and Mary Grace straggled along on the other side, and now they dropped back beside Mick McKernan's team of horses.

Lee slowed the oxen so the girls could catch up, but it wasn't soon enough. Mick's bellowing voice made his hands clench on the reins.

"Hey, girlie, you tell yer ma hello from this Irishman, will ya?"

Tess tossed her head and slipped an arm around Mary Grace's waist.

"You hear me?" McKernan whipped his team and pulled forward so his front wheels almost touched the Borland wagon. Jimmy Gumpert hurried Tess into a faster pace, while Mary Grace swung herself up into the wagon.

"Hey," Mick yelled again. "Tell yer ma she's the prettiest colleen in this train, even if she is in the family way."

Tess turned to make some retort, but the Gumpert boy yanked her back.

"Ya hear me, gal? You tell that to yer ma, and make sure she knows it's Mick McKernan that's sayin' it."

Jenna shot Lee a look. "Stop the wagon, Lee. I don't want the girls harassed."

"Better to keep moving," he called. "I'll outpace him." Jenna frowned, but she resumed walking steadily at his left.

"What's a colleen?" Ruthie piped.

Lee leaned toward her. "A pretty girl. Like you."

He started to add something, but Mick McKernan's voice stopped him.

"You tell yer ma she's a damn fine-lookin' female," the Irishman rasped. "Bet she's hungry for a real man 'bout now, and I'm just the—"

His words suddenly broke off. Lee twisted to check on the girls and found Mary Grace walking backward next to her sister, pointing Lee's revolver straight at McKernan's belly.

"You leave my stepmother alone!" she shouted.

Jenna gasped. "Lee, she has your gun!"

"Yeah." He was proud of the girl. "She knows how to fire it, too," he said. "Glad I showed her."

The McKernan wagon dropped back, and Lee released a long breath.

Jenna said nothing. She was astounded at Mary Grace's actions. Part of her swelled with relief and pride that the girl had come to her defense; another part questioned how long her stepdaughter's regard would last. Just when she thought the older girls were beginning to accept her, one of them said something mean and hurtful.

Lee had been right to teach the girls how to handle a weapon. It gave them a measure of safety on the trail. She supposed that was true of his teaching them to ride, as well.

When the wagons stopped for the night, Lee didn't bother to unhitch the oxen. Instead, he strode up to the

front of the train to talk with Sam Lincoln. When he returned, he climbed back up onto the box, lifted the reins
and drove the team forward in a huge circle and then pulled
in behind the McKernan wagon.

The minute he rolled to a stop, Tess and Mary Grace
stepped forward to unyoke the team. "You did well today,"
he said to Mary Grace.

She gestured at their new position in the train. "So did
you."

Supper was corn bread and beans that had been soaking
all day in a canvas bag tied to the wagon. They had replenished their dwindling supplies at the sutler's store at Fort
Caspar, and now there was plenty of cornmeal and coffee,
even a small sack of sugar. For dessert that night Jenna
concocted a pudding using eggs from Sophia Zaberskie's
chickens and milk from Emma Lincoln's cow.

Darkness fell. Crickets began to scrape in the silence,
and mosquitos whined about her head. Jenna smeared Ruthie's face and arms with citronella oil to repel them. The
older girls escaped into the wagon, but Ruthie insisted on
staying up to watch Lee carve another wooden figure.

"Is that a woof?" she asked.

"It's a dog," Lee answered. "He has a big tail, doesn't
he? Guess he does look a bit like a wolf, though."

"Woofs sound sad at night," Ruthie observed. "They
make howly noises. And they're scary, too."

Jenna jerked to attention. Was the girl frightened at
night? She plunged the tin plates into the bucket of hot
wash water. "Ruthie, are you afraid at night?"

"Y-yes, sometimes. Tess pokes me when I'm scared.
Could I sleep with you under the wagon, Jenna? Then I
wouldn't be scared."

Lee caught Jenna's eye and nodded. "I'll be on guard
duty all night," he said in a low voice. "Sam warned me
about some Indians he spotted."

"Indians?" she whispered.

"Don't worry, you're plenty safe under the wagon. I'll be three feet away from you."

"Oh."

"Disappointed?" he breathed.

"Relieved," she admitted with a laugh that just burbled out. "I don't know if I could stand another night with no sleep."

He sent her a look she couldn't read. "Didn't like last night, huh?"

She sloshed the last plate in the rinse water and picked up the huck towel. Lee stepped in so close she could feel his breath on the back of her neck. It sent a shiver of want through her entire body, and her hand faltered.

"Send Ruthie to bed in the wagon and let's go for a walk," he whispered.

Her face burned. "I…well, I…"

He laughed softly. "All right, I'll kiss you right here."

"Ruthie," she said quickly. "Go to bed in the wagon for now. Later you can sleep next to me."

"What about Mister Lee?"

Lee knelt in front of the girl. "Mister Lee isn't going to sleep tonight. He's going to be on guard duty."

"What's garduty?"

"That's when someone protects you while you're sleeping."

Ruthie flung her thin arms around his neck and smacked a kiss against his stubbly cheek. "Night, Mister Lee."

Lee found his throat so tight he couldn't answer. When Ruthie scampered up into the wagon, he rose to discover Jenna had disappeared. Well, hell.

He checked the hobble he'd attached to Devil's legs, then took his rifle and stationed himself between the Borland wagon and the one ahead of it, settled his back against the iron wheel rim and rested his weapon across his lap.

It turned out to be a long, long night. He thought a lot about Jenna, and about the girls, about the child Jenna was carrying. About the hundreds of miles they had yet to cross before winter would set in.

In the morning he was bleary-eyed, and his chin was bristly as a porcupine. Jenna fried bacon and poured his coffee with extra care, and Mary Grace and Tess yoked up the oxen on their own. Beaming, they pranced back into camp, and Jenna let them each have a mug of watered-down coffee.

Tess spit hers out immediately. "Ick! How can you drink this stuff, Mr. Carver?"

"Took me years to get used to the taste, but—" He halted as Sam Lincoln walked into camp, flanked by two tall, well-muscled Indian braves, their faces painted with red and yellow stripes.

Lee stood up. "Jenna, girls, get into the wagon."

"But—" Tess started to object.

"Now!" he ordered. He watched them climb through the bonnet, then turned his attention to Sam and waited for the wagon master to explain.

Chapter Twenty-Two

Jenna crowded together with the girls in the wagon bed, her heart pounding so hard her chest hurt. Ruthie whimpered in her lap, and both Tess and Mary Grace looked white as ghosts. Through the canvas bonnet she watched Sam and the painted Indians approach Lee.

Sam took Lee aside. "I know you speak some Indian lingo. Can you figure out what these two want?"

Lee lifted his right hand and spoke some words in that odd language he'd used before. Sioux, Jenna guessed. One of the braves returned the gesture; the other said nothing, just stared around the camp. He made a move toward the loaf of bread Jenna had baked, still sitting beside the fire, but the other one made a sharp cutting motion with his arm, and the bread-seeker focused elsewhere.

The first Indian held up two fingers and motioned toward the wagon. Lee shook his head and spoke a single word. The brave then held up four fingers.

Sam began to look uneasy. "What do they want?"

"They're looking for white women for wives. They offer two horses for Tess, four for Jenna."

"Good God!" Sam exploded. He spat onto the ground and shouldered his rifle. In an instant, Lee reached over and pressed the gun barrel down toward the ground. "For God's sake, Sam, don't shoot. Let them talk."

Jenna shot a look at Tess; the girl's hazel eyes were wide with horror. "Mary Grace," Jenna murmured. "Find Lee's revolver."

The girl rummaged in the large pocket sewn high up on the interior canvas wall and slid the weapon into Jenna's trembling hands.

"Now, take Ruthie and lie flat, all of you." She trained the gun on the Indian doing the talking. After a moment, Mary Grace reached up and released the safety.

"Aim at his chest," she whispered.

Jenna nodded and aimed.

Now the brave raised five fingers. Lee responded with a combination of chopping hand motions and Sioux words spoken in the harshest tone Jenna had ever heard him use. Then he jabbed at his own chest, poking his thumb on his own shirt.

Frowning, Sam looked from the Indian to Lee. "What's happening?"

Lee made no answer. Instead, he spoke more words to the braves. One grunted and gestured over his shoulder toward the west. His companion paced around and around the cook fire, dipped his forefinger into the still-warm skillet of bacon grease and jammed it into his mouth.

Lee pointed to the west and apparently asked a question. The Indian broke into a grin and nodded. He kept nodding as Lee rescued the skillet and offered it to him. The brave grunted, tipped it into his mouth and gulped down the greasy contents.

Jenna shuddered.

Abruptly both Indians pivoted and strode out of camp. Sam caught Lee's eye, shrugged and followed.

Jenna's hands were trembling so hard the revolver wobbled, so she handed it back to Mary Grace. "Fix that thing so it won't fire," she ordered. "And put it back into the pocket."

She patted a whimpering Ruthie, then climbed down from the wagon and ran to Lee. "What did they want?"

"You."

"Whaaat?"

"They offered five horses for you. I told them that wasn't enough."

"Oh! You didn't, not really."

"Yeah, I did. Then they told me they're fighting the Crow on the plain to the west. Unfortunately, west is right where we're headed."

Her knees felt weak.

He reached out and squeezed her shoulder. "I've got to let Sam know so we can reroute the train. Pack up."

Jenna's head spun. *Five horses?* The Indian thought she was worth only five horses? Her very next thought was one she couldn't stifle. What did Lee think she was worth?

The girls tumbled out of the wagon. "Are they gone? What did they want? Were those Indians mad?"

"Yes," Jenna said, choosing to answer only the last question. "They were…mad. Now, quick, wash up the dishes."

Tess's lower lip pushed out. "Jenna, do we have to? I'm sick of washing dishes."

Jenna clamped her jaw tight. For just one moment she thought of telling her oldest stepdaughter that the Indian braves had offered two horses to buy her. Some days, that seemed like a fair price.

The wagons rerouted to the south, and that night after supper Lee went off to Sam's camp to discuss the situation. Those Indians were obviously keeping track of where the wagon train was, and that pricked all his old soldiering instincts. He prayed they were more interested in attacking the Crow than in stealing white wives.

He found the men gathered around Sam's cook fire,

muttering among themselves. It looked to be a long night; Emma had made enough coffee for an army.

"Lee." Sam nodded at him. "I wanted you here while we talk over the situation."

"Don't tell them the Indians want white women, Sam. It'll make the men edgy and they'll be trigger-prone. Hot-headed action could be dangerous."

"Yeah," Sam agreed. "Relations with the Indian tribes are tense enough with thousands of settlers invading their hunting grounds. It'd be like tossing a match into a can of kerosene."

The wagon master then turned to the crowd and explained about the two Sioux braves who had ridden in to talk with Lee. The crowd's uneasy grumbling grew until Sam raised his hand for quiet.

"Carver here thinks it best we reroute the train even farther south."

"Oh, yeah?" Mick McKernan blustered. "Why's that?"

Lee moved into the firelight. "To avoid stumbling into the middle of an Indian war," he said calmly.

Emil Gumpert nervously stroked his salt-and-pepper beard.

"How ve know where iss dis war?"

"Huh!" Mick spit out. "How do we know there really *is* an Indian war?"

"Because," Lee returned, "the Sioux and the Crow have been enemies for generations. One of those Indians, a Sioux warrior, warned me to steer clear of their battleground."

"You'd trust a dirty savage to speak the truth?"

Lee clenched his fists. "An Indian isn't necessarily a savage, McKernan. In my experience neither the Sioux nor the Crow will lie. Steal, maybe, but not lie."

"You believe them, Carver?" Ted Zaberskie asked.

Lee accepted a mug of coffee from Emma. "Yeah, I do. No reason not to."

Mick McKernan flung the contents of his mug onto the

ground. "Why should we trust this Johnny Reb any more'n a dirty Indian?"

Sam faced the Irishman. "For one thing, this Johnny Reb speaks some Indian lingo. And for another, he's here on our wagon train, tryin' to get to Oregon just like the rest of us."

"Bull!" Mick shouted. "Carver's prob'ly in cahoots with them redskins."

Lee gave the Irishman a careful once-over. "You been drinkin', McKernan?"

Mick dragged the toe of his boot back and forth in front of him. "Not so's you'd notice."

"I notice," Lee said. He propped both hands on his hips and turned to Sam.

"What do you suggest, Carver?" the wagon master asked.

"I suggest we keep driving south ten or twelve more miles before we turn west."

"Might not be water out there," an older man said.

"Might not," Lee conceded. "It's a risk, all right. But it's better than running into a bunch of scalping knives."

"Hell," Mick jeered. "Yer nuthin' but a coward."

Lee ignored him, but Sam brushed past him to confront the Irishman. "Shut up, McKernan." Then he turned to the assembled men. "Gentlemen," he said quietly. "We will vote on it."

"Vote!" Mick scoffed.

"That's how we do things in this country," Sam said. "And that's how we do things on this wagon train."

"Yeah, take a vote," a few men echoed.

"All right, then," Sam said. "All those in favor of heading straight west on our original course?"

Only two men, Mick and his brother, Arn, raised their arms.

"Looks like we'll reroute south, like Carver said," Sam announced. "Make sure your water barrels are full. We'll pull out in the morning."

Lee turned to go, but Sam laid a hand on his arm. "How far south you figure we'll have to travel?"

"Don't know. I can ride out and scout ahead, see if I run into any Indian skirmishes."

"We're already into sagebrush country. It's likely real desert south of here."

"Yeah, you're right. I've ridden some of this area with the army. It isn't pretty."

Sam frowned and worked his lower lip with his teeth. "Lee, if you go off to scout, who's gonna drive Miz Borland's wagon?"

"Mrs. Borland herself."

"Think she can handle an ox team?"

"Yeah, I do think so. She's tougher than she looks. The girls can yoke up the team. But there's just one thing, Sam. I don't want McKernan slinking around their camp offering to help."

Sam gave him a long, steady look and then nodded. "Right. I'll keep an eye on her wagon."

"Could you move it up to the front of the train? Away from McKernan?"

"Sure, Lee. Glad to."

"Thanks. I'll saddle up and leave at first light. I might be gone most of the day, so just keep driving farther south until I can get back and report."

He didn't return to Jenna's wagon right away. The exchange with Mick McKernan had left a bad taste in his mouth, and he needed to blow off some steam. He tramped twice around the infield where the animals were penned, checked Devil's picket rope and stood for a long time studying the sky off to the west.

When he walked back into camp he could hear the girls arguing inside the wagon, their voices rising in strident tones. He closed his ears to the shrill accusations. If he was their father he'd put a stop to that squabbling right quick. Good thing for them that he wasn't.

Jenna sat beside the dying fire, Ruthie curled up on her lap.

"Thought you'd be asleep," Lee said.

"It's too noisy. Just listen. The minute I think those two girls are finally growing out of their yammering at each other, they're at it again."

Lee hunkered down in front of her. "What are they fighting about this time?"

"You."

"Me!"

"Tess insists she is a better horsewoman than Mary Grace, that you taught her more. Right now I wish you hadn't taught either one of them to ride."

"No, you don't, Jenna. You don't need helpless females out here on the prairie. Everyone has to pull his..." He hesitated. "Her own weight."

Jenna said nothing. Was she pulling her own weight? With her increasing waistline and swollen ankles she was beginning to feel more and more inadequate. Useless. She didn't want to be a helpless female, as Lee put it.

Lee rose and lifted Ruthie out of her lap. "Is Ruthie sleeping under the wagon with...um, you?"

"You mean with us? Yes. Do you have guard duty tonight?"

"Nope. I'm riding out at dawn to scout a new route for the wagons. We have to avoid the Indians. They're on the warpath."

"But what about the wagon?"

"You can drive the wagon, Jenna. If you're unsure about it, put Jimmy Gumpert up on the driver's box with you. But I'm pretty sure you can do it by yourself. You did it once before, when we crossed the Platte, remember?"

"I hardly remember crossing the river." Her voice wobbled.

Lee laughed. "Well, you did cross it. You drove the

wagon right into it, as I recall. You did well, Jenna, and you can do it again."

She worried her bottom lip until it was rosy and swollen. Fortunately, she picked up Ruthie and headed for the wagon before Jenna could see how she affected him.

He spent a tense night with little Ruthie snugged down between Jenna and himself. He sure wished the older girls would stop pestering the little girl so she could sleep in the wagon bed and he could lie close to Jenna.

An hour before dawn he reached up and quietly retrieved his rifle from its hiding place in the wagon undercarriage, rolled away from Jenna and walked out to saddle Devil. He stepped into the makeshift corral and stopped dead.

What the—?

His prize Arabian stallion was gone! The picket rope had been cut into two neat segments, but he'd heard nothing, not a single footfall or a whinny. Nothing. He gritted his teeth so hard his jaw cracked. No matter what that horse meant to his future, no matter how much he wanted to go after it, he couldn't do it now. He had to scout west for the emigrant train.

He swallowed back a groan. He felt sick inside. Devil was a thousand-dollar stallion, but it wasn't the money that mattered. That horse was the start of his herd, a herd he wanted so bad he could taste it.

Something didn't make sense. An Indian wouldn't cut the rope all neat and clean like that. An Indian would skillfully work the picket loose, take the horse and leave no trace.

He strode into the wagon master's camp to find Sam crouched by the fire, nursing a mug of Emma's coffee.

"My horse is missing," he announced.

Sam's thick eyebrows shot up. "Indians?"

"Don't think so. Picket rope was cut clean through. Sam, I'm going to have to borrow another mount."

"Wish I could give you one of McKernan's string," Sam growled. "Serve him right."

"Forget it. I wouldn't ride a McKernan horse."

"Take one of mine, then."

"Thanks, Sam. I'll be back sometime tonight."

"Be careful. I don't trust either the Indians *or* McKernan."

Lee saddled the bay mare Sam offered, touched his hat and rode out in widening circles, studying the ground for horse tracks on the off chance he could pick up Devil's trail. When he found none, he set his jaw and headed west.

As he rode he kept an eye out for smoke from Indian campfires. At the same time he searched for some sign of his horse, a hoof mark, a tuft of black horsehair, anything.

He kept moving west, but by noon he'd seen nothing. When the sun was straight up overhead, the back of his neck began to prickle. Hell and damn. He knew he could be seen. A lone rider on this flat, sagebrush-dotted plain would be visible for miles.

Suddenly he spied something off in the distance and drew his mount to a halt. Then he sat staring at a mesa some miles ahead. He didn't believe what he was seeing, but he sure believed what his stomach was doing. His gut lurched, then started to bunch up in a tight knot under his heart.

Chapter Twenty-Three

Jenna tightened her hands on the reins and tried to ignore the pain in her shoulders. She'd been hunched over on the driver's bench since early morning, afraid to loosen her hold for fear of losing control of the ox team, and now she felt worn down to a nub of gritty skin and burning muscles. Despite her floppy sunbonnet, her nose was sunburned and her eyes ached from looking into the sun. Perspiration slicked her fingers under the leather gloves.

She straightened and looked ahead. The wagon rolled past bleached animal bones turning to chalk in the merciless sun. She was beginning to hate this flat, barren country with its endless miles of nothing but gray-green sagebrush and stunted trees. On her right, Tess and Mary Grace trudged along, their bonneted heads bent. Both girls had worn holes in their leather shoes, and their simple dresses of blue homespun were stained and fraying at the hem. Her own faded blue gingham skirt was torn and ragged.

Choking dust billowed up from Sam Lincoln's wagon ahead of her. She was hot and sticky, and there was still supper to make, and then breakfast, and then more suppers, more quarrels to mend, and more dirty clothes to wash, that is if they could ever find water. Day after day it was the same, the heat, the drying wind, her squabbling stepdaughters. Sometimes she thought she would go crazy.

Still, she could not give up. The Borland girls were her responsibility, and soon there would be a baby. But Lord knew she was more frightened than she'd ever been in her life. Oregon was an unknown, and their future was cloudy. She swallowed over a moan of despair.

Then she straightened her backbone. No matter what, she had to see this through, had to be sure Mathias's daughters had the chance for a good life, that her own child was safe. She groaned under her breath. She had to keep going. She would do what she had to do.

But oh, God, not knowing *how* to do it made her want to cry.

She gazed up at the sky where the sun was sinking behind the mountains off in the distance, sending a blush of orange across the horizon. It was so beautiful it stopped her breath. Even Tess and Mary Grace grew quiet as the sky flamed crimson and then purple.

Beside her on the bench, Ruthie pointed a grimy finger. "Look, Jenna. That's real pretty."

"Yes," she said quietly, "it is." The sight lifted her spirits somewhat. They *were* going to reach Oregon. It was two thousand miles from Ohio, but they had to reach it. She clamped her teeth together to stifle a sob.

Out on the hot, barren plain, Lee swallowed hard and stared at the red-rock mesa in the distance. Was he hallucinating? His magnificent black stallion stood silhouetted against a haze of blue-gray smoke.

But there was something odd about the scene. For one thing, his Arabian stallion did not seem to be restrained in any way. No lead rope. No bridle. If Indians had taken it, wouldn't they keep it confined? And if that was an Indian camp, where were the Indians?

Instinctively he checked his rifle and very slowly

stepped his mount forward toward that mesa. Any minute he expected to be shot out of the saddle.

A movement ahead caught his eye, and then something twitched in the sagebrush. Lee lifted the rifle and kept moving. Sweat dampened his face and neck, dripped from his upper lip. He could taste it, warm and salty on his tongue.

Whatever was in the brush rustled, and suddenly he thought he knew what it was. He rolled out of the saddle and hit the ground, then belly-crawled into a shelter of sagebrush and waited.

An hour went by. The bay mare moved off, nibbling sporadically at sparse clumps of stunted dry bunchgrass, and still he lay quiet. If he didn't live through this, he hoped Jenna would understand.

He craned his neck to see the top of the mesa, where his black Arabian still stood. God, he wanted his horse back.

And he wanted some answers. Why was the animal still there? He could see it pacing back and forth, unrestrained by rope or hobble. If Indians were nearby, which nation were they, Sioux or Crow? Or Cheyenne or… Where was their camp?

He waited, batting away flies, until the moon rose and hundreds of Indian campfires glowed far across the wide plain. Duty nagged at him. He stood up slowly, caught the mare and led it away to the south, away from the mesa. Away from his horse. He'd never know what had twitched in the brush; if it was an Indian, he'd make no sound. Maybe he'd grown tired of waiting.

He counted a hundred or more campfires, and across the wide valley were a hundred more. He rode on until he saw no more sign of campfire smoke, then turned east and headed back toward the wagon train.

In the morning, the wagons would have to cut even farther south to avoid the Indian battle he knew was ahead.

He'd give anything to ride out to that mesa and look for Devil one last time, but...

Must be past midnight. He was so tired his vision was blurry. He kicked the bay mare into a canter, and before he knew it he'd blundered within thirty yards of another Indian camp. This one was dark, with no campfire. He pulled up short, and the horse stood trembling in the dark.

Very quietly he dismounted, slid his Winchester from the saddle holster and began to lead the mare away. He'd taken half a dozen steps when the crack of a rifle sounded, and a scorching bolt of fire bit into his shoulder.

He hit the ground, clawing at his flesh. His last conscious thought was that somehow he had to get back to Jenna.

"Sam? Sam, where is Lee? It's after midnight."

"I don't know, Jenna. He should have been back by now. Maybe he ran into an Indian skirmish and had to detour around it."

"Oh! What if—?"

"Jenna, the man's an experienced soldier. He knows how to take care of himself around Indians."

Her unease tightened her chest, but she had no choice but to walk back to camp. Halfway there she could Tess's raised voice. "Let go! Let go, Mary Grace! That's *my* ribbon."

"It is not, it's mine! It matches my dress."

Jenna marched to the back of the wagon and tore open the bonnet. "Stop it!" she screamed. "Stop this endless fighting. You girls argue over every little thing, things that are not important."

Tess turned a flushed, belligerent face to her. "What is it that's so important, Jenna? Tell me that!"

"Our survival is important," Jenna shouted. "Can't you see that? A ribbon is not important. It makes no difference whose ribbon it is. What matters is food! Water!"

Good heavens, her mother would never have recognized

that tone of voice from her properly raised daughter. Her mother, she thought with a stab of regret, would not recognize anything about her now.

"I wish we'd never started out on this wagon train!" Tess yelled. "I want to go back to Ohio."

"Me, too," Mary Grace said. "I'm scared out here, 'specially at night."

"Hush up, both of you," Jenna ordered. "I am scared, too. But we can't go back. We've come too many miles from home to turn back. Besides, we cannot travel alone, just one wagon. We have no choice," she said, her voice suddenly calm. "We must go on to Oregon."

Tess groaned. "What'll we ever do in Oregon? Tell me that, Jenna." She shoved her face up close to Jenna's and began to shout. "What are the three Borland sisters and a bossy old stepmother gonna do in some place we've never heard of?"

"I don't know," Jenna said. She was beginning to tremble, and she had to work to keep her voice steady. "Your father had thought of opening a store, but—"

"But Papa's dead!" Mary Grace screeched. "And we're all alone."

"Do you think I don't know that? That I don't wonder what we're going to do?"

"You're not even our real mother," Mary Grace sobbed.

"No, I am not. But you are *not* all alone. I am here. I am your stepmother, and I am doing the best I can…" She choked back a sob and took a deep breath. "The very best I can…" Her voice broke. She waited four heartbeats, then five more. "To…to be strong and think clearly and do what must be done. Now, you two, stop your arguing and think about helping me to—"

A horse whickered somewhere in the dark, and in the next instant she heard the thud of hoofbeats. They did not slow, but drew closer.

Jenna motioned the girls into the wagon and scrambled

in after them, then reached up to the canvas pocket for Lee's revolver. She gestured for the girls to keep down, raised the gun and pulled back the hammer.

"Jenna," a ragged voice called from the dark.

"Lee?" She handed the Colt to Mary Grace and climbed down as fast as she could manage. A horse stepped in close to the wagon and halted, flecks of foam dripping from its muzzle.

"Lee!"

He lay along the winded animal's back, clinging to its mane. "Jenna," he croaked. "Get Sam." He slid sideways off the mare and lay motionless. Blood soaked his shirt.

Jenna dropped to her knees beside him. "Tess, get Dr. Engelman. Hurry! Mary Grace, go find Sam. Move!"

Chapter Twenty-Four

Jenna started to tear away Lee's blood-sticky shirt, but his hand snaked out and caught her arm. "Gotta talk to Sam."

"I sent Mary Grace to get him, Lee. He's coming."

His hand fell back and his eyes closed. "Thirsty," he muttered.

She brought a cup of water, lifted his head and held it to his lips. When he'd drunk all he could, she went back to removing his shirt. The linen was stuck to the wound, and when she pulled it free, blood welled from a ragged hole in his shoulder.

"Who shot you?"

"Don't know. Tell Doc I want to see the bullet when he gets it out."

Jenna pressed the clean part of his shirt hard against the seeping blood and bit her lip. "Did you see any Indians?"

"Lots. Two camps, about three miles apart. Big battle coming."

Sam arrived, along with Dr. Engelman, who dropped his leather bag and squatted beside Lee. Jenna moved to one side as the graying physician leaned over to study Lee's wound.

"Close," he muttered. "Missed your artery by a hair. Take it from the back?"

"Wish I knew," Lee gritted.

"That bullet's gotta come out, you know," the doctor said, giving Sam a look.

"Figured that," Lee rasped.

"Isn't going to be fun."

"Figured that, too. Gotta talk to Sam first."

"Make it fast, son. You're losing a lot of blood. Boil some water, will you, Miz Borland? And have you anything to use for bandages?"

"Tess." Jenna caught the girl's eye. "Look in the chest inside the wagon. Find one of my petticoats."

Sam knelt at Lee's side while the doctor rummaged in his bag. "What'd you find out, Lee?"

"Two Indian camps dead ahead. Go farther south tomorrow, maybe ten more miles, before you turn west again."

"Right. I'm grateful, Lee. We all are. Sure sorry you got hurt."

"Better me and a bullet hole than twenty wagons and a couple hundred Indian arrows."

The doctor shouldered Sam out of the way and motioned for Jenna to bring a bowl of boiling water. He set it down near Lee's shoulder and reached for the petticoat Tess held out.

"Tess, take Ruthie over to Sophia Zaberskie, please."

"Sure, Jenna. Should I stay there, too?"

"No. I might need you here."

"Is…is he gonna die?"

"No," Lee muttered. "We're not finished with your riding lessons yet." He tried to smile at her, but the doctor dumped half a bottle of whiskey over his chest and he hissed in his breath.

"Oh," Tess moaned. "Don't hurt him."

"Sorry, miss. Got to hurt him to save his hide. Why don't you do what your stepmother said, go on over to the Zaberskies' with your little sister."

"Take Mary Grace with you," Lee added.

Doc dropped two steel instruments into Jenna's pot of boiling water. When the girls headed off, he motioned to Jenna. "You mind me ripping up your petticoats for bandages?"

She didn't answer, just tore off the bottom ruffle. Before she was half-finished, she heard an agonized groan slip from Lee's mouth. The sound cut into her belly like a jagged blade, and she turned away.

"Need someone to hold this and soak up the blood," Doc said.

Tess stepped out of the shadows. "I'll do it."

Jenna forced herself to continue ripping strips from her muslin petticoat, but Tess gave a little cry and she whirled around. Then another dreadful sound came from Lee, half scream and half choking, shuddery breath. Tears flooded her eyes.

"Damn," the doctor said. "Can't reach it. Gonna have to try once more, son."

Tess was crying, but she kept blotting away at the blood. Jenna tried not to listen to Lee's labored breathing, and when he cried out again, she gritted her teeth so hard her jaw ached.

"Got it!" the doctor exclaimed. "Press that cloth over here, miss. Don't worry that you'll hurt him, he's unconscious. Sure has lost a lot of blood."

Tess nodded and continued to work.

"Sam," the doctor said. "Think we could lift him into the wagon? I'd like him to ride inside tomorrow. He's running a fever."

Jenna scrambled to make up a pallet in the wagon, and the two men manhandled Lee inside.

"Can someone sit up with him tonight?" Doc asked. "With that fever, he'll need to be sponged off."

"I'll stay with him," Jenna said. "Tess, you and Mary Grace can sleep under the wagon." She glanced at the older girl. Her hazel eyes were huge and troubled, and Jenna laid both hands on her shoulders.

"He will be all right, Tess."

The girl nodded wordlessly. Jenna noticed that her eyes were wet.

"Ask Mrs. Zaberskie if she can keep Ruthie overnight, will you? I don't want her upset, and tell her that Lee, uh, Mr. Carver, looks…well, he looks…"

"He looks dreadful," Tess supplied. "I'll talk to Mrs. Zaberskie." She turned to go.

"Tess?"

"What?"

"You did well tonight. I'm proud of you."

The girl sent her an unreadable look, spun away and disappeared into the dark. Jenna climbed into the wagon and settled herself beside Lee's motionless form.

His face was flushed, and sweat stood out on his fore-head. She wiped it off. His eyes were still closed but all at once he began to talk. The words made no sense, something about that black horse of his and someone called Laurie. He sounded angry when he spoke of the horse, but when he mentioned Laurie, his words drifted into unintelligible syllables and he began to thrash.

Jenna pinned his arms, afraid he would open his wound, but he broke free. "Laurie," he muttered. Then "Never again. Never." His voice sounded so anguished it sent chills up her spine.

"Lee." She ducked under his waving arm. "Lee, it's Jenna. You're all right. You're here, on the wagon train."

"Jenna," he whispered. She sponged off his face and chest, careful not to disturb his bandage. His fist opened to reveal a small lump of metal, which she retrieved and stowed in her skirt pocket. When she looked up, his eyes were open.

"Jenna, get some sleep."

"I'm fine, Lee. You're the one who's been shot."

"You...drive wagon tomorrow. Get...rest."

Tess climbed in through the bonnet. "I can sponge him," she announced. "He's right, Jenna, you need to rest." She lifted the cloth out of Jenna's hand.

"Thanks, Tess," Lee rasped. "Appreciate it."

Jenna crawled under the wagon and stretched out her aching body next to Mary Grace. The girl murmured in her sleep and burrowed closer. Jenna wrapped her arms around her and closed her eyes.

In the morning after breakfast, Mary Grace helped Tess yoke up the oxen, then took over sitting with Lee. Jenna made sure that Jimmy Gumpert came to walk alongside the wagon with Tess; the girl was so tired she was weaving. Then she climbed up on the driver's box.

She drew in a shaky breath and lifted the traces. "I can do this," she muttered under her breath. She flapped the reins. "Walk on."

Mile after mile, the wagon jounced and bumped along the new route to the south the wagon master was following. Ruthie huddled next to her on the bench, leaning her sunbonneted head against Jenna's arm and chattering away as she always did.

"How come Mister Lee's riding in the wagon, Jenna? Is he tired?"

"He's... Yes, he is tired. He was awake very late last night, long after you went to sleep at Mrs. Zaberskie's."

"Can I talk to him?"

"Not yet. He's still asleep. Maybe when we stop for our nooning, all right?"

"I wanna show him my dolly's new dress. Missus 'Berskie made it for me."

After another five miles across the bleak, arid landscape, Jenna began to wonder if she herself would make it to the noon rest stop. She didn't know which was worse, the searing heat or the thick, swirling dust kicked up by the wagon wheels ahead of her. She tied her handkerchief over Ruthie's nose and mouth.

When noon came, and she finally brought Sue and Sunflower to a halt on a stretch of sunbaked sand bordering a dried-up streambed, she discovered that her palms were blistered. Weary to the bone, she climbed off the bench and lifted Ruthie down beside her. Then she stretched out in the only shade available, under the wagon, and closed her eyes.

She could hear Tess and Jimmy Gumpert getting out leftover biscuits and stuffing them with cold bacon strips from breakfast, but she was too exhausted to even think about eating. After a while Mary Grace brought her a cup of water from their precious supply of water.

"Be sure that Lee, Mr. Carver, drinks some water, too, Mary Grace."

"I will, Jenna, but he's more worried about you. He says driving the wagon into the sun can be punishing. What's that mean?"

Jenna sighed and swallowed a gulp of the lukewarm water. "Punishing means that it's very tiring. And hot. And…" She drank again.

"And he said to make sure you ate something." She withdrew a lumpy bacon-and-biscuit sandwich from the pocket of her homespun skirt. "So you hafta eat this."

Jenna held the girl's wide hazel eyes in a long look. "Thank you, Mary Grace." She heard the girl scoot away and call out to Ruthie, and she closed her eyes again, pulling off bits of bacon and biscuit and shoving them into her mouth.

Her temples throbbed. Her eyes stung as if sand scratched under her lids. Her arms felt so leaden she wondered if she would be able to lift them to take up the traces again.

When the noon rest was over, wagon drivers gathered their animals, lunch makings were packed up, and Jenna hauled herself back up onto the driver's box and pulled her best leather gloves on over her swollen fingers.

Tess deposited a sleeping Ruthie inside the wagon next to Lee, and she and Mary Grace took up their positions walking beside the rolling wheels. Doggedly Jenna lifted the reins.

The wagon wheels crunched over the sand, churned over the remains of bleached animal bones and clumps of desiccated brush. This land was barren as the surface of the moon, she thought. Or a burned-out planet a million miles from the sun.

She tugged her calico sunbonnet farther down to shade her eyes and set her jaw. *I can do this. I must.*

She drove for hours. The sun rose high in a sky white with heat, and it was tempting to shut her eyes and doze, letting the oxen plod along after the wagon ahead. She caught herself and jerked to attention.

Suddenly Lee emerged from the wagon interior, and an arm swept her to one side. "Move over," he ordered.

"Don't be absurd, Lee. You can't drive!"

"I can and I will. Move over." He grabbed the reins out of her hands. She noted that he favored his left shoulder, but when she opened her mouth to argue, he shushed her. "Quiet. You'll wake Ruthie."

"Oh, Lee, you shouldn't be doing this. I am fine, really I am."

He barked out a harsh laugh. "Neither one of us is fine, Jenna. I figure that you and I together probably make one whole person."

"Then we will drive in shifts," she announced. "We will trade off every hour."

"We'll trade off when I say so." But his voice was so gentle she had to smile.

"How about when *I* say so?" she countered.

"We'll arm-wrestle over it. On second thought, maybe

that's not such a good idea. With my bad shoulder, I might lose."

"Lee, you don't have to do this. Really, I am—"

"Hush up, Jenna. And move closer to me in case I start to tip over. I need to be here. Besides, I want to keep an eye out for Devil. Saw him yesterday, but I couldn't get to him."

At sundown, the wagon train bumped into a loose circle to camp for the night. Both Jenna and Lee were parched and half-sick from the heat, and the minute he pulled the ox team to a halt, they struggled off the bench and crawled under the wagon where they lay panting in the only available shade.

Lee knew he'd pushed himself too hard. His breath came in jerky gasps, and his shoulder hurt like a red-hot poker had been shoved into it. But he was even more worried about Jenna. She lay beside him, her eyes closed, her fingers knotted over her swollen belly.

"You all right?" he whispered.

"Yes, just worn-out." She didn't open her eyes, not even when Ruthie crept in next to them.

"Don't cry, Jenna," the girl said. "I'll take care of you."

Lee jerked to a half-sitting position. He hadn't realized Jenna was crying. He laid his hand on Ruthie's thin shoulders. "Where are the girls, honey?"

"Gettin' the oxes unhitched. Tess said she'd cook some supper when they're done."

Jenna sucked in a shaky breath and tried to sit up, but he pressed her back down. "Let her do it," he intoned. "You're done in and Tess isn't. Sometimes, Mrs. Borland, it's more blessed to receive, you know that? Besides, she's not pregnant."

"What's 'regnant'?" Ruthie inquired. Jenna laughed but said nothing.

"Well," Lee said, "it's when a woman is growing a baby inside her."

"You mean like another sister for me?"

"Or a brother."

Jenna laughed tiredly. "Which one would you like, Ruthie?"

"A baby brudder," came the instant answer. "Don't want no more sisters 'cuz they pinch me."

"Oh, dear," Jenna murmured. She looped one arm around the five-year-old and cuddled her close.

"Carver?" a gruff voice called. "Young miss said I'd find you under the wagon."

"Yeah, Doc, I'm here."

"What the hell? I told you to ride inside today, what with your fever. Give your shoulder a chance to heal. Come on out of there and let me take a look."

Reluctantly Lee moved away from Jenna and Ruthie and climbed out from under the wagon. "I think I'm okay, Doc."

"Huh! Until you get a medical degree, I'll be the judge of that. Siddown and let me take a look."

Mary Grace took one look at Lee and dragged the fruit crate out of the wagon for him. He nodded his thanks and sank down on it. His shoulder felt bad, but what worried him was that his legs were unsteady.

Doc hemmed and hawed and poked and prodded for a good ten minutes while Lee gritted his teeth and sweated. Finally, Doc handed him a tin cup of water.

"Need any laudanum?"

"Nope."

"Got enough water?"

"Sure hope so. Doesn't look like we'll find much in this desert."

"Where's Miz Borland?"

"Resting. Under the wagon. She drove the team most of the day."

"Good God," the doctor blurted. "Neither one of you has a lick of sense. You know, I could always ask Mick McKernan if he'd—"

"No!" Lee shot. "McKernan stays away from Jenna and the girls. Away from this wagon."

Doc's bushy gray eyebrows rose, but he said nothing, and at that moment Sam strode into camp. "Emma wants to know if you all would take supper with us?"

"Thank you, no," Tess's voice came from inside the wagon. "I am cooking supper tonight."

Doc's eyebrows went up again, and Sam's mouth dropped open. "Well, sure, Tess, if you say so." The wagon master turned to go. "You need anything, Lee, you just holler."

"Thanks, Mr. Lincoln," Tess called after him. "Mary Grace is helping me. We'll be fine."

Lee eyed Tess as she climbed out of the wagon lugging a skillet and half a loaf of bread. "Have any trouble with Sue and Sunflower?"

"Nuh-uh. Fed 'em and everything, just like you showed us."

The doctor bent and peered under the wagon at Jenna. "Hmmm. Sound asleep, both her and the little one." He snapped his medical bag shut. "Be sure she eats, Carver."

"I will," Mary Grace answered. "Jenna doesn't much listen to what Mr. Carver says."

Lee twitched. "Huh? Why do you think that?"

"Oh, that's easy. Jenna doesn't like you."

He choked on a swallow of water. "She tell you that?"

"Not exactly."

"Well, *what*, exactly?"

"Tess and me saw you dancing at that ball at Fort Caspar. You never even talked to each other."

"Tess and *I*," came Jenna's voice from under the wagon. She was laughing so hard the words came out unevenly.

Lee clamped his mouth shut for fear he'd do the same. "Right," he said when he could trust himself to speak. "We didn't…uh…talk much that night."

"So," Mary Grace said, "you don't like her either, huh, Mr. Carver?"

"Well, I—"

"No," Jenna burbled. "He doesn't like me. You are very observant, Mary Grace."

"I just hope you keep on driving our wagon, Mr. Carver. 'Cuz Jenna doesn't do it right."

"What?" Jenna yelped. "What don't I do right?"

"You go too slow and jerky."

Lee gave a weak laugh. "The wheels ran over lots of potholes and wheel ruts today," he managed. "Probably be worse tomorrow, so best not ride inside."

"Oh. Very well, I guess."

Lee was starting to feel dizzy, so he crawled back under the wagon with Jenna. "I can see how hard it'd be to be a stepmother to those two," he murmured.

"You have no idea," she said tiredly.

"Sure glad I'm not their father."

Half an hour later, Mary Grace bent down and handed two tin plates with bacon and slices of fried bread under the wagon. "Well, damn," Lee said with a chuckle. "Maybe there's hope."

Jenna poked a piece of bacon into Ruthie's mouth. "I have asked myself over and over and over again why Mathias took your horse. Where could he have been going? And why?"

Lee stared at her. "And?"

"I think I know," she said slowly. "I think Mathias was, well… This will sound crazy, I know. I hardly believe it myself. But I think he was running away."

"Running away? What are you talking about?"

"I think he was going back home, to Ohio."

"Alone? Without his family? What makes you think that?"

She waited some time before answering. "Because many times I have longed to give up and do the same thing."

"But you didn't."

"I think Mathias was frightened by how hard the trip turned out to be and by what lay ahead."

"You're just as scared, aren't you? I don't see you turning tail and running."

"I am scared, Lee. I'm terrified every single day, afraid we won't make it to Oregon. Afraid of what we'll find if we do get there."

"You'll make it, Jenna. I'll die before I see you fail."

She held his gaze, her blue-green eyes brimming with tears. "Don't say that, Lee. Don't even think it."

"Okay. Let's think about when we can make lo—"

"Hush!" She gave a significant glance at Ruthie, happily munching a mouthful of crunchy bread.

"Okay," he said with a grin. "We'll talk about it later."

"No, we won't. I've done a good deal of thinking about it, Lee. We have to stop."

"What?" Lee set his tin supper plate down and grasped Jenna's hand. "What the heck are you talking about?"

"Ruthie," Jenna said quickly. "Finish your supper and go help Tess."

"I dowanna. She'll pinch me!"

"You tell your sister that if she pinches you, I will make her sorry."

Ruthie's blue eyes grew wide. "You would, Jenna? Really? Nobody's ever stood up to Tess before."

"Well, it's about time, don't you think? None of you sisters should be mean to each other. We all need each other. Now, shoo! Off you go. Mr. Carver and I need to talk."

Chapter Twenty-Five

Jenna watched Ruthie crawl out from under the wagon and felt Lee's eyes bore into her. "You really want us to stop being together?" he asked.

She gulped in air. "Yes. Now, while we still can."

"Can what? Jenna, you're not making sense."

"While we can still walk away from each other."

His head jerked up. "Well, hell, Jenna, you can do that anytime you want. You know that."

"Yes, I know. And I know that when we reach Oregon you're going off somewhere to start your ranch."

He looked away. "I've wanted this ever since I went back to Virginia after the War. Everything was gone. Fields ruined. Stables burned. The house had been ransacked, and Laurie…she had died the year before. Even her gravestone was gone."

He swallowed. "Ever since then I've wanted to start a horse ranch. I need to take away the memory of killing and start over, get my life back. A ranch is where things can grow. I need that now."

"Then that is what you must do, Lee. No matter what."

"Jenna—" He broke off and stared at her. "You know I care about you."

"Yes," she said quickly. "But we can't go on, Lee. For

one thing, the girls… I am responsible for them. I must set a good example."

"Oh, hell, they've never noticed what goes on under this wagon at night."

"Perhaps not. But *I* notice." She cared for this man far too much. If she wasn't careful, he could break her already bruised heart.

"Also," she continued, "I am pregnant. Very pregnant."

"So?" He caught her chin in one hand and forced her to look at him. "That's not the real the reason, is it?"

"N-no, it's not."

"Then what is it? God, I feel like a horse just kicked me in the gut."

"I don't want to be in love with you, Lee. Loving someone makes a person…vulnerable. Once I thought I loved Randall Morgan, and that turned out to be the biggest mistake of my life."

"Yeah," he said, his voice rough.

"And I know that you loved someone once, too. You talked a lot last night. You were feverish, I know, but the things you said told me you don't want to love anyone again."

"Must have been raving about my wife, Laurie."

"Yes." She worked her fingers into a knot where he couldn't see it. "You don't want to be hurt by a woman again. And I wouldn't want to hurt you, Lee."

"Yeah," he said drily.

"That doesn't mean…" Her voice broke. "That doesn't mean I don't want you."

"Thank God," Lee breathed. Her words were sending razor-edged knives into his belly. "Jenna, I'll do whatever you want, but God, this isn't what I want. What I want is you, dammit."

"Yes," she murmured. "I understand."

"Then I guess we both understand. Doesn't make it easy."

Jenna nodded. "But we must try."

Lee rolled away from her. The look on her face was ripping up his insides. He didn't think he could stand being close to her on the driver's bench tomorrow, but doing all that walking beside the wagon wouldn't be good for her. And he knew from his experience yesterday, lying in the wagon bed, that enduring the jolts and bumps inside would be unwise for her. Dr. Engelman had warned him about it.

He'd have a hard time keeping his hunger for Jenna under control. He wasn't sure he could do it; he didn't even want to try.

Halfway through the morning it became clear that he couldn't. Not in a thousand years could he keep from wanting Jenna Borland. He listened for her voice as she spoke gently yet firmly to the girls and comforted little Ruthie when she skinned her elbow, watched her move around camp making coffee and frying bacon. He ached to touch her.

He spent more hours driving the wagon that day, just to keep her near him, but it was sheer agony sitting next to her on the driver's bench, feeling the warmth of her body through his jeans. He worked to keep his arousal hidden from her and from the girls.

He didn't want Jenna to drive the wagon; it tired her too much. That evening he offered to rub her sore back and shoulders, but she declined, and all night she kept a foot of distance between them. Hell, he might as well sleep with his rifle!

The next night Tess and Mary Grace allowed Ruthie back in the wagon, apparently having taken to heart Jenna's warning about teasing their youngest sister. But without the girl's small body between them, it was even harder. Lee tried to keep himself from moving close to Jenna, resisted laying his arm across her body when she sighed or moaned in her sleep. It kept his jaw tight all night.

For the next three nights he lay awake, eaten up with

wanting her. In the morning he was so groggy he could scarcely drag himself over to hitch up the oxen.

The wagons detoured twelve more miles to the south, then turned west once more. On the fourth day out he noticed occasional clumps of huckleberry bushes and cottonwoods along the streams. But the air was hazy with blue-gray smoke. Dust, maybe. But it was an odd color. He raised his head and drew in a deep breath.

It wasn't dust—it was smoke! At that moment the wagon train came to an abrupt stop and Sam Lincoln suddenly appeared beside the Borland wagon.

"What's up, Sam?"

"Indians. Battleground, I guess. Dead ahead. God in heaven, that's the last thing we need."

"I'll saddle up and go check it out."

"No. It's too risky, Lee. We'll hold up here and wait until dark. There's some trees up ahead, maybe a river. We could use some fresh water. Nobody's had a bath in over a week."

They located a narrow river, drew the wagons into a loose circle and settled down to wait for dark. The sky grew more smoky, but now it was tinged with brown. Dust. Somewhere ahead of them a battle was going on.

He watched Jenna and the girls go off to the river to take baths and do some laundry. The men bathed downstream, and Lee even managed to lather up and shave his growth of beard.

He spoke again with the wagon master, and that night after a quick supper, he saddled up Sam's bay mare and rode west toward the smoky sky to scout ahead. After an hour he came up over a gentle rise and caught the scent of something he never in his lifetime wanted to smell again.

Death.

He stepped the mare carefully forward, his way lit by a sliver of a moon. When he could make out the battlefield, he drew rein.

Dead Indians lay everywhere, both Crow and Sioux warriors. His stomach tightened. Under cover of darkness, the braves would return for their dead, but for now the corpses lay like so many inert logs.

Except for one. A movement caught his eye, and then he saw an arm thrash near a shadowed bush. Cautiously he drew his rifle and stepped the horse nearer. When he heard a guttural sound he dismounted and walked closer.

A young Indian, Sioux, he guessed, lay faceup, his bloody scalp laid open, his chest heaving. Lee uncapped his canteen, knelt and held it to the boy's chapped lips.

Hooded black eyes watched him warily as he trickled water into the boy's mouth. Then he folded the young warrior's scarred hands around the canteen and left it beside him. He had to get away before the braves returned for their dead. After a cautious look around, he mounted up and kicked the mare into a trot.

When he reached camp, Jenna took one look at him and brought a mug of coffee laced with whiskey. It was more than an hour before he felt like talking to anyone. Then, when he finished his coffee, he went to find Sam.

Emma pressed another cup of coffee into his hands and disappeared into their wagon. "Looked like a slaughter on both sides," he told the wagon master.

Sam shook his head. "What a waste."

"Yeah," Lee agreed. "Just a few years back men in blue and gray uniforms weren't much smarter. Makes you wonder, doesn't it?"

"Wonder what?"

"Why it seems more important to kill each other instead of sitting down and talking."

Sam shot him a glance. "You tell Jenna what you found?"

"No."

"Any reason why not?"

"Yes." When he said nothing more, Sam pursed his lips and gave him a long look.

"Protecting her, are you?"

"Mind your own business, Sam."

The wagon master just smiled wryly.

"The tribes will remove their dead tonight," Lee continued. "By tomorrow morning the field should be clear. Except for dead horses, nothing should prevent the wagons from traveling across this valley. Just to be sure, I'll leave before you pull out and scout ahead."

"Thanks, Lee. Appreciate it. All of it."

Lee touched his hat brim. "Tell Emma thanks for the coffee." He tramped back to Jenna's camp, where Tess handed him a plate of beans and a hunk of corn bread. He didn't see Jenna anywhere.

"You make supper tonight, Tess?" he asked.

"I helped," the girl admitted. "Mary Grace made the corn bread."

He wanted to ask about Jenna, but he bit his tongue. Instead, he sat on the apple crate and absently shoveled food into his mouth while Tess and Mary Grace heated water to wash up the dishes.

He couldn't get that injured Indian kid out of his mind. He wanted to tell Jenna about him. He needed to lie next to her tonight, feel her body against his, hear her soft breathing. More than anything he just needed to see her. Talk to her.

"Aren't you hungry, Mr. Carver?" Mary Grace eyed his half-eaten plate of food. "Or maybe my corn bread isn't any good?"

"Your corn bread is just fine, Mary Grace. I'm just… preoccupied, I guess."

"Yeah. Jenna's hard to get along with, huh?"

"Kind of," Lee said. *Liar.* It was hard to get along *without* her. If he could figure out what was going on in her head, maybe he could survive the next five hundred miles.

"Did Jenna eat any supper?"

"Some," the girl responded. "Not very much, though. And her eyes looked real funny."

That did it. He rose, handed his plate to Mary Grace and headed for the wagon.

"Jenna?"

She lay curled up on a quilt underneath the wagon. "I'm awake, Lee. I'm glad you're back. I was beginning to worry."

He knelt beside her and poured it all out, about the battlefield he'd stumbled across, the young, half-dead Sioux brave, about his conversation with Sam when he returned. It felt good to talk, get it off his chest. "Tomorrow I'm going to—"

"No, you're not," she said quietly. "I know you want to look for your horse, but..."

"But what? Jenna, you know what that stallion means to me."

"Yes, I know. But I don't want you to risk your life getting it back. And the girls don't, either. I—I don't want to watch you ride off into God knows what and wonder if you're ever coming back."

He let out the breath he'd been holding and stretched out beside her. Well, damn. He bent forward, pressed his lips to the back of her neck and tried to keep the smile out of his voice.

"I have to go. But the day I don't come back to you, Jenna, is the day you'll know I'm dead."

She shot upright and conked her head on the undercarriage. "Ow! Now that's a *big* relief, Lee Carver!"

He reached up, grasped her shoulders and pulled her back down beside him. "At least you'll always know..." he slipped one arm under her "...where I'm sleeping nights."

She made a choking sound. "Lee, do not joke about it!"

"I'm not joking! If I'm not dead, I'll be right here under this wagon with you."

But in the morning when he left, Jenna was so upset she would not look at him. Mercy, he was so anxious about that horse of his he didn't even eat breakfast!

The girls yoked up the oxen, and the wagon train finally got under way. Jenna drove with Ruthie on the seat beside her, and as they creaked and groaned their way slowly westward, she scanned ahead for any sign of Lee.

The ground looked as if it had been picked clean except for scraps of cloth and a few broken lances scattered here and there. They rolled across the flat plain, and by their nooning the train had reached a slightly elevated valley of green trees and thick grass. A lazy river meandered beside the trail.

While the girls waded in the river, Jenna cobbled up a meal of cold bacon and corn bread. After lunch Tess took Ruthie and her carved doll over to Sophia Zaberskie's wagon, and Mary Grace lay down to rest in the wagon bed while Jenna washed up the dishes.

She had just dried the last tin plate when a shadow fell across the wash bucket. Clutching the huck towel, she spun to find a tall, unwelcome figure in front of her. Her heart thudded behind her breastbone.

"Randall! Where did you come from? What are you doing here?"

"You asked me that last time, Jenna." He sent her a cold, sneering smile. "I've been following this wagon train for weeks. I came for you."

She just stared at him.

"I came," he continued, his voice silky, "to take you away from this." He gestured at the wagon.

"Leave me alone, Randall."

He moved a step closer. "Leave you alone? I can't do that, now, can I, Jenna?"

"I want nothing to do with you. I made that clear back in Roseville."

He eyed her swelling stomach. "I think that baby says otherwise." He took another step toward her.

"No! Leave me alone," she said, her voice rising. "Go away and leave me alone."

Quick as a snake he grabbed her forearm and dragged her forward, but she managed to wrench free.

"You damn little— Come here." He lunged for her and caught her around the waist.

"Let me go!" she screamed.

He dragged her around to face him. "You're mine, by God." He yanked her forward, and she cracked her hand against his cheek as hard as she could.

Without warning he drew his arm back and backhanded her across the face. The blow sent her to her knees. Morgan swore and started toward her.

And then a gunshot rang out. Jenna saw a look of surprise cross Randall's face. A crimson stain spread over his shirt, and then his knees buckled and he pitched forward.

Afraid to breathe, Jenna could only stare at him.

Suddenly Mary Grace leaped out of the wagon, tossed Lee's Colt revolver onto the ground and raced toward her.

"Is he dead?" The girl's teeth were chattering.

Jenna pulled the girl down beside her on the ground and folded her into her arms. "I hope so."

Mary Grace began to shake, and then Sam Lincoln appeared, with Ted Zaberskie pounding at his heels.

"Jenna!" Sam yelled. "I heard a shot. Are you—?" He stopped short at the sight of the motionless form on the ground. "My God."

Ted bent over the body. "He's dead, Sam. Bullet went right through the heart."

Mary Grace let out a wail. "I killed him! He was after Jenna, and I—"

Sam went down on one knee before her. "It's all right, honey. It's all right." He shot Jenna a glance. "Good Lord, Jenna, you're white as milk."

"I—I—" She couldn't get a single word past her throat. Mary Grace began to sob, and then Emma Lincoln bustled in and knelt beside them.

"Mary Grace," the older woman said. "Hush up, now.

You did what you had to do, so hush. Hush!" Over the girl's head she spoke to Jenna.

"Are you hurt?"

Jenna could only shake her head. An instant later Tess ran up and stood frozen at the edge of camp, her face whey-colored.

After the men carried Randall's body away, Jenna felt Emma's calloused hand on her shoulder. "Can you stand up?" the older woman asked.

"Don't know," Jenna mumbled. "Mary Grace?"

The girl looked at her, tears spilling from her hazel eyes. "I… I'm all right, Jenna, but I was so s-scared."

"You two, come on over to our wagon," Emma ordered. "I've got some hot coffee and maybe a little whiskey, if I can find it. Come on, now." Emma helped Jenna to her feet and propelled her past the wagon.

"Give some whiskey to Mary Grace, too," Jenna murmured.

"And me," Tess said, her voice shaky.

"You're t-too young," Mary Grace said.

At that, both Jenna and Emma looked at each other and burst into laughter.

But it wasn't a laughing matter. Jenna shuddered. A man lay dead. A man who had wanted her. Or wanted to control her, always demanding her time and attention, insisting she act a certain way, dress to please him, and on and on. Why, she wondered now, had she put up with it? True, she had been young and infatuated with him, and that had been her downfall. Never again would she let herself be enamored of a man.

She compressed her lips to keep them from trembling. The men she'd known had always wanted to control her. But now she had three young stepdaughters to raise and a baby on the way. From now on she would be her own master.

She ran one hand over her belly. Randall Morgan might

have given her this child, but he would never be part of its life. If she could choose a father for the babe, it would be someone like Lee.

But that, she acknowledged, was the worst thing she could do to a man who never wanted to love anyone or marry again.

Chapter Twenty-Six

Lee dismounted at the Lincolns' camp. "Sam, Jenna's camp is deserted. What's going on?"

Emma Lincoln pushed him down onto a wooden box and shoved a glass of something into his hand.

"What's this for? Where's Jenna?"

"It's whiskey," Sam said at his elbow. He tipped his graying head toward his wagon. "Jenna's resting in our wagon."

"Why?"

"Lee! Oh, Lee." Mary Grace flew at him. "Lee, I shot him! I k-killed him dead. It was horrible!"

He leaped to his feet, and Mary Grace flung her arms around his waist. "Shot who?"

Sam pressed him back onto the crate. "That fellow Morgan. He sneaked into Jenna's camp and accosted her. Mary Grace shot him. Used your Colt. Nice shot, too, right through the heart."

"Jenna? Where is she?" Lee started to stand, but Sam again shoved him down.

"She's fine, Lee."

"Oh, Lee," Mary Grace sobbed. "I feel sick. Just awful."

He lifted her onto his lap and nestled her head against his shoulder until she quieted down. "I know, Mary Grace.

It feels terrible when you take a life. But sometimes it's the only thing you can do."

She clung to him. "I—I didn't w-want to, but he hurt Jenna, and he was gonna do it again, so I—" She gulped a shaky breath. "Am I gonna go to hell?"

"Well, if you are, honey, so am I. We'll keep each other company, all right?"

The girl nodded. If he wasn't mistaken, she smelled of spirits. He sent an inquiring look to Sam, who tipped his head toward Emma.

"I gave them all a teensy bit of whiskey to settle their nerves," the older woman confessed.

"Jenna had more than a teensy bit," Mary Grace sniffled. "She drank two whole glasses."

Lee didn't know whether to laugh or curse. He sent Sam another questioning glance.

"Buried him," Sam growled. "You'll see where tomorrow morning when we pull out."

Mary Grace raised a tearstained face. "Are we gonna drive the wagons over his grave, like we did Papa's?"

"Yep," Sam said. "You don't have to watch if you'd rather not. You can detour around the place."

"No, I want to see. He was mean to Jenna."

Lee slid her off his lap, stood up and climbed up into the Lincolns' wagon to see Jenna.

She lay staring up at the canvas interior, her face white. "Lee? Did you find your horse?"

He knelt beside her. "No. It's not important, considering what happened here."

"It ish too important." She was slurring her words. Must have had more than two shots of Sam's whiskey.

He lifted her hand into his own. "No, it isn't important. I'll just have to find another stud horse."

"Whatsa stud horse?"

Lee chuckled. "Uh, well, it's a male horse, a stallion, that covers a female horse and…uh…makes a colt."

Her eyelids popped open. "What does that mean, 'cover'?"

"It means…" He began to perspire. "Jenna, don't you know anything about horses?"

"Not a thing," she admitted. "Mama never allowed me to ride."

"Well, 'cover' means to mate. When a stallion and a mare, uh…"

Her cheeks grew pink. "Oh," she said, her voice drowsy. "Emma said I could stay here tonight. Can you stay here, too?"

"Don't you think Sam and Emma might wonder what I was doing here?"

"Yes, but I don't care."

"What happened to setting a good example for the girls?" he said with a laugh. "Besides, someone should stay in camp with them."

"Oh. You're right."

"Damn," he managed. He leaned down to kiss her and got a big whiff of spirits. But she kissed him with enthusiasm. Twice.

Early the next morning Sam brought around Randall Morgan's horse, a roan mare with a fancy tooled saddle. "I figure this belongs to you, Lee."

"Give it to Mary Grace. She's earned it."

When Sam left, Lee made coffee and Tess fried up a skillet of bacon and scrambled six of Sophia Zaberskie's eggs. Jenna stumbled over from the Lincolns' camp, and Lee sat her down on the apple crate and wrapped her hands around a steaming mug of coffee.

"I'm driving the wagon today," he announced.

Jenna nodded, then wished she hadn't. Whiskey was dreadful stuff, really. But it had softened the shock of seeing Randall and… She closed her eyes. Watching him die.

Poor Mary Grace. What a harsh way to grow up.

After breakfast, Lee tied Mary Grace's new roan mare onto the wagon and went to yoke up the oxen. Before the train pulled out, Mary Grace climbed up onto the box next to Jenna. "I don't want to see that man's grave," she confessed, burying her face in her hands.

"I do!" Tess announced from beside the wagon. "I want to stomp on it!"

Jenna and Lee exchanged glances. "Maybe you'll find your stallion today," she said. "If you see him, I'll drive the wagon and you can go after him."

Mary Grace raised her head. "I'll go with you, Mr. Carver," she announced. "I've got a saddle and everything."

They drove steadily all morning, drawing nearer and nearer to the jagged purple mountains that loomed ahead. It didn't seem possible to Jenna that twenty wagons loaded with food and furniture and tools could climb over such towering peaks. But other trains had done it, and Sam said it was the only way to reach Oregon.

The wagons climbed gradually into the foothills, where groves of fir and maple and aspen trees, their leaves nipped by frost, glowed scarlet and orange against the hillsides. The oxen rumbled over marshy patches and splashed across rushing brooks, and with each passing hour the trail climbed higher. The sky was so blue it looked painted, and the air smelled sweet and pungent.

All at once the lead wagon jolted to a halt. Lee hauled on the reins to bring the oxen to a lurching stop just in time to avoid ramming the Zaberskie wagon. "What the—?"

He looked up to see Sam running toward him, waving his battered hat. "Lee! Come quick!"

The hair on his forearms prickled. He set the brake, jumped down off the bench and followed the wagon master to the head of the train where he stopped dead, unable to believe his eyes.

A stone's throw from Sam's wagon four Indians sat their mounts, one of them obviously a chief from the cascade of feathers on his headdress. At the end of his braided leather lead rope danced Lee's black Arabian stallion.

He thought his heart would leap into his throat and choke him. He walked slowly toward the man, making the sign for peace.

The chief dismounted and met him a dozen paces in front of Sam's wagon. Using sign language and what few Sioux words he knew, Lee gradually pieced together an incredible story.

The chief said he had found the horse wandering free, and one of his braves led it to their camp, high on a mesa near Little Dog Valley. He did not hobble it, believing its owner was a Sioux warrior, and that he would come for it. But no one did.

The next day he and his warriors fought a battle against the Crow. The chief's son, Black Lance, fell on the battlefield, and that night when the braves returned to retrieve their dead, they found the boy alive, with Lee's army canteen beside him.

The old chief stepped forward and offered the lead rope to Lee. Then he signed that he wished to thank the White Eyes soldier for his son's life.

Lee couldn't speak. The chief motioned to him, then laid the lead rope in his hand and spoke a single word. "Friend."

The chief remounted, motioned to his braves and wheeled his horse away to the east.

A buzzing started inside Lee's head, and it was a few minutes before he realized a crowd had gathered behind him. Above their murmuring he heard Mick McKernan's sneering voice.

"Now that's what I call the luck of the devil. A beautiful woman and a prize stallion, too."

"Shut up, McKernan." He moved to step past the Irishman, but Mick blocked his path.

"Hey, Johnny Reb, why don'tcha keep the stallion and let a real man have the wom—"

Lee dropped the lead rope and slammed his right fist into McKernan's soft belly. When the Irishman straightened, Lee drove his left into the man's jaw. Pain spiraled into his injured left shoulder, but McKernan went down like a clobbered bull.

"What d'ya do that for, you coward?" Mick's brother, Arn, yelled.

"You have anything to say?" Lee grated in the younger man's face.

Mick groaned, and Arn dragged him upright.

"Get this straight, McKernan," Lee said, his voice quiet. "I don't ever want to see you or hear you anywhere near the Borland camp or the Borland women."

Mick nodded, nursing his jaw.

"But, Mick," Arn interjected. "You said—"

"Shut up, boyo. Just shut yer trap."

Lee picked up Devil's lead rope and strode back to Jenna's wagon. When he walked in with his horse, Mary Grace squealed and threw her arms around the animal's neck. Tess rubbed his muzzle, and even Jenna risked a small pat on the stallion's nose.

For the rest of that day Lee nursed his scraped knuckles and his left shoulder, and the train moved farther into the foothills of the Rockies. Every few minutes over the fourteen miles the wagons covered that day he found himself staring at his handsome black Arabian stud horse, securely tied to the corner of Jenna's wagon.

Chapter Twenty-Seven

At first the ascent into the Rockies was so gradual the emigrants scarcely noticed the change except for thickening stands of dark green conifers. Towering pines and Douglas fir trees were punctuated with groves of blazing maples and aspens, their leaves gold and brilliant orange in the sunlight.

"This reminds me of fall back in Ohio," Jenna said over supper one night. "I always loved this season. I used to press those beautiful red leaves in my poetry books."

Lee set down his plate of venison stew and caught her gaze. A needle of jealousy niggled under his breastbone. Had Randall Morgan read poetry to her? On fall afternoons did they sit before the fireplace embers and...

He swallowed hard. He had to get his mind off whatever Jenna and Randall had done before he'd met her, otherwise he'd go crazy. He couldn't stand the thought of any man touching her, much less a snake like Morgan.

He'd never felt so possessive about a woman before, not even Laurie. He'd never felt so protective, either. Maybe it was because he'd taken on responsibility for the Borland wagon and its occupants. Or maybe it was because, in his mind at least, Jenna belonged to him.

Whatever it was, she was looking at him now with a question in those green eyes of hers.

"How early did it snow back in Ohio?" he ventured.

"Some years as early as October."

"One year it snowed on the first day of school in September," Mary Grace added.

"It's almost September now," Lee said. "Sure hope winter doesn't hit until we're over those mountains."

Jenna cast an uneasy look at the steep blue-green hills that rose ahead of them. "How can our heavily loaded wagons ever reach the top of such a mountain?"

The question hung in the air. Lee couldn't come up with an answer other than the obvious one. "We just put one foot in front of the other and cross over the pass one wagon at a time."

Disbelief was written all over Jenna's face, but she said nothing, just worried the ruffle on her apron with her fingers.

"I wanna go to school in 'tember," Ruthie blurted.

"You're not smart enough," Tess said.

"Am too!"

"Are not!" Tess then caught Jenna's frown and patted Ruthie's drooping head. "Well, maybe you will be smart enough by the time we reach Oregon. I was really smart when I was your age."

"Smart enough to learn French?" Lee teased. He figured the girls' somber mood could use some lightening. His own thoughts could use some distraction, as well. Thinking about Jenna made his jeans feel too tight.

"Sure," Tess said. "I guess so."

"Me, too," chimed Ruthie. She climbed up onto Lee's lap. "Teach me."

He tugged one blond curl. "All right. Are you ready?"

The girl nodded vigorously.

"Okay, here goes. *Bonjour*, Mademoiselle Ruthie."

"I bet that means 'I'm hungry,'" Mary Grace said.

"No," Tess shot. "It means, um, today is, uh, Monday."

Lee chuckled. "Jenna?"

She met his eyes and nodded. *"Comment ça va?"* she said, followed by the first smile he'd seen all day. Nothing made him happier than seeing that smile, especially when it was directed at him.

"Tres bien," he responded.

She smiled again, so he guessed her mood was lifting. She'd been oddly preoccupied all day, and while he worried about it, he figured he had to let her work whatever it was out on her own. He hoped it wasn't about that Morgan fellow. He clenched his fists. He wanted Jenna to think about *him*, not Randall Morgan. And no one else.

The girls looked from one to the other with fascinated, puzzled expressions. "Are you talking about us?" Tess snapped.

"Always," Lee quipped.

"Never," Jenna said in the same instant.

"What were you saying?" Mary Grace demanded.

Again Lee caught Jenna's gaze. "I think we've discovered a private language."

Her eyebrows went up. "Do we need one?"

His pulse began to race. "We might." He stroked the stubble on his chin and tried to look thoughtful.

Her green eyes widened. "What on earth for?"

Oh, Jenna. Beautiful, maddening Jenna. There are a thousand things I'd like to say to you, in English or French or Swahili.

"For…" he lowered his voice "…private conversations."

Her cheeks flushed. *"Bonsoir, monsieur,"* she said, her voice crisp. She rose, brushed the biscuit crumbs off her apron and headed for the wagon.

Lee laughed softly.

"What's funny?" Tess demanded. "Are you laughing at us?"

"No, I'm not laughing at you. But sometimes adults can be funny."

"I am most certainly *not* funny!" Jenna shouted from inside the wagon.

Lee gave a hoot of laughter. He guessed one way to take Jenna's mind off whatever was bothering her was to tease her. Seemed to be working. Mad was better than preoccupied. It was also arousing as hell.

"I wanna learn more 'rench," Ruthie pleaded. "Please?"

Lee leaned forward and whispered a single word in her ear. *"Dormir."*

She repeated it in a whisper. "What's that mean?"

He swept his gaze from Tess to Mary Grace. "Any guesses?"

"Buffalo," Mary Grace cried.

"Donkey," Tess countered. "They both start with a *D*."

Lee lifted Ruthie off his lap, set her on the ground facing the wagon and pointed. "Here's a hint," he whispered. "It means 'to sleep.'"

"I know, I know!" Ruthie chortled. "It means time to go to bed!"

Jenna's soft laugh floated from the wagon. "Ruthie, you get an A."

Mary Grace and Tess stared at him. Quickly he seized his advantage. *"Va dormir,"* he ordered.

The two girls looked at him blankly, then gazed at each other, their expressions questioning. All at once Tess's face lit up. "I bet *va dormir* means go to bed! Come on, Mary Grace."

"You get an A, too, Tess," Lee called as she disappeared into the wagon. Mary Grace slowed and sent him a withering look. He gestured for her to wait, then murmured another word in her direction.

"Vite! Try that one out on Tess."

The girl grinned. "Thanks, Lee. I love being smarter than Tess."

"Me, too," said Jenna as she exited the wagon, her quilts piled in her arms. She gave Mary Grace a pat. *"Moi aussi,"* she murmured. "That means 'me, too.'"

Lee motioned her under the wagon. *"Vite,"* he muttered.

Jenna laughed. "You," she said softly, "get an F."

"What? Why?"

"Because you have been ordering me around all day. 'Sit here.' 'Don't walk.' And I…" she tossed her loose, just-brushed hair over her shoulder "…strongly object to taking orders."

Lee couldn't take his eyes off her. He rose and moved toward her, but she quickly turned her back, threw her quilts under the wagon and crawled in after them.

"Hey." He bent to peer underneath. "Come on out of there."

"You're giving orders again, Mr. Carver. Besides, why should I?"

"Because it's almost September."

"So what?"

"And we've climbed to over three thousand feet."

"So?" she said again.

"So you should lay a waterproof ground cover underneath your bedroll."

"Why should I?"

He blew out an exasperated breath. "Because at this elevation it gets cold at night."

"I have been sufficiently warm at night."

"Jenna…"

"Don't 'Jenna' me, Lee. Just spread your old ground thing where you want it and leave me and my quilts alone."

All right, by God, he would. Jenna was one headstrong woman, and she could sure be stubborn about things. She wasn't usually this testy. Something was sure bothering her. One minute she was smiling at him, the next she sounded as snappish as Tess. Maybe she wasn't feeling well.

Or maybe she was feeling just fine, but she was worried about something. But what? God, the woman was a mystery.

Without another word, he retrieved his rectangular piece of gutta-percha, spread it out next to Jenna and rolled himself up in his wool blankets. But his conscience pricked him.

He should have insisted she use a ground cover, but for some reason she wasn't taking any advice from him. Well, it wouldn't hurt her to be cold for one night. Might even make her more friendly, since he'd be warm as toast and right next to her, so close she could touch him.

He closed his eyes and tried to think of other things, the mountain passes they'd have to cross, for one. He prayed the weather would hold.

In the morning, he took one look at Jenna's pale face and felt a stab of guilt. He should have insisted on the gutta-percha ground cover, whether she liked it or not.

The trail before them wound up one slope and when they crested the top, there was another, steeper hill facing them. And then another. Foot-deep ruts that had been cut into the rock marked out the route. On foot beside the wagon, Jenna stared at them. "Look! How did those tracks get there?"

"Those cuts were worn by hundreds of wagons that went before us."

"Oh, glory," she breathed, her eyes widening. "How did all those wagons manage to get over these mountains?"

Lee pointed. "Look around you."

Beside the trail lay discarded tables, chests, carved wooden bedsteads, even a piano. "Those wagons had to lighten their loads to make it up the grade."

"Do you think our wagon will make it?"

He sure hoped so. He'd hate to see Jenna have to discard what little she carried. "Bet you never saw mountains like these in Ohio," he quipped to take her mind off what they faced. "I know I hadn't until I came out West with the army. But my patrols just looked at the peaks. We didn't try to climb over them."

He pressed his lips shut. *Until now.*

The oxen were slowing down. Their labored breathing told him the high altitude was affecting them, and he worried about Jenna, walking beside the wagon with one hand gripping the wooden frame. She was working hard, hauling her own weight plus the extra weight of the baby she was carrying.

He leaned down. "Jenna, are you all right?"

She didn't answer right away, and when she did her voice sounded hoarse and breathy. "Yes. But my legs feel…shaky, as if they…" after a few words she gulped a big mouthful of air "…are going to give out."

He pulled the team to a halt. "Get into the wagon," he ordered. "And don't argue."

She clung to the wagon frame with both hands, panting, her head down. "Could I…ride up there…with you?"

"The trail is too rough. We're bumping up over rocks and dropping down into potholes. On the bench there's nothing to hold on to."

"But—"

"It's not safe for you up here. Ruthie's riding in the wagon, so just get in, Jenna. We've got to keep moving."

She sent him a dark look, but she climbed in through the bonnet, and the wagon rolled on. Jimmy Gumpert moved up a few yards, and Tess and Mary Grace walked steadily along beside him.

Just when Lee began to relax, Sam appeared, signaling a halt, and he knew something was wrong.

"Lee!" the wagon master yelled. "I need you!"

Chapter Twenty-Eight

"Sam?" Lee shouted. "What's wrong?"

The wagon master puffed out his cheeks and didn't answer. Sam never lacked for words, and Lee knew then it was serious.

"Got something to show you," Sam said at last. Lee set the brake, climbed down and followed Sam to the head of the train.

"Look down there."

Beyond the lead wagon, the trail came to an abrupt stop. Sam pointed ahead to a steep drop-off, then gestured across a wide canyon where the wagon tracks picked up again. The two men stepped to the near edge and stood looking down an incline too steep for a wagon to negotiate.

Lee whistled. "Lord, how'd they get across?"

"Dunno," Sam breathed, "but they did."

"Yeah? What'd they do, fly?"

Other men from the wagon train started to gather at the cliff edge, and a low muttering of unease rose.

"Got any ideas?" Ted Zaberskie said at Lee's elbow.

Emil Gumpert and two other men, one of them a sweating Mick McKernan, paced back and forth some yards away, studying the situation. Sam removed his hat and scratched his graying head.

"Only way across that I can see is to lower the wagons on ropes."

"Huh!" McKernan exploded. "Not *my* wagon. I got anvils and blacksmith tools loaded inside. Damned if I'm gonna risk spilling them down some mountainside."

"Got any other suggestion?" Sam snapped.

"Well, no," the Irishman admitted.

"Then shut your mouth!"

Lee stepped up beside the wagon master. "We could attach ropes to all four axles and snub them around trees, then winch one wagon down at a time."

"Could," Sam agreed. "There's a switchback trail yonder." He pointed a quarter of a mile off to the left. "The women and children will have to walk down."

"The horses and mules and Zaberskie's cows could be walked down, as well," Lee added.

Sam turned to him. "Pretty steep incline. Think you could get Jenna's ox team down that trail?"

Lee wasn't worried about the oxen; Sue and Sunflower were plenty sure-footed. He was worried about Jenna. She was moving more slowly every day, and with her expanding belly she was easily unbalanced. And she got tired quickly, and with all the switchbacks, that trail down the canyon side looked to be over a mile long.

"Let's pick out some trees," he said. "I'm going to take Jenna down that trail myself, so wait 'til I'm back before you drop the first wagon over."

Sam nodded, and Lee went to talk to Jenna and the girls.

"Walk?" Tess screeched. "Down there?" She jabbed a forefinger at the trail snaking its way down the side of the canyon.

"Walk," Lee repeated. "And lead one of the oxen."

"I can't!" the girl protested.

Mary Grace stepped up beside him. "I can," she said calmly. "But what about Jenna?"

"I'll walk Jenna down myself," Lee said. "She's unsteady on her feet, and I don't want her trying to lead one of the oxen."

Ruthie grasped his hand. "Can I come with you, Mister Lee?"

He nodded. He'd thread a light rope through his belt and tie the other end to Ruthie in case she stumbled. But Jenna... He shot a look at her, standing some yards away and staring over the canyon edge. He'd keep a tight grip on Jenna all the way down.

"What about Devil?" Tess asked.

"We'll need Devil up top to help anchor the wagons when we lower them."

"It won't hurt him, will it?" Mary Grace said quickly.

Lee shook his head. "Girls, I want you to climb inside the wagon and lay everything out flat."

Jenna started issuing orders, as well. "Take all the drawers out of the clothes chest, then unload the cooking pots from the pantry box and lay it down on its side."

Lee's frown had deepened, and that worried her. Lee frowned only when he was angry about something she'd said. But he couldn't be angry now. He was worried about something.

"We're last in line again," she said. "How much time do we have?"

"I figured it'll take over an hour per wagon, and there's twenty wagons. It'll be full dark in another three hours, so your wagon will go over in the morning. Yours and the Lincolns' wagon will be last. We'll take the oxen down now."

Jenna nodded but said nothing, just peered across the canyon. She hoped what Lee would be doing wouldn't be dangerous, but that had never stopped him before. Her heart began to pound and she clasped both hands over her breasts. Exasperating man.

"Zaberskies' wagon will be first. Sophia said she'd give you supper down on the valley floor tonight."

Jenna nodded and bit her lip. "Tess, load that slab of bacon into a sack. We'll take it down to Mrs. Zaberskie."

Lee and Mary Grace unyoked the oxen, and each girl took a lead rope and started off toward the narrow trail, walking slowly with the other women and children, who led cows and mules and the extra horses. Ted Zaberskie tramped on ahead, balancing a wire cage filled with Sophia's chickens on his shoulder.

When Lee tied Ruthie to his belt the girl giggled with delight. Then he gripped Jenna's elbow and started down the long, well-worn path snaking down the cliff side. She was thankful he was holding on to her; these days she lost her balance easily, and the touch of his hand was steadying. Every time she had been afraid or uncertain on this journey, Lee had been there, offering his strength and good sense.

She didn't want to think about how much that meant to her. She didn't want to be dependent on him. On anyone. After her experience with Randall and then Mathias, both of them turning out to be inadequate and unreliable, she'd resolved never again to rely on any man. If she'd learned anything during these past awful months it was that to be truly safe she had to stand on her own two feet.

The long line of emigrants zigzagged down the steep trail with no mishap except for when one of the Zaberskies' cows got rambunctious and butted Jimmy Gumpert's backside. But all the way down to the bottom of the canyon, Jenna worried about Tess and Mary Grace and the two oxen plodding after them.

As they completed the last switchback, Jenna glanced up at Lee. "Where will you sleep tonight?"

"Up on top."

She felt an odd jolt of disappointment. "Be sure to—" She broke off.

He unhooked Ruthie from his belt. "Be sure to what?"

"Keep warm."

He laughed aloud, and chuckled all the way back up the

cliff to Devil and the wagons. He'd be a lot warmer with
Jenna sleeping beside him, even if he couldn't touch her
like he wanted to. Each night when she fell asleep, he laid
his arm over her, but she never stirred so he guessed she
never knew about it.

Safely down in the flat valley, Jenna clasped her arms
across her belly and stared upward as the first wagon was
tipped over the top and dangled, supported by ropes attached to each wheel axle. Her neck grew stiff from peering
up, but she watched, fascinated, as the cumbersome load
inched lower and lower while the men on the ridge above
payed out the rope they'd snugged around sturdy fir trees.

As soon as the Zaberskie wagon had descended, the men
rolled it to one side and Jenna let out a long breath of relief. Then she and Sophia set about putting the interior to
rights, scattering feed for Sophia's precious chickens and
constructing a fireplace.

Tess and Mary Grace tied Sue and Sunflower to a thick
pine tree and rambled about picking ripe blackberries. Before thick darkness fell, four more wagons were slowly
lowered off the cliff. Each one came down accompanied
by gasps and murmurs, and when all four locked wheels
finally settled onto the ground, relieved cheers broke out.

By nightfall, after a supper of beans and bacon and
blackberry cobbler, Jenna was so exhausted she felt light-
headed. Sophia sent her a sharp look.

"What iss wrong, Jenna? Are you not well?"

"I just realized most of our menfolk are up there." She
gestured toward the cliff above. "And we are alone down
here."

"Nonsense." Sophia laughed and patted her arm. "You
worry over Mr. Carver, eh? Do not. We haf five big strong
men who stay to guard us. Go sleep now. We haf big day
tomorrow."

The girls and Ruthie curled up on quilts by the blazing
fire. Jenna lay down beside them and closed her eyes. She

had to think ahead to what she—and her stepdaughters
and the new baby—would do when they reached Oregon.
The wagon train's destination was the Willamette Valley,
mostly farms and small towns. Her small stash of money
was running out; she had to think what she could do to earn
a living. Mathias had planned to run a store, so she supposed she could work as a clerk in a mercantile. Or maybe
she could give piano lessons? Mathias often hadn't thought
things through. When they had started out, he'd had no idea
of how difficult traveling to Oregon would prove to be.

She groaned and rolled over. She couldn't stop wondering about Lee up on the ridge. What was he thinking
about? Probably that horse ranch he wanted to start when
they reached Oregon. Such an ambitious undertaking, and
with only one horse. Why could he not do as Mathias had
planned to do, start a little business in a town? Towns were
civilized. Ranches were…out in the unprotected country.

She sighed. But she already knew the answer to that.
A business, a shop, or a store in a town—that wasn't Lee.
He had his heart set on his ranch. No doubt in his mind
he already had a corral laid out and fence posts dug. She
was learning that Lee Carver thought about things far in
advance.

Well, so did she. She had three daughters, and girls
needed certain things: a school, friends, and clothes and
fripperies and…civilization. Things that were not available on a ranch out somewhere in wild, untamed country.

She had to think about her children's future, and her
own, and how to earn a living in a town. But she would
miss Lee when they got to Oregon.

"That's far enough," Sam yelled.

Lee wrapped a length of thick rope around the trunk of
a pine tree, one on either side of the cliff edge, and looped
one end around his saddle horn. At Sam's signal, he stepped
Devil backward until it pulled taut.

Beside him, Arn McKernan, mounted on one of his mules, did the same. The two men stood ready to secure another rope tied to each of two front wagon wheel axles. Sam and Emil Gumpert attached the other two ropes.

Sam raised one arm. "Let 'er roll!"

Two men kicked away the blocks under the front wheel rims, and four more joined in pushing the wagon forward until the wheels tipped off the cliff edge. Immediately the two front rope handlers went into action, pulling with all their strength to keep the wagon from hurtling headfirst down the steep slope.

The men grunted and shoved until the rear wheels disappeared over the edge.

"Now!" Sam shouted. "Keep it level."

Lee felt Devil stiffen as the weight dragged at him.

"That's it! Keep those wheels up." The wagon master swiped his shirtsleeve over his sweaty face.

Lee stepped Devil forward with Arn's mule. The horse dug in his hooves, and he hoped to hell the rope wouldn't snap. The wagon gave an unexpected lurch, but he managed to advance the horse steadily, paying out line as needed. Arn was doing the same.

The ropes scraped marks around the two thick tree trunks until suddenly all four lines went slack and Lee knew the wagon had settled on the canyon bottom. A cheer rose from below. Within minutes the axle ropes were untied, and the men on top drew them up, hand over hand.

Sam waved one arm. "Next wagon."

Wagon after wagon was laboriously lowered to the canyon floor. It went on all day, and by suppertime, Jenna's wagon and then the last one, Sam's, came dangling down the canyon face and Lee rode an exhausted Devil down the steep switchback trail to find Jenna. Maybe he could talk her into giving him a shot of that medicinal whiskey she kept stashed somewhere. He prayed the bottle was still intact after the wagon's bumpy ride over the cliff.

She surprised him. When he rode in, she climbed into her wagon and emerged in the next minute to hand him the whiskey bottle. An hour later, pleasantly fuzzy-headed, Lee sat down to a supper of fried rabbit and biscuits. Then he took a swim in the bracingly cold stream, downed another shot of whiskey and spent a drowsy hour underneath the wagon, listening to Jenna's voice reading about Lancelot and Guinevere.

Poor old Lancelot, he thought lazily. What he should have done was scoop Guinevere up and ride off to his castle, never mind King Arthur. But in the next moment he recalled that Lancelot had done just that, and it brought the lovers nothing but heartache and a doomed kingdom.

He rolled over and closed his eyes. "It was good while it lasted," he muttered.

"What was?" Jenna asked. When he didn't answer, she scooted closer and repeated the question.

He was half-asleep, but he managed to mutter a reply. "Lancelot and Guinevere. Star-crossed."

Jenna studied his face in the flickering light of the campfire. She guessed it wasn't any easier to love a man in Guinevere's time than it was today. Men always wanted to go kiting off on adventures. She'd bet Lee would risk every cent he owned on his horse ranch. Once they reached Oregon there would be no stopping him. She pulled her quilt over her body and closed her eyes.

For the next six days the wagons climbed steadily higher and higher. Pines and firs grew more sparse and finally turned into low scrub and wind-twisted bushes above the tree line, and still the wagons climbed.

It grew harder and harder to breathe. The girls didn't appear to suffer, but for Jenna, carrying the additional weight, every few steps she had to stop and pant.

"We're at seven thousand feet," Dr. Engelman said as he checked her heart rate one night after supper. The gray-bearded physician surveyed her with somber eyes. "Not only that, Miz Borland, but you're closer to delivery than I'd originally thought."

Jenna sucked in a panicky breath. "Surely not before we reach Oregon?"

"Probably not, no. But just to be on the safe side, I want you to stop hauling buckets of water and lifting heavy kettles. Let your girls do it."

Jenna groaned under her breath. The cooperative spirit that touched Tess and Mary Grace was sporadic. One day they were all smiles and "let me helps," and the next they sniped at each other from sunup until dusk and refused to lift a finger. Even Ruthie was disgusted with them.

"When I go to school," she announced, "I'm not gonna listen to my sisters any more. Ever."

"Well, go on, then," Tess jeered. "Get Lee to teach you some more French words, like *s'il vous plaît*."

Ruthie's wide blue eyes sparkled. "What's 'silly play' mean?"

"That's for me to know and you to find out," Tess taunted. "Come on, Mary Grace, let's practice our French."

"I wanna know now!" Ruthie clamored.

"Good heavens," Jenna murmured to Lee by the campfire. "I hope their schooling will include some lessons in manners. I am certainly wasting my breath trying to instill some gentility in the Borland girls."

"Gentility?" he queried with a wry smile. "They're plenty genteel around Jimmy Gumpert."

"And around you," she returned. "They're oh-so-polite around you. What is it that makes girls so catty to each other and so nice to men?"

He chuckled. "Competition."

"I was never, *never* mean to my friends like that," Jenna said.

"You probably didn't have to be."

She propped her hands at her thickened waist. "What does that mean?"

He rose and lifted the kettle of bubbling stew off the fire. "You going to make biscuits tonight?"

"Don't change the subject."

"Dumplings, maybe?"

"Yeah!" Ruthie clamored. "Do dumplings, Jenna. I'll help." She clung to Lee's leg. "Make her do dumplings, Mister Lee."

He detached Ruthie's small hands from his knee and bent down. "You really think I can make Jenna do anything?"

"Yeah," Ruthie blurted. "Jenna listens to you."

"Not much," he said.

"I do, too!" Jenna exclaimed.

He straightened and pinned her with tired gray eyes. "Not much," he repeated. "And not often enough."

"Oh! Oh…" Her brain didn't work right at this altitude, and her usual words of rebuttal didn't come. Instead she seethed in silence, climbed into the wagon and scooped out a bowlful of flour from the barrel. "Dumplings," she announced when she returned to the fire.

"Oh, not again," Tess groaned.

"Yeah," Mary Grace added. "I'm sick of lumpy old dumplings."

"Well," Jenna said carefully. "Maybe Jimmy doesn't like them, either."

"What's Jimmy got to do with dumplings?" Tess asked.

Jenna smiled. "I've invited him to join us for supper tonight."

Tess's hazel eyes widened. "You have?"

"Well…" Jenna hesitated, hiding a smile. She caught Lee staring at her, his lips twitching. "Perhaps Jimmy would rather not come, since—"

"I'll help you with supper," Tess interrupted.

"I make good dumplings," Mary Grace added. "Better than you," she sneered at Tess.

"Wanna bet?" Tess grabbed the bowl of flour out of Jenna's hands. "Watch me!"

The girls donned aprons and bustled about the camp and Jenna dusted off her hands and shot Lee an I-told-you-so look.

He rose from the apple crate, signaled her with his chin and strode out of camp. She met him at the corner of the Zaberskies' wagon, where Sophia and Ted sat eating supper.

"Jenna, Lee." Sophia rose and extended her hands. "Join us, please. Iss plenty."

"No thanks, Mrs. Zaberskie," Lee said. "The girls are making stew and dumplings."

Jenna studied the swelling under Sophia's gingham apron and sent her a secret smile. "The doctor thinks maybe twins," Sophia whispered.

Lee touched her arm. "How long do dumplings take to cook?" he whispered.

"About ten minutes. Maybe longer at this altitude." She pointed at a skinny figure slipping past the wagon. "There goes Jimmy."

"Love is a great motivator," Lee murmured. "Poor kid."

Jenna wondered why she went from furious to introspective within seconds. Dr. Engelman said her mood swings were perfectly normal, but she wasn't usually like this.

In fact, the physician had advised, *women in the later stages of pregnancy tend to pull into themselves.* He went on to describe it as being "broody, like a hen." The analogy made her teeth clench.

"I'm going for a walk," she announced.

Chapter Twenty-Nine

Mary Grace and Lee had washed and dried the tin plates when Jenna dragged back into camp, looking preoccupied and unusually downcast. The minute Lee saw her, he picked up the ladle and bent over the still-warm kettle of stew. "Want some supper, Jenna?"

"No," she said, her voice weary. "I am not hungry."

"Might want to eat some anyway," he said. "Pretty good stew. Besides, you need to keep your strength up."

She spun, her green eyes full of tears. "Don't tell me what I need to do, Lee. I am perfectly capable of thinking for myself."

Carefully he laid the ladle back in the kettle. "Then do some of that thinking," he said quietly. "And start now."

Her lips trembled. "What does that mean, exactly?"

"It means start taking better care of yourself, exactly."

"Oh. Dr. Engelman said I am perfectly healthy, and—"

"No, he didn't," Lee interrupted. "Doc said your pulse is too fast and you're letting yourself get overtired."

"He did? He told you that?"

"He did," Lee said, keeping his tone matter-of-fact.

"Well!" she said, narrowing her brimming eyes. "I'll have you know that my pulse is none of your business."

"Jenna, for God's sake—"

"Please don't lecture me, Lee."

He stepped in close and laid one hand on her shoulder. "We're all tired and on edge. We're making a long, tough trip, but your stubbornness isn't making it any easier."

Without warning she turned into his arms. "I don't know wh-what's the matter with me," she sobbed. He pressed her head against his shoulder and motioned the girls off. Mary Grace grabbed Ruthie's hand and all three of them walked off toward the Zaberskie wagon.

"I can guess what's wrong," Lee said at last.

"What?" Her voice sounded muffled against his shirt.

"For one thing, you're having a baby."

She tipped her head back and looked up at him. "That is perfectly obvious, isn't it? I'm as big as a house and clumsy as…as a cow."

"Yeah, you're big. And maybe you feel clumsy, but—" He stopped suddenly and sucked in a breath.

"But what?"

"Nothing. I was… Nothing."

"But what?" she pursued.

He shook his head. "Come on, crawl under the wagon and roll out your quilts. I'll tell you a bedtime story."

She laughed in spite of herself. "A story? What kind of story? About King Arthur and Guinevere?"

"You'll just have to wait and see."

She did as he suggested while he put a lid on the stew kettle and banked the fire. Then he lugged two buckets of water up from the stream and dumped them into the water barrel.

The girls straggled back into camp and dutifully went to bed, grumbling when they found Jenna was not reading to them tonight. Lee fed Devil and Mary Grace's roan mare some of his dwindling supply of oats, checked the hobbles on both horses and crawled under the wagon next to Jenna.

He noted with satisfaction that she was using a water-proof ground cover under her bedroll, but he was smart enough not to mention it. One thing he'd learned about Jenna—she did not like to be proved wrong.

Making no noise, he shucked his boots, laid his hat and gun belt aside and rolled himself up in his wool blankets. He half hoped she'd be asleep so he could lay his arm across her body. It made him feel good, like he was taking care of her. He'd just closed his eyes when he heard Jenna's subdued voice.

"Lee?"

"Yeah?"

"I'm sorry I'm so hard to get along with. To be honest, I—I think I'm a little frightened."

He rolled toward her and propped up on one elbow. "There's plenty to be scared about, Jenna, that's for sure."

"But I've been scared ever since we left Ohio."

"All of us on this train have been scared at one time or another. Any reason in particular?"

She was quiet for a long moment, and he reached over and smoothed an errant strand of hair off her forehead.

"I think," she said, her voice almost inaudible, "that up to now in my life I have not done one thing well."

"Yeah? What, for instance?"

"Oh, you already know, Lee. First it was Randall, and then Mathias. I am finding I am not able to raise the girls the way they should be brought up. They're growing up with no discipline, no manners. I feel responsible for them. And…and I'm afraid I'm making more mistakes."

She started to cry, and Lee bit his tongue to keep himself quiet and just let her talk.

"Then," she said in a low voice, "there is you."

God, here it comes. "What about me?"

"You're a good man, Lee. You owned up to shooting Mathias, and then you volunteered to drive us on to Oregon. And…and…"

"And?" He found he was holding his breath.

"And, well, you are helping with the girls. Teaching

them things. They like you. They don't like me, except maybe for Ruthie. Oh, Lee, I—I feel I've failed at everything."

"You haven't failed with me, Jenna."

She lifted her head. "I haven't? Really? I thought when you learned about Randall... And then after we... I mean, after that night..."

"Jenna, listen. After that night I couldn't stop smiling. Sam said he thought maybe I'd drunk too much whiskey. All I wanted was to have another night with you, and I've got to tell you, Jenna, I'm still thinking about it."

She gave him a shaky smile, and Lee saw that tears sheened her cheeks. He settled back and pulled her head onto his shoulder.

"You ready for your bedtime story?"

She nodded, her hair brushing against his neck. "All right, here goes." He took a deep breath. "Once upon a time..."

What the hell story could he tell a scared, very pregnant woman? He swallowed hard and started over. "Once...once upon a time, there was a beautiful, brave butterfly and, um, a cowardly woodpecker. He was so cowardly he was afraid to even talk to the beautiful butterfly for fear she would fly off and he'd never see her again."

"Mmmm-hmmm," she said, her voice drowsy. "Go on."

"One day the brave butterfly got lost between a rosebush and a...uh...a morning glory vine. The woodpecker watched her flutter here and there, trying to find her way home, and after a while he said to himself, 'I could let her climb up on my back and take her to a safe place.' So he flew along beside her and said, 'Land on me, beautiful butterfly, and I will take you home.'"

He looked down and smoothed his thumb over Jenna's wet cheek. "What did the butterfly do?" she murmured.

Lee weighed possibilities for the wacky story he was

spinning. He couldn't make it too obvious, or too simple; Jenna would see right through it.

"Well, you remember that the butterfly was very brave. But she didn't trust the woodpecker to take her home, so she refused his offer. The cowardly woodpecker puffed up his chest feathers and said, 'Trust me.' And the butterfly asked, 'Why should I?'"

Jenna gave a soft, sleepy giggle.

"'Because,' the woodpecker said, 'you need to find your way home, and I like being useful.' The butterfly asked, 'Aren't you scared *you* will get lost?' 'Yes, I am,' said the woodpecker. 'But I'd like to try anyway.'"

"Then what happened?" Jenna murmured.

Lee thought for a moment. "The butterfly hemmed and hawed, but finally she climbed up on his back and they flew off."

There was a long silence, and he glanced down to find Jenna sound asleep. Thank the Lord. He wasn't used to making up stories, and he sure didn't know what happened next. He leaned over and pressed his lips against her forehead. "Night, Butterfly."

The wagons labored on toward the pass at the top of the mountain, and the closer they got, the harder Lee found it to push the ox team onward. The trail was rough, strewn with rocks and pitted with holes deep as half barrels. He prayed the animals wouldn't drop dead in their tracks.

Jenna had given up walking beside the wagon and now rode on the bench beside him, her blue shawl wrapped tight around her shoulders, as they slowly lurched upward. The air was cold, too cold for August, Lee thought. A sharp wind whipped around them, sending showers of bright-colored aspen leaves onto the ground.

Ruthie was riding with Sophia Zaberskie, and the two older girls were warm inside the wagon. Their quarrelsome voices rose like the jabbering of angry birds.

"I did not!"

"Did too. I saw you. Jimmy saw you, too."

"I didn't take your dumb old ribbon, Tess."

Jenna twisted toward the canvas opening behind the bench. "Stop it, both of you! Find something better to do than argue with each other."

Lee turned up the collar of his sheepskin jacket, folded his chilled hands around the traces and urged the team forward.

All at once a sharp crack sounded, and one side of the wagon tipped sharply. Jenna yelped and clutched his arm to keep from sliding sideways off the bench.

He brought the wagon to a halt.

"What happened?" Tess screeched.

Lee set the brake and climbed down to inspect the wheels. When he saw what had occurred, he swore under his breath. "Broke an axle," he called. The iron shaft had snapped completely free of the wheel hub. Damn bad timing.

He reached up for Jenna, lifted her down and watched the last of the wagons in the train lumber on up the mountainside toward the pass.

"Lee, what will we do now?"

"Fix it." He knelt beside the back wheel and studied the break. "I'll have to make a new axle."

"Can you do that?"

"Yeah. I can make a new one out of wood."

"There aren't many trees up here," she observed.

"All I need is one. A small sapling will do." He scanned the landscape and spied a sparse stand of dark green conifers half a mile back.

"Tess," he called. "Find the ax."

After a few minutes Tess poked the wooden ax handle through the bonnet; Lee shouldered it and tramped back down the trail.

He felled a young pine tree, limbed it and peeled the

bark off a six-foot length, then hoisted it and the ax on his shoulder and hiked back up to the wagon. There was plenty of daylight left; it shouldn't take too long to shape a new axle. He'd run the wheel up onto a rock to lift it off the ground, and...

The thought died when he caught sight of Jenna, her body bent over the back wheel, both hands locked onto the iron rim.

"Jenna?"

She tipped her head sideways to look at him. Her face was pasty, her lips white around the edges. Lee dropped the ax, rolled the sapling off his shoulder and began to run.

Chapter Thirty

"Jenna? Jenna, what's wrong?"

She tried to smile, but her mouth twisted oddly. "Lee," she panted. "I think…the baby…" She caught her breath and her voice trailed off.

"God!" he gripped her shoulder. "Are you sure?"

"N-no. I've never…" she tightened her hold on the wheel rim, bowed her head and hissed in air "…had a baby before."

Lee peered up the trail, but the wagon train was already out of sight. "Mary Grace!" he shouted. "Get your warm coat on."

The girl popped her head out the bonnet. "What for? It's nice and warm in here."

"I'm going to saddle up Devil. I want you to ride after the wagon train and bring Dr. Engelman."

Mary Grace jumped down, a bulky wool coat over one arm. "Why? What's wrong?"

Lee walked her off a few yards. "It's Jenna. The baby's coming."

The girl's hazel eyes rounded. "Now? But it isn't time yet, is it?" She shot a look toward Jenna, gripping the wagon wheel.

"I guess it *is* time," Lee said quietly. He bent to retrieve his saddle from the wagon undercarriage and strode toward his stallion.

"Couldn't I take my own horse? The roan?"

"No. Devil is stronger. Get some gloves on."

By the time Mary Grace reemerged from the wagon, he had Devil saddled and waiting. He heaved her up and laid the reins in her hands.

"Lee, I'm scared." Her young voice shook.

"So am I," he confessed. "Just do your best." He slapped the animal's rump and the horse trotted up the trail.

Tess's head appeared through the bonnet, and Lee motioned her down.

"Jenna's baby is coming. I need you to build a fire. A big one." Before she could question him, he grabbed the ax and ran back to the stand of pine trees. Twenty minutes later he staggered back with a huge armload of firewood to find that Tess had rolled three stones together and was dipping water from the barrel reservoir into one of the water buckets.

He shaved kindling, added dry leaves and dropped a match onto the pile. When a tiny flame showed, he moved to Jenna's side.

"I wanted the baby to be born in Oregon," she said through gritted teeth.

"Don't think so," he replied. He pried her fingers from the iron rim. "Can you walk?"

She nodded.

"Come on, then, into the wagon."

Tess took one look at her stepmother and clasped her arms across her waist. "Oh, Jenna," the girl breathed. "Are you sure? I mean, is the baby really coming now?"

"Yes," she said, her voice thin, "I'm sure. I probably joggled it up when the axle broke."

"What should I do?"

"Make sure the fire doesn't go out," Lee said. "Boil some water. And find Jenna's scissors."

"And pray," Jenna added.

"Scissors," Lee reminded as Tess moved away. He lifted Jenna through the canvas bonnet and settled her on the quilts and then bent over her. "You warm enough?"

"Yes. Actually I feel…" She closed her eyes abruptly. "Too hot."

Lee leaned out the back end of the wagon. "Tess, dip out some water and bring me a rag."

"I'll sponge her," Tess said. "We can take turns."

Lee traded places with the girl, made sure a full bucket of water sat heating over the fire and tried to talk his nerves into some kind of sanity. Women had babies every day. They'd been doing it for thousands of years.

But Laurie had died having their son.

He clamped his jaw shut. *Don't think about that now. Just do what needs to be done for Jenna.*

He straightened and went to chop down another small tree. They'd need a lot of firewood before the night was over.

At dusk, snow began to spit out of the sky, the wind driving big white flakes that coated the ground. A dark cloud covered the pass above them, and Lee knew it was snowing even harder up there, probably closing the trail. If Mary Grace did reach the wagon train, she would never be able to get back over that pass with the doctor.

He and Tess were on their own.

Dammit to hell. He'd fought Yankees and battled Indians, but he'd never felt this helpless.

It grew darker. And colder. The swirling snow began to stick to the ground, then pile up in drifts. Every hour Lee chunked up the fire and checked on Jenna. Tess had helped her remove her shoes and her dress; now she lay on top of the quilts in just her chemise and petticoat.

He knelt on one side of her, Tess on the other, and they took turns sponging off Jenna's sweat-sticky face and dribbling small sips of water past her cracked lips.

Hours dragged by and it began to grow dark. Lee could tell Jenna was trying to contain her cries, and when Tess went out to replenish the cup of water, Lee leaned down and smoothed Jenna's hair off her forehead.

"Yell if you want to," he said.

"Don't…want to frighten Tess," she whispered. "Someday she may…wonder about having her own child. Not good to be…frightened."

"God, Jenna, yell anyway. Tess is tougher than you think."

She laughed, then caught her breath, and a low moan escaped. "Lee?" she said after a long moment.

"Yeah?"

"This is…taking a long time, isn't it?"

"We've been here about nine hours, I'd say. Maybe longer. It doesn't matter."

She slept off and on, waking when the pains came, then drifting off. An exhausted Tess stretched out beside her. Much later Lee checked on the fire and then lay down on Jenna's other side. In the dark she grabbed on to his hand and held on so tight he thought his knuckles would break.

Toward morning, Lee slipped out for more water for Jenna to sip. He'd just dipped some into the cup when a guttural scream broke the silence.

"Lee?" Tess's voice sounded frightened.

He bolted forward and met Tess as she tumbled out of the wagon. "Lee," she sobbed. "She's hurting so much. Is it always this awful? I can't stand to watch her."

He pressed the girl's shoulder. "Listen, Tess. It's almost light. I want you to wrap yourself up warm and go for a walk, away from the wagon. Maybe back to those pine trees I chopped down."

She turned a tear-streaked face up to his and nodded. He watched her move away, and then Jenna screamed again, and he turned back to the wagon.

She was panting, her face contorted. She reached for

him, and he grabbed her hands and held on. She writhed and groaned, pulling against him. "Talk to me, Lee," she whispered. "Please."

He worked to keep his voice calm. "How about I finish that bedtime story?"

"Yes. Anything." Again she squeezed his hands and pulled with such strength he had to brace his arms. His knuckles ached.

"Well," he said when she relaxed her hold. "You remember our woodpecker? He's—"

She cried out, arching her back off the quilts. "More," she gasped after a long minute. "More story."

He couldn't do it, couldn't think while he watched her suffer.

"Story," she begged. "Now."

"Okay." *Think, Carver.* He cleared his throat. "So the woodpecker, he, uh, he put the beautiful butterfly on his back and off they flew."

"Then what happened?" Jenna whispered. The contractions were coming every minute or so now, and he could see she was tiring.

"Um…well, they got lost. The woodpecker flew back and forth between the rosebush and the morning glory vine, but nothing looked familiar. 'I can't see from way up here,' the butterfly said. 'Can you fly lower?'"

He stopped to wipe the perspiration from Jenna's face. "And?" she muttered.

"And…the woodpecker thought about lying to her, but he decided he couldn't do that. No matter how much he wanted her to admire him, he couldn't lie to her. 'I can't fly any lower,' he said. 'I'll crash into the ground. But you could flutter off on your own. Is that what you want?'"

Jenna grabbed for him again. When she relaxed back onto the quilts she tugged at his shirt. "More."

Oh, Lord. "Well, let's see. The butterfly didn't answer

for a long time, and the woodpecker, he, uh, he thought she had forgotten all about him."

Her body convulsed and her hoarse cry made his blood run cold. "But she hadn't, had she?" Jenna whispered when it was over.

He gripped her hand. "Nope. The woodpecker figured she would leave him, so he landed on a huckleberry bush and waited for her to fly off. He waited and waited, but nothing happened."

"I just knew it," Jenna said between clenched teeth.

"You did?"

She nodded. "More," she groaned.

He racked his brain to focus on Jenna and to think up more of the story. And to not show how damned scared he was.

"Finally," he said, trying to keep his voice steady, the woodpecker asked, 'Are you still there?' And the butterfly said..."

Oh, God, he couldn't think with Jenna groaning and panting like that. "The butterfly said, 'Yes. I am thinking about what I should do.'"

"Go on," Jenna urged, her voice guttural.

"Well..." he grasped her hands and let her pull hard "...the woodpecker waited. And waited. Summer turned to winter, and still he waited. At last, when the snow was thick on the woodpecker's back, the butterfly flew away."

"And the woodpecker?" Jenna asked, her eyes closed. "What happened to the woodpecker?"

"Oh, yeah, the woodpecker. Well, the woodpecker spread his wings and tried to fly, but he found he couldn't move."

"Why not?" She bit down hard on her lower lip.

"Um... He couldn't move because...because his feet had frozen to the ground."

"Oh, no," Jenna murmured after the next contraction. "Did he...did he die?"

"I don't know, honey. What do you think happened to him?"

"I think the butterfly felt very sad about the woodpecker. I think he was very brave." She caught her breath and jammed her fist against her mouth.

"That butterfly was not brave at all," she muttered when she relaxed again. "The woodpecker gave his l-life for her. He was the b-brave one."

Lee thought his heart would crack in two. He leaned over and briefly pressed his lips against her sticky forehead.

She jerked away and cried out, arching her back off the quilts. "Bottom drawer," she gasped when it was over. "Baby blanket."

He reached over and slid the drawer out, rummaged inside and pulled out squares of soft blue flannel with embroidered edges.

The contractions built so rapidly Jenna could scarcely catch her breath between them, and Lee began to pray in earnest. With her next pain she clawed at his sleeve.

"I can't," she gasped.

"Yes, you can." Then he shouted for Tess.

"Quick! Bring the scissors and some warm water."

The enamelware bowl and the scissors appeared through the bonnet, and then Tess's face. "Anything else?" she asked, her voice quavery.

"Go for another walk," he ordered. "A long one."

Jenna thought she would split in two, but through the fog of pain she tried to concentrate on what Lee was saying.

"Push," she thought he said. As if she wasn't already. She took a deep breath and bore down with all her strength, and then she was tearing... Oh, God... Oh, God...she was ripping right up the middle.

Lee yelled something, and she could hear Tess sobbing

outside the wagon. One more long, clenching push and suddenly she felt a gush of liquid and she was free. A funny, faint squall sounded.

Oh! Was it finally over?

Lee was busy doing something with the scissors, and then she heard water splashing and the funny noise got louder. And then Lee was laughing and holding up something, a blue bundle that was moving. A tiny pink fist waved.

"It's a boy, Jenna." He lifted his head. "Tess," he called, "it's a boy!"

The sobbing outside stopped. "Is…is Jenna all right?" a small voice asked.

He pulled the soaked quilt out from under her and rolled it up into a ball. "Jenna is fine," Lee called.

To Jenna he said some more words. "What do you want to name your son?"

She thought his voice sounded odd. Choked, somehow.

She drew in a long, tired breath. "His name," she said, her voice tired, "is Robert E. Lee Carver Borland."

Chapter Thirty-One

Lee left Tess in the wagon with Jenna, exclaiming over the baby, counting fingers and toes and admiring the fuzz of dark hair on his tiny head and his big blue eyes. Lifting his head, Lee stumbled across the snowy ground for a good half mile up the trail until he stopped shaking.

Jenna had more courage than he did, enduring the endless hours of pain and exhaustion while he worried and sweated and tried to sound calm. His hands ached from Jenna's wrenching grip, and his legs felt rubbery. Women were tough. Men were cowards.

The beautiful, brave butterfly and the cowardly woodpecker. He would never forget that ridiculous fairy tale he'd concocted, and he hoped to God he never had to think up another one.

The sun broke through a puffy white cloud, bathing the mountain in warm golden light. Good God, it was morning! Late morning, from the angle of the sun. He had to fix that broken axle and get over the pass before dark.

From the wagon he heard Tess crooning nonsense words, punctuated by Jenna's laughter. Robert E. Lee Carver Borland, huh? Big mouthful of a name. He was flattered. Hell, he felt poleaxed.

The axle. Focus on the axle.

He cut the pine sapling to the length he'd need, skinned off the bark and went back to the stump he'd left. He chopped it off close to the ground, rolled it up to the wagon and wedged it under the rear wheel. Then he backed the ox team up until the axle hung up on the stump and the wheel could spin freely.

He shaped one end of the pole into a point, removed the wheel and pounded the makeshift axle into place. He prayed it would hold long enough to catch up to the wagon train.

Just as he drove in the last nail, he heard a horse. Two horses. No, three. He looked up to see Mary Grace galloping toward him on Devil, and behind her... He squinted against the snow glare. It looked like Doc Engelman and... Emma Lincoln? He blinked to make sure.

Mary Grace reined up, slid off and launched herself at Lee. "Is she all right? Did she have the baby yet? Was—"

"Hold on, honey. Catch your breath. Jenna is fine, and yes, she's had the baby. You have a brother."

The girl yelped and whirled away toward the wagon, but Lee snagged the back of her wool coat. "Wait! Let Doc look at her first."

Lee went to greet Dr. Engelman. The physician dismounted and shook his head. "Got here as quick as I could, Lee. Snow closed the pass. How's Jenna?"

"Jenna's fine, I think. Baby seems fine, too. But, hell, I don't know what's fine and what's not fine."

The physician nodded, lifted his leather bag off his horse and started for the wagon. Lee moved to help Emma dismount.

"Never seen you on a horse, Emma. Didn't know you could ride."

"I don't ride," she huffed. "That's why I can't get down off from this darned animal! My legs won't work."

Lee managed to lift the woman off her mount, and she

stood on the ground, patting herself all over. "Hurts everywhere," she said with a laugh.

"Jenna has some whiskey inside."

"You mean you didn't drink it all up during her labor last night?"

"There wasn't time," Lee said drily.

Emma touched his arm. "Are you all right, Lee? You look like something's clobbered you good."

"It's been a long night. Broke an axle and then…"

"I can guess," the gray-bunned woman said. "Mary Grace told us. When Sam wouldn't let her ride back over the pass she cried and carried on something fierce."

Tess and Mary Grace walked off arm in arm, talking so fast it sounded like the chatter of squirrels. The doctor climbed out through the canvas bonnet and dropped his medical bag to the ground with a clunk.

"Emma? I expect Jenna'd like to talk to a woman about now."

Lee swallowed. "Is she okay, Doc?"

"Son, Jenna is fine, just fine. You ever want to give up this idea about a horse ranch, you let me know. You'd make a fine physician. A whole lotta men wouldn't have any notion how to deliver a baby. They'd have just caved in."

A laugh of sorts burst from Lee's mouth. "Hell, Doc, you think I knew what I was doing? What Jenna went through was enough to give a man religion."

"Yep. I can guess what it must have been like for you, Lee. I hear she named the baby after you. Good choice."

"Got to fix that axle, Doc," Lee said quickly. "Help yourself to the whiskey, if Emma and Jenna have left any."

Emma poked her head through the canvas bonnet and called to the girls. "Jenna says she's hungry! That's always a good sign. So let's cobble up some breakfast." She climbed down out of the wagon and headed toward the fire.

Lee worked all afternoon on his improvised wooden axle while the girls flitted in and out of the wagon with biscuits and bacon and hot coffee for Jenna. He ignored the squeals of excited laughter from inside, and late in the afternoon he got the axle fitted through the wheel hub and nailed in place.

Doc and Emma mounted their horses. "Lee," Emma called. "The wagons will wait for you to catch up." The two riders headed back over the pass, and Tess and Mary Grace came to stand beside him.

"Are we gonna go now?" Tess asked.

"Maybe," Lee said. "Any coffee left?"

Tess's eyes widened. "Oh, Lee, I forgot you haven't eaten anything all day. There's biscuits and—"

"Any of Jenna's whiskey left?"

"Oh!" Mary Grace clapped her hand over her mouth. "I think Mrs. Lincoln and Jenna drank it all up!"

"Well, hell."

Both girls sucked in their breath, but Lee just sighed. "Come on, then. Get in the wagon. Mary Grace, do you want to ride Devil?"

"Uh, no. I want to ride inside the wagon and hold Baby Rob."

"Baby Rob, is it?"

"Well," Tess said with a giggle. "It'd be confusing to have two males named Lee, wouldn't it?"

Lee bit his tongue and went to feed the animals and shovel dirt over the remains of the fire. When he'd stowed his saddle and the tools under the wagon, he climbed up onto the driver's bench and lifted the traces.

He hadn't seen Jenna since morning. And, he had to admit, he missed her. He didn't want to think how he'd feel when they separated in Oregon.

Chapter Thirty-Two

They caught up to the rest of the wagons just before full dark. Lee was so tired he considered sleeping right where he sat his horse while Tess and Mary Grace cooked up some supper. But he decided he couldn't stand one more hour without seeing Jenna. He climbed up into the wagon bed.

She was propped up, holding a tiny bundle of blue blankets in her arms. She looked up and smiled.

"Jenna, I—" His voice failed.

"Oh, Lee, just look at him! Isn't he beautiful?"

Reluctantly he forced his gaze away from her glowing face and peered down at the baby she held. A fuzz of dark hair covered the small head, and his eyes were a unique blue-green, like Jenna's. Yeah, he was beautiful, all right. *Really* beautiful. Like her.

"Have you eaten?" she asked.

"Not yet. The girls are cooking something."

"I know," she said with a laugh. "I can hear them arguing over whether to make stew or beans. Nothing changes, does it?"

"Everything changes. You. Me. Everything." He looked everywhere but at her. She was so incredibly lovely he could scarcely speak.

"You know," she began, then bit her lip. "When you first

came to drive our wagon, I thought you were pushy and… um…maddening."

"Yeah? What do you think now?"

She laughed softly. "I think you are still maddening. But…"

He closed his eyes. "But?"

"But," she said shyly, "I think you are the bravest man I've ever known. You are not afraid of anything."

That brought a snort of laughter. "You think I wasn't scared last night?"

"No," she said quietly. "*I* was the one who was frightened. Really, really frightened. I have never felt such pain."

He caught her hand. "Jenna, I thought you might die. Or else *I* might. You're so, well, small."

"Oh, that." She blushed scarlet, then held out the blanket-wrapped baby. "Would you like to hold him?"

Lee froze. Hold him? Another man's child? A man he detested?

"Lee?" she urged. "It's just a baby."

"Yeah, but he's… My hands aren't clean," he said abruptly.

"Here." Jenna thrust the baby into his arms. He weighed about as much as a pan of oats. He spread his fingers around the tiny body and tentatively reached out his forefinger and grazed the soft cheek. The little mouth opened in a yawn and something strange happened inside his chest.

"Jenna." His voice shook.

"Don't talk, Lee. You don't have to say anything."

He couldn't talk even if he wanted to. But what he could do, what he couldn't keep from doing, was bend over and catch Jenna's soft mouth under his.

"Butterfly," he murmured after a long moment.

Lee's homemade axle held for the next five days as the wagon train descended into broad valleys and climbed over more mountains until they reached Fort Hall on the Snake

River. They replenished their dwindling supplies and Lee found a forge and a blacksmith to make a new axle.

The following day the train forded the river with no mishap other than when one of Mick McKernan's mules got mired in a quicksand bog. Lee drove the Borland wagon past him, then went back on horseback to help pull the animal free.

Four families split off to follow the trail to California; the sixteen remaining wagons continued on to Farewell Bend, where they turned south to follow the Free Emigrant Trail that skirted the foothills of the Cascades.

Four days later they dropped down into the Willamette Valley, and Jenna steeled herself for what she knew was coming.

Chapter Thirty-Three

When the wagon came up over the rise Jenna gasped. She could see all the way to the valley floor. Everything was so green it looked painted.

"I've never seen grass so lush," Lee said. "Not even back in Virginia."

His excitement sent an odd pang through her chest. She cuddled Baby Rob closer and listened to the girls' laughter as they pointed their fingers down at the place they had struggled so hard to finally reach—Oregon.

That night the wagon train celebrated. Emil Gumpert brought out his squeezebox, and then instruments began popping up from ragged, dust-laden wagons like jack-in-the-boxes—two fiddles, guitars, and a banjo played by aging Jan Ronning. The girls and Ruthie skipped off to join the dancing, and Jenna walked over to visit Sophia Zaberskie, grateful for a place where she could sit and nurse the baby in peace and relative quiet.

"Your baby so pretty," Sophia remarked when Jenna folded back the flannel blanket. The other woman patted her expanding belly. "I hope for girl. Maybe," she added with a laugh, "my daughter and your beautiful son, they will grow up and get marry."

"You are fortunate that your baby will be born in a

town. I don't even know what state we were in when Robbie came. Wyoming? Nebraska?"

"I think Idaho. Ted showed me on map."

Idaho! And now they were dancing and singing in Oregon. She hugged the baby close. They had arrived safely, thanks to Lee Carver. She was glad she had named the baby after him. Without Lee, she might not have borne a healthy child. Mercy, if Lee hadn't been with her, she might not have lived through the birth at all.

"What troubles you?" Sophia asked suddenly.

"N-nothing. It's just that, well, now that the journey is over, I hope we will settle close enough to be neighbors."

Sophia squeezed her hand. "Yes, sure. Ted has job waiting with newspaper." She pointed down to the town that lay in the pretty green valley below. "I t'ink we all be neighbors."

Lee appeared carrying Ruthie on his shoulders. "Mrs. Zaberskie."

Sophia nodded. "Mr. Carver, welcome. Would like coffee?"

"No, thanks. I was wondering if you'd look after Ruthie for half an hour or so." He handed Ruthie down, lifted Robbie out of Jenna's arms and deposited him on Sophia's lap. "And the baby, if you don't mind. I'd like to talk to Jenna in private."

Sophia smiled. "Sure. You go, Jenna. Baby is fine."

"Well…" Jenna hesitated, but Lee grasped her hands and pulled her to her feet.

"Come on, Jenna. Tomorrow we'll be going into town, and then it'll be too late." He slipped his arm around her waist and walked her off a dozen yards.

"Too late for what?" Jenna asked.

"Too late for what I want to say now that our journey is over."

Jenna waited, aware of a tension about him she'd never

sensed before. Her insides tightened. "What is it, Lee? You have never hesitated to speak your mind before."

"Yeah, well, I… It's like this, Jenna. I want to keep going north. Find a place to start my ranch."

"Yes. I know how important that is to you."

He let some time pass before he spoke again. "Something else is important, too. You and the girls and the baby." He took a breath and plunged on. "I want you to come with me, Jenna. All of you. We could…um, we could get married."

"Oh, Lee," she breathed. "I know you don't want to marry again. It scares you to death."

He said nothing.

"Doesn't it?" she repeated.

"Yeah, it does scare me. Even so, I want you to come with me."

She looked up into his unsmiling face. "But it *does* matter, Lee. I have always known what you wanted."

"Jenna—"

"Wait. Let me finish. We have all depended on you. And you and I have grown close these past months. Very close. But that is not reason enough to marry."

He pulled her into his arms and rested his lips against her forehead. "Jenna, I care about you. You know I care what happens to you and the girls and the baby."

"I do know that, Lee," she whispered. "I care about you, too. But when Mathias died, and after that awful business with Randall, I realized what a mess I had made of everything. Now I distrust my judgment. I let Randall seduce me against my better judgment. I let Mathias talk me into marriage, also against my better judgment. It's too late for me, Lee. I will never marry again."

He huffed out a choked laugh. "How old are you, twenty-four? You're too young to give up like this."

"It's too late for me," she repeated. "I feel as if I've lived three lifetimes this past year."

He grazed her mouth with his. "It's not too late. Marry me, Jenna. Come with me."

She reached both arms around his neck and kissed him. "I can't, Lee. I just can't. It would be a disaster for both of us."

He tightened his hands around her shoulders. "Dammit, Jenna, yes you can."

She shook her head. "I no longer trust myself to make good decisions. I would hurt you, Lee, and you don't deserve that." She stepped back and turned her face away so he wouldn't see her tears.

From the crest of the last gentle, grass-covered hill, Jenna looked down on the pretty little town nestled between a wide, slow-moving river and a thick stand of fir and maple trees. As the wagon drew closer, she spied a large painted sign. "Heavenly, Oregon. Population 743." This was the emigrants' chosen destination.

A big white-painted church with a pointed steeple perched at one end of the main street; at the other end stood a redbrick schoolhouse. Heavenly seemed like the perfect name for such a lovely place. It looked peaceful and orderly and clean, a different world from the one they had inhabited for the past five months.

Horse-drawn wagons piled with bulging sacks of feed rumbled past the storefronts. First County Bank. Springer's Mercantile. The sheriff's office, Morning Glory Hotel, a newspaper office, a dressmaker with fancy hats in the window. Women in starched shirtwaists and flared skirts swept along the board sidewalks, some leading young children by the hand.

Suddenly she realized how uncivilized she and the girls must look to the townspeople; the emigrants were worn-out and sunburned, their clothing frayed from skirt hem to collar. They had traveled two thousand miles to start a new life, rolling over wildflower-strewn plains and across towering mountains, over rivers and through sandy, sage-brush-dotted deserts. Their ordeal certainly showed.

The wagon rolled past a manicured, tree-shaded park with a white gazebo and a raised bed of bright yellow roses. Lee's eyes shone. "This country is perfect for horses. Devil will get fat within a week."

"I am more concerned about its being perfect for three girls and a baby. Lee, I need to look for a place for us to live."

Without a word, he turned down a wide street lined on both sides with chestnut trees and trim houses, some with beautiful gardens—orange zinnias, blue bachelor buttons, and red and yellow roses everywhere.

"Is this where we're gonna live?" Ruthie asked.

"Maybe," Jenna said. Over the girl's head she exchanged a long look with Lee.

"Stop!" she shouted suddenly. Lee pulled the team to a halt in front of a brown two-story house with a hand-lettered sign in the bowed front window that read Board-ers Wanted.

She thrust the baby into Lee's arms and was off the bench in a flurry of petticoats. The girls poked their heads out of the wagon and watched her march up the steps onto the porch and ring the bell.

The door opened, and a diminutive, silver-haired women in a crisp black dress looked at her inquiringly.

Jenna cleared her throat. "Excuse me, your sign said you are looking for boarders?"

"Oh, my stars, yes." The sharp blue eyes moved past her to the wagon. "I see you have a family."

"There are five of us. Three girls and a baby."

The woman tipped her head toward the wagon. "And a husband?"

"Oh, no. We are not married."

The silvery eyebrows went up. "Living in sin, are you?"

"Oh, no, I—"

"Makes no never mind to me, dearie. I could use a good man around the place. I'm getting too old to chop wood, and my last boarder, a preacher man, moved on to Portland. Said there were more souls to save in the city. Fact is, I was just about to give up and move back to Iowa."

Jenna introduced herself and waited politely.

"I'm Della Bueller. Been a widow for nineteen years, I have. Been renting out rooms to make ends meet, but with Reverend Snell gone…"

"Perhaps my older girls could help with the chores."

The woman's eyes brightened with interest. "Could they, now?"

"Yes, and I… I could share the cooking and run errands and…"

"Why, you've been sent from heaven, you have."

"Could we move in right away? We have traveled all across the country, from St. Louis, and my girls need to start school."

"Mrs. Borland, you come right on in, and make yourself at home. Bring your girls, too. You can have your pick of the rooms upstairs. It's two dollars a week, including meals. Might charge less if you help out and the girls spend some time in the kitchen."

"Well?" Lee queried when she returned to the wagon.

"We have rooms!" Jenna was so excited her voice shook. She climbed up onto the bench and lifted Robbie out of his arms.

Ruthie tugged at her sleeve. "Can Mister Lee have a room, too?"

Lee laid his hand on the girl's shoulder. "Mister Lee is moving on, honey. He's going to find some land and start a ranch."

"Why?" Ruthie's face clouded. "Don't you like us?"

He caught Jenna's eye and his mouth tightened. "Yes, I like you," he said, his voice rough. "All of you. I like you a lot."

"But," Jenna interjected, "Mister Lee can't raise horses in a town, can he? He has to find someplace with lots of room and grass and…well, grass."

"Oh." Ruthie studied the toes of her raggedy leather shoes. "I don't like grass."

Lee sucked in a gulp of air. "How about I help you unload the wagon and take it on down to the livery. Then maybe we could all eat supper together at the hotel before I leave. What do you say?"

"Yes!" Tess sang from inside the wagon.

"Can I have a steak?" Mary Grace shouted.

"Me, too," Ruthie said. "I want steak."

Lee's gray eyes sought Jenna's. "How about it, Jenna? Now that we're finally here, maybe we should celebrate."

"Yes, thank you, Lee. That is a lovely idea." Her words sounded stiff, even to her. The truth was she *felt* stiff. In fact, she felt frozen inside at the prospect of a farewell meal with Lee Carver.

Jenna and the girls lugged all their belongings upstairs while Mrs. Bueller busied herself in the kitchen, storing the extra food Lee carried in. Jenna insisted that Lee keep the skillet and the kettles and all the cooking utensils.

"You will need them on your ranch, Lee. Take them."

Jenna chose an upstairs room with two tall windows that looked out on the street, flanking a narrow bed with a crocheted coverlet in blue and cream. She especially liked the wallpaper, sprigged with tiny blue and white flowers. At Mrs. Bueller's direction, Lee wrestled an old hand-carved cradle down from the attic and installed it next to the bed.

Tess and Mary Grace chose the large room across the hall with two beds separated by a large walnut armoire and a small cot with a ruffled yellow quilt for Ruthie.

When everything was unloaded from the wagon, Lee drove off down the street and Mrs. Bueller began heating water for the first hot baths Jenna and the girls had enjoyed in months. Afterward, Jenna fed Robbie, dressed slowly in her best gingham frock and brushed out her hair.

She dreaded supper with Lee. It would be the last time she would see him. Ever.

A fist-sized lump lodged in her throat.

Chapter Thirty-Four

"Just look!" Tess exclaimed that evening, her hazel eyes widening. "Real tablecloths!"

"And napkins," Mary Grace added in an awed voice. "Real cloth napkins." The older girls seated themselves at the center table in the Morning Glory Hotel dining room and Ruthie climbed up next to Mary Grace.

Lee's hand pressed gently at Jenna's waist, guiding her forward. He settled her in the upholstered chair and maneuvered Baby Rob's wicker basket onto the empty seat beside her. Then he pulled up his chair next to her and folded his long legs under the table.

He'd shaved, she noted. She wished he hadn't. He was too attractive without the dark stubble she had grown used to. She swallowed and dropped her gaze to the menu in front of her. Looking at him made her throat feel tight.

"Steak," all three girls announced when the waitress came for their orders.

"Small ones," Jenna murmured as the girl scratched her pencil across the pad.

"I'd like the meat loaf," Jenna decided. "With mashed potatoes and gravy. And some tea, please."

"And for you, sir?"

"Steak. Large. Medium rare. Lots of fried potatoes. And coffee. Oh, and milk for the girls."

"I guess we haven't been feeding you enough, have we?" Jenna observed with a tight smile.

Lee didn't answer. In fact he said nothing until the waitress returned with Jenna's tea and his coffee. After his first gulp, he leaned toward her. "Not near as good as yours," he whispered.

"Maybe you should ask her to add some medicinal whiskey," Jenna murmured. She wouldn't mind a generous dollop of whiskey herself right about now; her insides were feeling more cold and heavy with every passing minute. She sipped her tea, and the diners lapsed into an awkward silence.

"While you were getting settled today, I heard some news," Lee said at last. "About our fellow emigrants."

Instantly Tess perked up. "Tell us! Is it about Jimmy Gum— Uh, the Gumperts?"

"Some of it. Emil Gumpert has a job at the bank. He and Hulda will be living just three blocks from your boardinghouse. I bet Jimmy could walk you girls to school."

"What about me?" Ruthie asked. "I wanna go to school, too."

"You're too little for school," Tess grumbled.

"Am not!"

"Are too!"

Jenna rapped her knife sharply against her plate. "Girls, what did I say about arguing in public?"

"In private, too," Ruthie added. "Mister Lee, I'm not too little for school, am I? I already learned some 'rench."

"I think Jimmy will walk with you, too, honey," Lee said with a grin. "Now," he added quickly, "you all want to hear some more news?"

"Yes!" three voices chorused.

"All right, listen up. Sam and Emma Lincoln have

bought a small farm just outside of town. Mary Grace, Sam said he'd board your horse for you."

"He won't need to," Mary Grace said, her voice quiet. "Lee, I want you to take Red for your ranch. You'll need more than a stallion to start a herd. You'll need a mare, too."

"Oh, honey, I couldn't—"

"I want you to have her, Lee. To remember us by."

Jenna shot a look at his face. His mouth twisted, and his eyes looked suspiciously shiny.

"I will always remember you," he said, "horse or no horse." His voice sounded raspy.

"What other news do you have?" Jenna asked quickly.

Lee cleared his throat. "Let's see now. I ran into Ted Zaberskie at the mercantile. He'll be working at the newspaper office. He and Sophia will live in the apartment upstairs. And Mick McKernan…"

He stopped and waited until he had the girls' complete attention. "I want you to stay away from McKernan's blacksmith shop, understand?"

Jenna and the girls nodded. "I don't like him," Tess announced. "Or his brother, either. We won't go anywhere near their shop."

Lee grinned at her. "Doc Engelman's setting up his practice next to the dressmaker. Can't recall the lady's name, but she said… Can't remember what she said, either."

Everyone laughed and then lapsed into a gloomy silence. The waitress brought their meals, but one by one the girls put down their forks and stared at their plates.

Lee frowned. "What's wrong?"

"N-nothing," Mary Grace said. Tess gave a little choked sob, and Ruthie's blue eyes flooded. Even Jenna looked stricken.

Carefully he laid his fork on his plate. "What is it?"

"You're going away," Jenna said, her voice quiet.

"Yeah, I am. But I don't want you to leave three good steaks uneaten just because of that."

"I'm not hungry anymore," Ruthie said, her eyes swimming.

Lee touched her shoulder. "You remember how hungry we got on our journey? Seems to me that we shouldn't waste good food. Besides," he said, bending toward Ruthie, "if you eat up all your steak, you'll grow up faster and then you can go to school."

"Oh." Reluctantly Ruthie picked up her fork, and Lee leaned over to cut her meat into small bites.

"And," he addressed Tess and Mary Grace together, "steak makes girls grow up to be beautiful."

Both girls looked at each other and reached for their knives.

"What about meat loaf?" Jenna couldn't resist asking.

"What about it?" he said, his voice bland.

She rolled her eyes.

"Meat loaf," he murmured near her ear, "makes a woman love a steak-eating man."

"Oh, Lee, I don't need meat loaf for…" Her voice wobbled. "Oh, dear." She pressed her fingers over her mouth.

Under the table he sought her hand. "Jenna," he breathed. "For God's sake, don't cry."

She nodded, her eyes wet.

When supper was over, Lee lifted Baby Rob's basket and ushered Jenna and the girls out onto the board sidewalk where he'd left Devil tethered to the hitching rail, saddlebags bulging.

"Is that all you're taking?" Jenna managed, eyeing the animal.

"Nope. Got a pack mule loaded up and waiting at the livery."

She lifted her chin. "Oh."

Lee folded Tess into a hug, and when she let out a shuddery breath he smacked a kiss on her cheek. Then he turned to Mary Grace. "I'll give your mare the best feed I can afford. And I'll name her first foal after you, shall I?"

The girl nodded, unable to speak. She reached up and touched his cheek.

Ruthie clung to his pant leg with both thin arms, tears bathing her cheeks. Lee gently pried her fingers away from the denim. "You have to let go, honey. I need to speak to Jenna."

He entrusted the baby's basket to Tess, took Jenna's arm and walked her around the corner out of sight of the girls.

"Lee…"

"Don't say anything, Jenna. Just kiss me." He took her in his arms and covered her mouth. God, it was hard to stop kissing her. It was even harder to let her go.

"Don't forget me," he whispered.

"You know I won't. Ever."

"Do you need any money?"

"No. Mrs. Bueller is reducing our rent in exchange for help in the kitchen, and besides, I have some money saved up. And if we run short I can always give piano lessons."

"Be happy," he breathed. He kissed her again, walked her back around the corner and moved to his horse. "Goodbye, Jenna." He touched his hand to her cheek. "I wouldn't trade these past five months with you for anything on this earth."

He stepped into the stirrup, reined away with a single backward glance and was gone.

Jenna waved until she could no longer see the tall, lean figure on the black horse, pressing her lips together hard to keep them from trembling.

"I feel awful," Ruthie complained.

"Too much steak," Tess observed.

"No," Mary Grace contradicted. "Not enough of Lee."

"You," Jenna murmured to her middle stepdaughter as they headed toward the boardinghouse, "are getting to be wise beyond your years."

"And you," Mary Grace whispered back, "are gonna miss Lee more than any of us, and you know it." She slid her arm about Jenna's waist and laid her head against Jenna's shoulder.

Jenna opened her mouth to reply but found she couldn't speak. She knew she was doing the right thing, for Lee and for herself, but her heart felt like it was shattering into a million tiny, sharp-edged pieces.

Chapter Thirty-Five

With the crisp days of fall, Tess and Mary Grace started school, walking the short distance to the red-brick schoolhouse each day with tall, gangly Jimmy Gumpert, who tactfully divided his attention between the two girls. Ruthie had daily lessons with Jenna in reading and sums, and little Robbie nursed and slept and cried and nursed some more, as regular as clockwork.

Jenna couldn't shake her lethargy or her sadness. She attributed both to the demands of motherhood, taking care of Ruthie and guiding the two older girls, and helping Mrs. Bueller in the kitchen as much as possible. And then there was Tess's occasional grumbling and Mary Grace's quarrelsome attitude. Both girls had sweetened considerably, but some days they seemed unusually out of sorts. Sharp-eyed Della Bueller just observed the goings-on with her birdlike blue eyes and smiled to herself.

November came. Ruthie clamored for more words in French, and then one rainy afternoon she discovered Mrs. Bueller's upright piano. Jenna began to teach all the girls music, but it was Ruthie who excelled. She could pick out any tune she heard, and she remembered the words to every song and she sang it on pitch. Her favorite was

"Frère Jacques," Jenna suspected because the words were in French.

Baby Rob grew round and bright-eyed and was starting to make happy gurgly sounds. Jenna enjoyed the hours spent playing peekaboo with him, but at night, after she fed him, she lay on her narrow bed and stared up at the ceiling for hours.

Had Lee started that horse ranch he wanted so much? Did he have enough to eat? A warm jacket to wear now that winter was coming? If it was snowing here in Heavenly, it must be blowing blizzards farther north, with bitter wind and perhaps sleet and frozen rivers.

She prayed he was all right, safe and well and warm. Had he built a barn? A house? Oh, she hoped he had a big fireplace and plenty of firewood.

Christmas was two weeks away, but Jenna felt oddly disinterested in the festivities. The girls decorated a tall Douglas fir that stocky, bearded Ted Zaberskie dragged into the house and set up in the front parlor. Tess and Mary Grace made chains of colored paper and looped strings of popcorn and cranberries over the fragrant branches, but Jenna noticed that both girls were subdued.

A few days before Christmas, Jenna's feeling of emptiness bloomed into an uneasy depression. What was the matter with her? She had everything she needed—food, warm clothing for the girls and herself, a safe place to stay at the boardinghouse, but…

But what? One rainy afternoon she sank to the floor beside the decorated tree and buried her face against her knees. What on earth was wrong with her?

You miss Lee.

Yes, she admitted. She did miss him. His absence had left an unexpected Lee-shaped hole in her heart.

Ruthie slipped into the parlor and plopped down beside her. "How come you're crying, Jenna?"

"I guess I'm just sad, honey. It's wet and cold outside and…"

"I want Mister Lee to come back," the girl announced. "You want Mister Lee to come back, don'tcha, Jenna?"

"Yes." She wiped her snuffly nose on an already sodden handkerchief. "But we must make the best of things. We will all celebrate Christmas and give thanks for the good things we have."

The day before Christmas, Della Bueller invited Emma Lincoln, Sophia Zaberskie and Hulda Gumpert to join Jenna and herself for afternoon tea at the boardinghouse. Jenna had made an apple-brandy cake, peeling apples until her fingers smarted and taking nips of brandy while she soaked the finished layers. The whole house smelled wonderful.

The girls had been invited to a church social, and they walked out the front door dressed in their very best starched gingham shirtwaists and woolen skirts, escorted by a blushing Jimmy Gumpert and his brusque, no-nonsense father, Emil.

Mrs. Bueller's afternoon guests arrived, and Jenna tried her best to feel festive. "Ladies," Mrs. Bueller announced when everyone had gathered at her lace-covered dining table. "Thank you for coming. My stars, I haven't had a proper tea since I left Iowa."

Sophia shared a platter of what she called sand cookies and made a breathless announcement. "Doctor say baby come maybe early," she stated, her face beaming.

"How early?" Emma inquired.

"Not early enough," Sophia said with a laugh. "I feel like big fat cow." Her dark hair was coiled at her neck. Jenna had never seen it unbraided.

"Jimmy vas three veeks late," round-faced Hulda Gumpert admitted. "I thought I had swallowed a whole barn with the cow inside!"

Della Bueller poured tea into flowered china cups, and

Jenna cut slices of cake and passed out silver forks. Talk moved quickly to the Heavenly town newspaper, the *Star*, and its latest articles on the Oregon senate race and the suffrage movement.

"Ted says vote for women will come soon," Sophia offered.

"Good!" Della exclaimed. "I'm getting too old to let those young pups make all the decisions for me."

Gray-bunned Emma Lincoln changed the subject. "Have you ladies heard about the blizzard up north?"

Jenna choked on a swallow of tea. "Where exactly up north?"

"Can't say for sure. Sam heard about it when he went to Portland last week to pick up his new plow."

"Jenna!" Sophia said suddenly. "You look white like cream. You maybe have worry about Mr. Carver?"

"What? Oh, no. Not really."

"You mean 'oh, yes,' don't you, dearie?" Della Bueller interjected. "That man must be on your mind. I hear you tossing and turning at night."

Emma peered at her. "You have heard from Lee, haven't you, Jenna?"

"No, I… We agreed not to…" Her voice trailed off and she focused on her teacup.

"Hmmmm." Emma studied her face so long Jenna felt her cheeks flame. "Only one reason why a man and a woman agree 'not to' something," the older woman observed.

"What reason?" Sophia and Hulda asked at the same time.

"Oh…" Emma paused to lick apple cake from her fingers. "When the man and the woman want to be together but can't for some reason."

"What reason?" Hulda and Sophia chorused again. Hulda fanned her round, flushed cheeks.

Della watched Jenna so closely it made her insides

jumpy, and Emma's pale blue eyes sought hers. "I take it you haven't written to him?" Emma queried.

"I don't know where he is, Emma. I have no address for him."

Emma huffed out a breath. "And I gather he hasn't written to you."

Jenna shook her head, her vision blurring. "No. We agreed that we... That is..."

"Is foolish thing," Sophia blurted, shaking a work-worn finger at Jenna.

"Maybe," Emma countered. "Maybe not. Seems to me that's how a man and a woman act when they're in love with each other but they don't want to admit it."

In the ensuing silence Jenna closed her eyes and struggled for control.

"Is foolish," Sophia repeated.

"More tea?" Della offered quickly.

"I think," Emma began, holding out her cup, "that Lee Carver is waiting for a signal from you, Jenna."

"Good!" Hulda Gumpert exclaimed. "So, vat iss problem? Jenna she not vant signal?" The woman's dark purple dress fluttered over her generous chest.

"Oh, no," Sophia said. "Jenna maybe is wait for Mr. Carver to make signal?"

Della set her silver teapot down with a clunk. "Jenna? Is that true?"

Numbly, Jenna managed to nod. "I told Lee that I will never remarry."

"Remarry is not question," Sophia sputtered. "Question is whether love is there."

Four pairs of eyes focused on Jenna.

"Well?" Emma said gently. "Is love there?"

Della Bueller rose abruptly, rummaged in the walnut sideboard and withdrew a fat bottle of brandy. "For courage," she announced. She dribbled a hefty shot into each teacup. Into Jenna's she poured two extra-generous shots.

Jenna gulped down a swallow, coughed and held out her cup again. The assembled ladies laughed and waited. The silence grew.

"Jenna?" Emma prompted. "Do you love Lee Carver?"

"I— Well, you see, there is more to it than that."

"Vat 'more'?" Hulda queried in a piercing tone. She leaned her ample body forward.

"Um… I don't want to force Lee's hand. He lost his wife and son during the War, and he is wary of being hurt again. And…and I have made such awful mistakes in my life. I don't want to hurt him."

Emma held her gaze with unwavering directness. "But Lee *is* being hurt again, Jenna. By you."

Sophia touched her hand. "And you not want to make again big mistake and hurt more, iss so?"

"Is so," Jenna whispered. She downed another gulp of her brandy-laced tea.

"Iss not so," Sophia challenged. "Man love woman. Woman love man. Iss simple."

The burst of chatter set Jenna's teeth on edge. Had she been wrong? Was it really as simple as Sophia suggested?

Yes, it was that simple, she realized. She loved Lee Carver. Nothing else mattered.

But still, even if she wanted to, she could do nothing. Lee had not let her know where he was or how to reach him.

Oh, her head was beginning to ache, and her heart hurt, as well. She listened to the women's talk with half an ear and let her thoughts stray far away to the north.

Finally the afternoon tea drew to a close. The ladies agreed it had been a fine party and immediately made plans to do it again next month.

The following day Tess and Mary Grace helped Mrs. Bueller stuff two roast chickens for supper that night. Jenna baked four apple pies. It snowed all day, big white flakes that floated past the front windows, turning the yard into a frozen fairyland. Tonight was Christmas Eve.

When the meal was ready, Della turned down the lamps and lit the candles on the table. Jenna and the girls gathered at the long walnut table in the dining room.

Except for Ruthie, who stood at the front window, watching the snow drift down. The girl had been blue all day. Nothing seemed to interest her, not even the parlor piano.

"Ruthie," Jenna called. "Come and sit down. It's time to eat."

"I dowanna, Jenna. I'm not hungry."

"What? I thought you loved roast chicken and—"

Suddenly the girl gave a yelp and gripped the lace curtains. "Somebody's coming!"

"What do you mean, 'somebody'?" Tess questioned. Her hazel eyes snapped with impatience. "Well, who is it?"

"It's…it's…" Ruthie gave a little jump.

"Well?" Mary Grace shot. "Cat got your tongue? What *is* the matter with you, sister?"

Footsteps pounded up the porch steps. Mrs. Bueller refolded her napkin and laid it on the table, then patted her gray hair. In the next instant Ruthie raced to the door and yanked it wide-open.

Chapter Thirty-Six

A tall, snow-dusted figure came in, shaking white flakes from his dark hair. His arms were full of brightly wrapped packages.

"It's Mister Lee!" Ruthie crowed.

Jenna half rose from her chair. Lee? Here?

"It *is* Lee!" Mary Grace and Tess launched themselves at him, and Ruthie glommed onto one leg. "Mister Lee! Mister Lee!"

Lee laid the packages on the upholstered settee, scooped Ruthie up and spun her around and around. Then he set her down and snaked an arm around Tess and Mary Grace to hug them tight. Behind him, he heard Mrs. Bueller close the front door.

"Mr. Carver," she said, a smile in her voice. He planted a big kiss on both the woman's leathery cheeks.

"Merry Christmas, Mrs. Bueller."

The old lady blushed a lovely shade of rose, so he kissed her again.

Jenna stood by the dining table across the room from him, her eyes wide, one hand at her throat.

"Hello, Jenna." Lee reached her in three strides, folded her into his arms and kissed her until he thought he'd explode. When he released her she opened her mouth to speak, but he laid his forefinger against her lips and brought his mouth near her ear.

"I'm so damn glad to see you I could…"

"I—I'm glad to see you, too, Lee. So glad I can't talk," she whispered. "Where on earth did you come from?"

"From my ranch. It's a little over a hundred miles north of here, near Maple Falls. I've been riding for two days."

"Take off your wet things, Mr. Carver," Mrs. Bueller urged. "And sit down and join us." She hung his hat and his snow-covered jacket on the coatrack in the hall and added another log to the fireplace.

All through supper Lee couldn't take his eyes off Jenna. Ruthie crawled into his lap, and the girls told him all about school and church socials and Jimmy Gumpert. The baby slept in his wicker basket, and even when he whimpered, Jenna couldn't stop staring at Lee.

Finally, Lee decided it was time. "Guess I should tell you why I'm here," he began. Across the table from him, Jenna carefully laid down her fork and studied him.

"I have my ranch. Three hundred acres of the best grass in the state. I have a barn for my horses and a big ranch house."

"Ooh," Ruthie breathed. "A real big house?"

"A real big house. It has six bedrooms."

"Why so many?" Mary Grace asked. "Who else lives there?"

"I have three ranch hands who work for me, but they sleep in a bunkhouse. The bedrooms in the house are for you. At least I hope so."

Jenna's head came up and her eyes rounded into an unspoken question.

"I need a wife," Lee said, looking straight at her. "And now I have something to offer her." He moved to her side and bent to hold her gaze. "I want a family, too," he continued, looking deep into her blue-green eyes. "I figure three girls and a baby boy ought to be about the right size. What do you think?"

No one said a word. Then Ruthie flung her arms around Lee's leg. "I wanna come live with you, Mister Lee."

"There's a school a mile away. And the Gumperts are buying the ranch next to mine, so Jimmy can walk—"

"Yes!" Tess screamed.

Mary Grace blinked. "Can I ride Red to school?"

"And me?" Ruthie chimed. "Can Jimmy walk me to school, too?"

Lee paused and studied the woman at the head of the table. "I also need a cook for the hired men and for the house. Mrs. Bueller?"

The old lady spilled her coffee. "You want *me*? To cook for you and the... Why, my stars, yes. *Yes.* I never did want to go back to Iowa, not really. I'd much rather look after these children and the baby and you and..."

Della Bueller's gaze fell on an openmouthed Jenna.

"Jenna?" Lee took her hand and tugged her to her feet. "Come," he said softly.

"Oh, Lee..." Tears pooled in her green eyes. "Oh, Lee."

He bent and murmured what he'd been waiting months to say to her. "I love you, Jenna. I need to be with you. And I want you so much I ache at night. You have to come. For God's sake, say yes. Because if you don't, I—"

"If I don't, what?" Jenna whispered.

"If you don't, I'll have to sell the ranch and move here to Heavenly." He lowered his voice and again held her eyes. His heart was hammering so hard he could scarcely speak.

"The truth is, Jenna, I want you more than I want the ranch."

Then, right in front of everyone, he tipped her face up and kissed her.

No one said a word for a long, long time. And then Ruthie gave a little yelp. "Oooh," she sang. "I think kissing means yes, doesn't it?"

Jenna lifted her head and smiled up at Lee. "You know something, Mr. Carver? I think Ruthie is smart enough to go to school right this minute."

"Open your presents," Lee urged.

For Tess he had brought a handsome sewing kit with a quilted blue satin lining. Mary Grace received a book about horses, and she immediately knelt on the floor to pore over the pages while Ruthie squealed over her present, a beautiful china doll with real hair and a pink lace dress and petticoat.

The girls launched themselves at him. "Oh, Lee, thank you! Thank you." Inexplicably, Mary Grace began to sniffle.

"I knew you'd come back," Tess said. "I'm going to sew you something special, Lee. A shirt."

For Mrs. Bueller he'd brought a carved walnut recipe box and a thick leather-bound recipe book with blank pages. For Baby Rob there was a chased silver drinking cup and a plush teddy bear.

At the very bottom of the pile lay a tiny package wrapped in red ribbon. With trembling fingers, Jenna peeled back the tissue paper and snapped open the velvet case.

Inside lay a wide gold wedding band.

Suddenly sunshine flooded her whole being. "Oh," she murmured. She looked up at him with eyes blurry with tears. "Oh, Lee." Her breath caught. "I love you so much," she whispered. "Yes. Yes! I will marry you. I can't stand not being with you."

Epilogue

Three weeks later, Lee returned to Heavenly and he and Jenna were married in the front parlor of the boarding-house. Jenna wore a gown of deep lavender silk, and Tess and Mary Grace served as bridesmaids in matching blue dresses with deep flounces. Ruthie sprinkled rose petals down the staircase when Jenna descended. A grinning Ted Zaberskie gave the bride away.

Sam Lincoln stood up with Lee, who wore his blue military jacket and dark wool trousers.

Jenna found herself so choked up she could barely speak her vows. Was this really happening? Her throat stung and tears rose in her eyes. She felt so happy and shaky she thought she would float away.

Lee slipped his arm around her waist and pulled her close. His touch gave her courage and her voice trembled only a little.

Lee's words were spoken in a voice that was sure and strong, and his kiss following the ceremony was the same.

Hulda Gumpert and Sophia Zaberskie had baked a four-layer wedding cake, and Emma Lincoln and Della Bueller served tea and a potent brandy punch that a half-inebriated Emil Gumpert swore was his German grandmother's old recipe.

After the reception, Lee went off to the livery stable to rent horses for the wagon they would need for their journey north to his ranch, and then he and Jenna climbed the stairs to the bedroom and closed the door.

Lee snapped the lock and turned to find Jenna standing in the middle of the room, looking at him. Her face shone as if lit up from the inside.

"Damn, honey, you're not going to cry, are you?"

"Yes, I probably am," she said with a soft laugh. "I always cry when I'm happy."

He moved close enough to touch her but kept his hands at his side. "Are you happy, Jenna? I want you to be. I'll always want you to be happy. I'll work like hell to make you—"

"You don't have to do a thing, Lee. Just be with me."

He reached for her, folded her tight in his arms and buried his face in her hair. "Jenna." His voice shook.

She lifted her face and he caught her mouth under his, gently at first, and then with deepening intensity.

"Don't stop," she whispered against his lips. "I've missed you so much, Lee. Ever since that night under the wagon I've wanted you. Wanted to be with you."

He gently touched his forehead to hers and closed his eyes. "My darling girl, you don't know how hard I worked to keep from touching you. A thousand miles of restraint is enough to kill a man."

"Well, we're here now. We're together. And I don't care if we're married or not, Lee Carver, if you don't take me to bed right now, I'm going to—"

He stemmed the flow of her words with his lips, and then he scooped her up into his arms, tossed her onto the bed and followed her down.

A long, long kiss later, Jenna felt his hands at the top button of her dress.

The next morning the girls were up early. They gobbled a breakfast of pancakes and bacon provided by Mrs. Bueller, then sat at the dining table, bursting with excitement, and waited for Lee and Jenna to come downstairs.

"Why are they so late?" Tess wondered. "Lee was always up before me, so what's taking him so long?"

Mary Grace sipped her hot chocolate. "Maybe Jenna's got a headache. Or she's feeding Baby Rob. Or—"

"I know, I know!" Ruthie cried. "They're kissing!"

At last Lee and Jenna appeared, the baby's wicker basket swinging from one of Lee's hands. The other was entwined with Jenna's.

An hour later, all six members of the Carver family packed up their belongings, loaded them into the horse-drawn wagon and started off for Lee's ranch and home.

Ruthie thought they smiled an awful lot.

* * * * *

If you enjoyed this story, you won't want to miss these
other great reads from
Lynna Banning

HER SHERIFF BODYGUARD
PRINTER IN PETTICOATS
SMOKE RIVER FAMILY
THE LONE SHERIFF
SMOKE RIVER BRIDE

COMING NEXT MONTH FROM

⊕ HARLEQUIN®

ℋISTORICAL

Available January 17, 2017

THE COWBOY'S CINDERELLA (Western)
by Carol Arens
Ivy Magee's life changes when cowboy Travis Murphy arrives with the startling revelation that she's inherited a ranch. Could Travis be the prince to this unlikely Cinderella?

THE HARLOT AND THE SHEIKH (Regency)
Hot Arabian Nights • by Marguerite Kaye
Prince Rafiq must save his desert kingdom's pride in a prestigious horse race. But he's shocked when his new equine expert is introduced...as *Miss* Stephanie Darvill!

A MARRIAGE OF ROGUES (Regency)
by Margaret Moore
Sir Develin Dundrake is surprised by nothing. Until the woman whose dowry Develin has claimed in a card game proposes a solution that will rescue her from ruin: a wedding!

MISS BRADSHAW'S BOUGHT BETROTHAL (Regency)
by Virginia Heath
Having escaped her evil stepmother, heiress Evelyn Bradshaw finds herself trapped with brooding Finn Matlock when her fake fiancé disappears...

Available via Reader Service and online:

THE DUKE'S SECRET HEIR (Regency)
by Sarah Mallory
When the Duke of Rossenhall meets Ellen Tatham at a ball, the tension of their shared past comes alive. What will Max do when he discovers Ellen's secret...and his heir?

SOLD TO THE VIKING WARRIOR (Viking)
by Michelle Styles
Sigurd Sigmundson knows that passionate Eilidith should merely be a means to an end. But beneath her ice-cold shield there's a sensual woman who longs for his touch!

SPECIAL EXCERPT FROM

H·HARLEQUIN®

HISTORICAL

Prince Rafiq must save his desert kingdom's pride in a prestigious horse race. But he's shocked when his new equine expert is introduced...as Miss Stephanie Darvill!

Read on for a sneak preview of
THE HARLOT AND THE SHEIKH,
the third book in **Marguerite Kaye***'s*
sizzling quartet **HOT ARABIAN NIGHTS***.*

Prince Rafiq could be wearing tattered rags and still she would have been in no doubt of his status. It was in his eyes. Not arrogance but a sense of assurance, of entitlement, a confidence that he was master of all he surveyed. And it was there in his stance, too, in the set of his shoulders, the powerful lines of his physique. Belatedly garnering the power to move, Stephanie dropped into a deep curtsy.

"Arise."

She did as he asked, acutely conscious of her disheveled appearance, dusty clothes and a face most likely liberally speckled with sand. Those hooded eyes traveled over her person, surveying her from head to foot with a dispassionate, inscrutable expression.

"Who are you, and why are you here?" Prince Rafiq asked when the silence had begun to stretch her nerves to breaking point. He spoke in English, softly accented but perfectly pronounced.

Distracted by the unsettling effect he was having on her while at the same time acutely aware of the need to impress him, Stephanie clasped her hands behind her back and forced herself to meet his eyes, answering in his own language, "I am here at your invitation, Your Highness."

"I issued no invitation to you, madam."

"Perhaps this will help clarify matters," Stephanie said, handing him her papers.

The prince glanced at the document briefly. "This is a royal warrant, issued by myself to Richard Darvill, the renowned veterinary surgeon attached to the Seventh Hussars. How do you come to have it in your possession?"

Stephanie knit her fingers more tightly together, as if doing so would stop her legs from trembling. "I am Stephanie Darvill, his daughter and assistant. My father could not, in all conscience, abandon his regiment with Napoleon on the loose and our army expected to go into battle at any moment."

"And so he saw fit to send his daughter in his place?"

The prince sounded almost as incredulous as she had been when Papa had suggested this as the perfect solution to her predicament. The enormity of the trust her father had placed in her struck her afresh. She would not let him down. Not again.

Make sure to read
THE HARLOT AND THE SHEIKH by Marguerite Kaye,
available February 2017 wherever
Harlequin® Historical books and ebooks are sold.

www.Harlequin.com

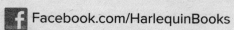
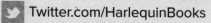